ALICE

S. M. Nuse

Title: Alice
Author: S. M. Nuse
Cover Art: Seerendip Publishing
Publisher: Seerendip Publishing
Edition: First printing, 2024
ISBN: 978-1-965273-09-8 (Paperback)
Printed in the United States of America

To My Cain,

Bossy I like it,

and I love you Always and Forever.

Contents

Prologue

Derrick Caruso sat back; his lazy boy creaked under his weight. His feet felt the dirty carpet under them as he tried to watch the Giants lose to the Eagles; screw you, Philadelphia, he thought bitterly.

His whore of a wife, Mary, sat at the kitchen counter reading a magazine and twirling her hair in her fingers. Erin, the "ginger wonder," was playing in her room, being quiet for the first time all day, not that she would stay put long. Irish-looking brat. He sat, and he stewed about everything that was going on.

Damn, Marino leaving with Bonetti in charge! Damn, his boss at the warehouse for firing his ass for getting in a parking lot scuffle. The other guy wasn't even hurt that bad. Damn, his Mary for stepping out with a newly promoted Don of all people! In the family, real leaders don't sleep with their guys' wives. Derrick was an enforcer; he was a tough guy, and this pansy world wasn't cut out for men like him anymore. Don Marino had been the leader of the Marino crime family for ten years after taking over for his old man. Marino liked the nitty gritty lifestyle of the Mafia and had brought back organized crime at a time when the Feds thought they finished them all.

Now Marino has left to take over the floundering area of Nevada because, he says "Sin city, is the place where we can have more power and control." Just abandoned Queens where it all began for them. New York is where the real Mafia lived.

Marino's second, Joey Bonetti, was taking over, and he had a different approach, or so he said. He didn't have use for enforcers as much as Marino did. He put Derrick on fucking collections. Waste of his talents. He should be used for high-level jobs, he should be used to expand and intimidate.

Before Marino left, he handcuffed Bonetti by making an agreement with the Irish that for two years, there would be no conflicts and the Italians would not grow their areas. Bonetti needed the time to acclimate. The bastard should focus on making a name for himself, not minding his manners and being a pussy.

Derrick threw back another drink as he flipped the channel from the post-game bullshit. He wanted something distracting when his daughter came running in and out of the room. What was she so happy about, damn brat.

"Shut it," he hollered at the girl as she raced back into the room to show her bitch of a mother a picture she drew.

He was under orders, he couldn't touch his wife as long as she was pregnant with this bastard child of Don Luca. Not that the Don would be taking the brat in, no. Derrick was expected to raise him. The Don was off to

Arizona with his own family, leaving this mess for him to clean up. At least he would be getting support for the brat. He was bitter that he hadn't been selected to move with Marino or given a higher status for all his hard work. He had been left behind and all but forgotten.

When Erin got too close, he kicked out his leg and tripped her, making her smash into the coffee table and come up with a bloody mouth. Tears leaked out of her eyes, but she would stay quiet now, wouldn't she? His wife glared at him from the kitchen table, and he glowered back. She hated him now, thought he was worthless, Bitch, he thought bitterly. When Erin moved to her mother for comfort, she was shoved away for obstructing the light over her mother's magazine.

"You wait until that brat pops out of you. I'll be all over you too. Can't lose practice for when the Don needs me back in fighting shape." Mary looked away with fear in her eyes. He could break her of that. The best way to break someone wasn't even hitting them; it was psychological. That was his secret; he could beat someone, then turn around and let them know what could be worse than the pain they were feeling now.

Maybe he would try that on the girl at some point… depending on how pissed she could make him. After all, it's always satisfying to know you've broken someone so completely that they will feel like the worthless dogs they are.

CHAPTER ONE

ERIN

*A*fter eighteen years Erin Caruso was finally free…
of one obligation. She had her GED and was ready
to make the break from her parent's apartment.
No more of the constant fighting and tension. No more
aggression from sun up to sun down. No more hiding
her lifestyle and pretending to be a high school student.
Her only regret was leaving her younger siblings at home
with **them**. She had a plan to get them out but it was
going to take a little time.

This was going to be a whole new chapter. Erin smiled
to herself as she thought of her people that depended on
her. She may even be able to come out in the open soon
if she plays her cards right. Now wasn't the time, she
needed to think about the details, that's how she had
become so successful.

Erin had a part-time job that she could now drop and
focus on her profitable side businesses. Her parents had
taken all of her paychecks from the part-time job, so it
was lucky she had her side businesses to handle anything

she needed. Thankfully, her friend had helped her get her driver's license, and she had a plan. She was going to purchase a truck that she could use for her business and move her siblings and their belongings. It was an older truck and something someone her age could likely afford, so it wouldn't draw too much attention. Then again, living in Queens and frequenting New York, kids there younger than her were driving BMWs.

At five foot two inches with long red hair and bright blue eyes, Erin looked every inch the small-town girl she wasn't. She looked young and naive, and she would play on that; it meant she would be underestimated. This was also why everything she did was in the shadows. No one showed respect to a woman in her industry, and an eighteen-year-old was barely a woman in the real world. She still couldn't legally drink or rent a car, at least with her legal name and identification. Her fake ID, on the other hand, had her at twenty-four.

Walking into the auto shop off Main Street, she smiled sweetly at the older man across the counter. His gray mustache was just slightly droopy from the sweat of the day. His face lit up at the sight of her, and he sat up straight, his back cracking with the effort. "Erin," the gravelly voice crunched out like he was chewing her name with his chaw.

"Eddie," She said back, bouncing up to the counter with the coating peeling from the tops like a bad sunburn. She had taken to popping into the shop after taking an auto shop class in school and having Eddie as her teacher. The shop was old and dirty like a good shop should be. "I would like to buy the F-150," Erin said, slapping a hand down on the counter. His eyebrows rose slightly, but he smiled down at her.

"You've been saving Erin?" he asked, opening a drawer and pulling out the shiny pink title slip from his desk. Like he knew she was going to be asking for it.

"Yes, I have, cash ok?" Her grin was so big it hurt her face. The excitement coursing through her was exhilarating. She pulled the five thousand dollars out of her bag and set it on the counter.

"Cash always works," Eddie said, twinkling at her. He had always been kind, and she knew he operated under Bonetti. She thought of her own small organization, granted, only thirty people currently, but with her GED now, she would be turning her focus to it and growth.

"You work with Bonetti, right?" She asked as he filled out the pink slip and tapped a few keys on his computer. His eyebrows rose as he glanced at her in surprise. Not many people openly talked about Bonetti if they wanted to stick around.

"I know Bonetti." Eddie said stiffly, "You know Bonetti, your Dad works for him too." He didn't sound happy or unhappy with Bonetti, but she hoped that if she could get the business to side with her, it would be a clean sweep for the neighborhood. It was a little rash to open herself up to speculation, but Eddie had been a friend for over two years.

"Yes, you know I have never met him. My Dad says my Irish will offend him." Eddie scowled at this, and she laughed lightly. "What is Bonetti like?"

"He's good for the neighborhood. Necessary and helpful. You know I don't pay protection like most of these other fools." Eddie leaned on the counter conspiratorially, her money still between them. "I took out a loan from Bonetti, and I am paying it back. Though we do have an arrangement that I will work on his cars even after the debt is repaid on the house. That's what I like about Bonetti. He does trade out, and he seems to care." Eddie leaned back and looked at Erin as though he was viewing her differently.

"Why are you asking? Are you going to work for Bonetti?" Eddie looked both concerned and disappointed."

Erin smiled slowly. "No, I'll never work for Bonetti. What if some new group came into town? Would you work with someone new?" Erin waited with bated breath for Eddie's answer. This was important for her to know; she liked Eddie, and it would help cement her plans to move forward and take over Bonetti's area to taunt Marino out of his hole in Nevada.

Marino was the real target; he had destroyed any chance of a happy childhood for herself and her siblings. Poor Theo and Josie had never known parents who loved them. She had lost that at three years old and only had vague images of her mother baking her cookies and sitting on the floor to play with her. That all ended when Marino abandoned them.

At that moment, the bell over the door dinged, and a shuffling footfall sounded behind her. Eddie glanced up, placing his hand on the cash on the counter and sliding it into the drawer.

"Erin!" The harsh word sounded behind her, and her blood ran cold. Erin turned to see her father. He was tall with dark hair and darker eyes. The alcohol on his breath was evident from across the room. His once full chest looked caved in as he took in the room around him. The smell of cheap vodka and whiskey brought so many cruel and painful memories into her mind, but she clamped down on them. All he felt for her was hate and disdain, so she could not feel anything but the same in return. She had decided that when she was a small child.

"Where did you get that money?" her father's voice was harsh. His eyes stared at where Eddie had shoved the cash. "Get your hands off her money!" He demanded of Eddie.

"Dad, I worked for this money and saved it to buy a truck," she said, trying to block the counter with her body. She shuttered and flinched and cursed herself. This, she reminded herself, was why she never got physically close to anyone in her organization. She could not flinch like a pansy in front of them whenever a man came near her. She needed to start working on this fear. She knew Eddie had not missed her flinching; she had hit the counter hard, and she blushed as she moved away quickly. She could feel her chest tightening as she fought panic at being in public with her father.

"Why didn't this go to the family? What do you need a truck for?" he demanded, stalking to the counter. "Put that back she doesn't need no truck" his voice was harsh as he reached out and grabbed her arm hauling her to his side, all the while glaring at Eddie.

"Now, Derrick," Eddie began to stand. "She worked hard for this money, and a girl needs a vehicle. She's old enough to go to college soon."

"Mind your own," Derrick shouted at Eddie, reaching for the drawer of cash. "She is my daughter, not yours; she doesn't even have a license, so she doesn't need a damn truck." Erin backed away from her father and shot Eddie a warning look. Her license. This was the first big deception that would be coming out in the open. Erin thought frantically of a way out of this. She wasn't ready to play her hand so soon. If her Dad searched her bag, he would find cash and weapons along with what little clothes she wanted to keep.

"What are you talking about?" Eddie said, fighting off Derrick's hands from the drawer. "I took her to the test for you three months ago." She closed her eyes as her heart stuttered, and all motion stopped from the desk. Her father turned slowly to her, rage apparent on his face. Well, Erin thought solemnly, one more beating for the road.

"What?" he demanded as she made herself as small as possible. Eddie looked bewildered as Erin closed her eyes. She knew if she showed any sign of attitude or defiance, it would be ten times worse, and he may use the cord if he got her home. "Give her the money back," Derrick said evenly. "We are going home." Erin's eyes opened wide as she watched Eddie pull the cash back out of the drawer, and her father swipe it into his pocket. She had to do something, this was her escape. She had her plans made, and this would throw everything off schedule.

"No," she said, "I got my license and GED. I'm leaving," she said, stepping towards her father. Keep your voice strong, she thought to herself, "Give the money back to Eddie for my truck." Her voice sounded desperate, not strong, as she stared at Eddie for any type of help, knowing he wouldn't do anything against her father. Eddie sighed deeply and put the pink slip back in his drawer with sad eyes. He handed Derrick the cash, which was shoved in his pocket quickly.

"If you ever talk to my daughter again, I'll call the boss," Derrick said to Eddie before grabbing her arm roughly and hauling her from the shop. She looked back at Eddie with fear and anger burning inside her. Tonight was going to be a rough night, but she couldn't let Derrick go back to her siblings with the anger that was directed at her. She needed a new plan. One to get all three of them out at the same time. She was marched back to the apartment, and she glimpsed a tall man she thought she had recognized at the coffee shop across the street.

Derrick kept a firm grip up the stairs to the fifth-floor apartment in the crappy low-income housing. They had to live there because, on paper, they had no money. Both her parents got unemployment and would only get a job long enough to qualify again before getting themselves fired.

The money that the Bonetti family gave them for her father's services was under the table and wasted on booze, and when they were feeling frisky, her parents would buy whatever drugs they felt like embracing. Derrick slammed her into the door and she was flung directly into the kitchen area.

"Mary" Derrick yelled out for Erin's Mother who was sitting at the table with the two younger kids' homework spread wide, Theo and Josie had terror in their eyes. Bad day for them to be home from school for a doctor's visit, Erin thought bitterly.

"Mary, the little bitch has been hiding money. Tried to buy a truck, and she dropped out of high school." he shoved her against the wall, and she stared back and forth as her parents started taking turns yelling and hitting her.

"Stop, you can't blame her for wanting to leave, can you?" Theo demanded all teenage rebellion, and Derrick lunged for him. Erin jumped up and knocked Derrick into the wall.

"Get in your room and lock the door," she said to both of them. "Hide." Derrick was up and grabbed her hair.

"Get the cord," he demanded, ramming Erin's face into the wall. She let out a whimper as she heard the whistle of the electric cord come through the air and slice her back. When he had tired himself of that, she started to move away, and that seemed to anger him more. She didn't scream, and she knew that made him angry. He loved to hear her scream when he beat her. She had stopped giving him the pleasure years ago.

"Derrick, don't kill her," Mary said, anxiety spiking her voice. "She's still our girl."

"She ain't my girl, with this red fucking hair. She's Irish like your ass." He spat, grabbing the old Irish family crest that hung on the wall right next to the Italian one that shined with pride. The Irish one was slightly dusty and made of iron. He turned the burner on the stove and grabbed the mass of red hair, pulling Erin to the kitchen,

"Derrick" Mary sounded alarmed as he dragged the now kicking and fighting Erin to the kitchen. He pulled his gun and held it to her head.

"Don't you move, you little bitch." Erin stared at her father, knowing at that moment he would kill her. Fear was there, but anger held her still as he heated the family crest until it was red hot. He held it up for her to see and pressed it to the unmarred skin on her shoulder blade that her bra had protected. She screamed long and loud and heard her mother rush over as she passed out.

Two hours later, Josie was wiping Erin's face, tears running down her face. "Hey, kid," Erin said, smiling up at her little sister. "It's going to be ok," she said softly. "I won't leave you here all alone," she promised. Josie was ten years old and the youngest of the three children. Her blonde hair hung around her face, and the red mark on her chin showed that she had been hit for the first time. Rage flowed through Erin as she looked at her sister's face. This was unforgivable, something she never considered raced through her mind. A more immediate and final punishment for her parents was needed to protect her siblings.

Josie was the sweetest and most patient little girl. She was thoughtful and dedicated. Erin knew for a fact that the reason they had her mother at the table doing homework was because Josie had convinced her to help. Josie could convince anyone of anything. She made the best of every situation. Even in their home she always tried to be happy. Even her father loved Josie.

Erin couldn't consider leaving her siblings alone, and she couldn't leave them to face what she had endured, this beating had been bad. Erin looked over at Theo, who was standing leaning in the doorway like a guard watching over the girls in their shared bedroom. He stood there watching the hallway and glancing back at her repeatedly. Prepared to jump in the way should her father come back.

"I won't leave either of you here," Erin said loud enough for him to hear. "I'll think of something," she said softly.

"He took your money and went out with Mom," Josie said softly. Her short blonde hair looked a mess like she had taken a good smack for something.

"Oh yeah? How long ago?" she asked

"Ten minutes," Theo said, glancing back. "You good?"

"Solid," Erin replied, sitting up. Yeah, she definitely had a broken rib, but it would hold for now. Her raw back and the brand hurt and had her eyes filling with tears. "Did he go through my bag?" she asked.

"No, he tossed it in the trash outside," Theo said, pulling up his baggy jeans. It was a thrift store buy, so the clothes rarely fit well. She would fix that soon enough, she had never wanted to buy them clothes while living here because then it would show her parents she had other money sources and cause way more problems.

"Are you sure they are gone?" she asked.

"Yeah," said Theo, turning to her. "They won't be back tonight. Said they were having a high roller evening" They all knew that meant they would be back in a few days when all the money was gone.

"Good," she said "Go grab my bag" Theo saluted her and headed out of the room. When he brought the light purple bag inside she started emptying it of the clothes and pictures she had taken. She pulled out an old-looking pair of sweats and pulled out a wad of cash. "Do you want to leave tonight?"

"Yes," they both said.

"Pack one bag each that you can carry. Now," and the two immediately got to work. She pulled out a cell phone from another pair of pants in her bag. "Eddie," she said when the old man picked up, "tell me the truck is still there."

"Erin, I don't think I can sell it to you with your Dad all in a huff," Eddie said, sounding distressed. "He calls the boss on me, and it's all over" Damn, she thought bitterly; the truck had really been a favor for him to get the money, but now she had no vehicle for getting her siblings out. He was right he had more to lose than to gain. She could afford a newer car, but it would be suspect to those who knew her, and she still wanted to keep a low profile.

"Fine," she said with a curse and hung up. She couldn't call her people, they had no idea she was a teenager still living with her parents. She couldn't call Billy Senior her second in command; he knew about her situation, but he would see her at her weakest. They needed to get out of the town and away from her parents so her siblings would be safe. She went to her parents' filing cabinet and pulled out their birth certificates and social security cards. She pulled out the court paperwork from the three times social services had been called and been useless and packed it away.

Today was going to be the first day of the rest of their lives. She would make sure of that. When she heard the front door slam open, her eyes opened wide, and she knew decisions had to be made.

CHAPTER TWO

CAIN

Cain stood waiting by the door of Hansons Cafe, it was his job to ensure the boss's orders were followed. At twenty-three he was the youngest second in command in all the families. He knew his boss Joey Bonetti was judged for picking him. Truth was Cain felt underprepared for the job but that meant he had to be on point at all times. Observe the area, and be prepared to both lend an opinion, playoff Joey, or fight.

He was also smart enough to be loyal but look to the future as well. He would always be loyal to Joey, he had been raised by Joey after his father had died a year after Marino had left. That time had been a rough transition, but even though Joey was busy and very important, he had come to talk with Cain's mother, a drug addict. Who easily took the monthly money and did her usual routine. When she had passed, Cain had been fifteen and he had gone to work for Joey full-time. He had been popped for an assault at eighteen, and Joey had been his character witness. Two years later, Joey had been at the jail to welcome him home. From then on, Cain had been in all the high-level meetings and had officially been announced as second last week on his birthday.

He stood waiting outside the coffee shop facing the auto shop as he watched the redhead go in looking thrilled about life. She was cute, maybe twenty at most but her height made him think of the possibilities. She was short and compact, he bet he could lift her with one arm. He watched the drunk man, Derrick he knew, stumbled in after a few minutes as he listened acutely to his boss's conversation.

Hanson's Cafe was behind on payments and that was inconvenient, this entire block had been struggling lately so it was time for an in-person visit. His boss was smart. Don't be overt and flashy, small deals with lots of people to make a good amount of money each would ensure large profits overall. This was a civilized society, after all. He watched Derrick dragging the girl from the shop, her face covered by the sheet of red hair, but he knew there was no happy ending to that story. Too bad. She was cute. Getting mixed up with Derrick Caruso was no one's idea of a good time.

Hanson sat at the small, black, shiny table set for two. His white hair slicked back his light pink shirt and white pants against his old tan skin made him look like the most Italian that ever Italianed. He looked like he belonged at a winery in Venice. His wife hovered behind him, unsure of her place. She should walk to the back and let her husband handle this, Cain thought to himself as he followed the progress of Derrick and the girl to the corner where they turned off.

Pity, that was probably his daughter, he'd heard that he had three kids. Derrick never brought them around at the Family functions where most socialize their children; it was only Derrick and his wife. They always sat with the same group of disgruntled low-levels that had clung on since Marino had left. Joey still took care of them because of their loyalty to staying on, and they did what was needed.

"Cain," Joey called, pulling Cain back to his main task.

"Yeah, boss?" Cain said, his six-foot-seven frame filling the doorway. "You think we should up the price by ten percent for inconveniences?" Joey said, knowing that it was way too much money. The couple gasped, and his wife placed a hand on his shoulder. Hanson had anger and fear in his eyes.

"I don't know boss, these are nice people, how about three percent?" he said knowing his role in this conversation. The couple's eyes darted between Joey and Cain.

"Five?" Joey shot back

"How about four?" Cain answered slowly, his deep voice sounding calm and polite. "We can do four," the older man said eagerly, and his wife jumped away from the table to retrieve the money. Joey nodded at Cain, who turned back to the door to stand outside. This area had a small-town feel, but it was still part of Queens. "Joey, we have been having problems with this new crew in the area," the older man said.

"What crew?" Joey asked, Cain's ears perked up. This was Derricks area for collections and he was supposed to report any problems. He had reported that the people had been light two weeks in a row and that had been all.

"This gang of kids keep coming around to all the shops and robbing us. They hit us on Tuesday, the liquor store yesterday, and last week, they trashed Santiago's furniture store when he refused to pay him." Hanson said, sounding both angry and tense. You were never supposed to take an angry tone with a Don, and Hanson looked terrified that he might be making it worse for himself.

"Why didn't any of you call me?" Joey asked with concern in his voice. "That is what I am here for to protect this community." Cain watched Joey's look of concern and turned to scan the streets. No one had called, Derrick had not reported it. How long has this been going on?

"I called Derrick and he said he would get back to me, said the same thing to Tony and Santiago," The old man said hesitantly "I don't want to get anyone in trouble" Cain shook his head lightly while he scanned the street again. Fear of Derrick was just as high as fear of Joey, pitiful.

"No, I'm glad you told me," Joey said hastily. "I'll talk to Derrick, and I will have some guys come around more. Here, this is Cain's number. If something happens, you call him directly." Cain turned around and handed the man his card a blank business card with a number on it with a C on the back.

"Mr. Hanson, I will come by tomorrow morning with a few guys. Is it ok if they hang around here since you are on the corner? Maybe put a table out front?" Cain asked.

Mr Hanson looked up at Cain with old blue eyes shining with relief. Yeah, Cain thought we actually care about holding up our end.

"Yes, whatever you like," Hanson said, his eyes crinkling. "Joey, thank you," he said to Joey as his wife handed him an envelope full of cash.

"When Cain comes tomorrow, I want you to give a full report of this crew to him and the guys so they know who they are looking for," Joey said easily. "Now, Mr. Hanson, thank you for the visit. I will take my leave now, and do not hesitate to call". Cain followed Joey out the door and looked at his boss.

Joey was in his late forties and graying around the temples. He was fit and tall, his Italian heritage showing in his tan skin. His sharp eyes never missed a thing, and he was from an old family. He had brought back an old-school mob family to New York, no more violent crime running rampant; they took care of the entire neighborhood. In 2023, who would have thought things could go back to the old ways? "When society starts to crumble, and law enforcement isn't enough, good people will turn to less ethical people of the world for protection. So we will be the ones to rely on," Joey always said. The cops left them alone for the most part, as they knew organized crime was better than what they had been going through. When Marino had run things, they had been attacked on all sides. Various street gangs from the West to the North, The Hispanics to the East. It was constant cloak-and-dagger attacks.

When Marino left, he forced the Irish into a truce for two years. The Hispanics had been beaten back, and a truce had been struck, and the street gangs had agreed on territory but had no truce laid out. Now, the streets were crowded with their people, families, and tourists. Queens was a beautiful place to be. Joey had maintained his truce with the Irish through good faith, and the Hispanics had been quiet for the last two years. Joey had beaten back the most prominent of the street gangs five years ago, so these should have been easy days. *Sit back and get rich days*, is what Joey had called them.

"When was the last time you heard from Derrick?" Joey asked as they headed for the car.

"Been a while since I talked to him, but I saw him pulling some young redhead out of the auto shop earlier. Probably his daughter, he says she's always causing him trouble and she looked like trouble." Cain nodded across the street. Joey stopped short and turned to go to the shop. The little bell jangled as they entered, and an old man with gray eyes and handlebar mustache looked up at them. He looked uncomfortable, to say the least, when he realized who was standing in front of him.

"Joey, how are things?" he asked, rifling in the drawer in front of him and pulling an envelope out. "You're a few days early" he sounded nervous.

"I'm not here about that, Eddie," Joey said, smiling lightly. What was Derrick in here for?" Eddie paled. Well, that got a response, Cain thought humorlessly, he hated Derrick, he was too much like his old man. He enjoyed inflicting pain and violence, and he enjoyed bullshitting too much. Self-inflated and over-opinionated, Cain preferred to sit back and listen and plan.

"Derrick? Did he complain because I swear I thought she had permission from him" Cain sat down in one of the overstuffed chairs in the lobby with the stuffing coming out. These chairs were always comfortable he thought as he watched the older man.

"Haven't heard from Derrick; why don't you tell me what happened?" Joey said, leaning on the counter. He could have been asking about the weather with how light he was keeping his tone. Cain wondered if Joey realized how imposing he looked when he did that.

"His girl, the oldest, Erin, came in to buy a truck from me that she's been saving for. She comes in at least once a week to talk to me ever since she was in my class. I helped her get her driver's license because she said that Derrick was too busy.

"Well he came in today when she was buying the truck and he took the money and when he found out about the license he dragged her out of here and threatened me with you" Cain was shocked at the nerve of that. Threatening someone with Joey usually or should mean that Joey had approved of it. Cain knew for a fact Joey wouldn't approve of a threat to Eddie. Joey looked confused and glanced at Cain.

"You know Derrick's kids?" he asked Cain.

"Never had the pleasure," Cain said, thinking of the redhead being dragged off.

"Did you have any trouble with this new gang we are hearing about?" Joey said changing the subject. Eddie's eyebrows shot up and he nodded.

"Yeah, they hassle me about parts they want for cheap. Said they are running this block, I called Derrick and he said it was being handled" Eddie sounded surprised that Joey had asked.

"They trying to charge for protection or are they just ripping people off?" Joey asked, thrumming his fingers on the countertop.

"Just ripping people off from what I hear. They threatened me, and Eddie Jr said they knew where he went to college and where Maggie works since they wanted me to order parts." Eddie was scared; why wouldn't he be? His kid and his wife had been threatened, and the people he thought he could rely on hadn't come through. It was no wonder the people on this block were upset. Cain wondered idly how far this new crew was impacting things for them. One thing was plain, Derrick was in trouble.

"We will take care of this, we are setting up some guys outside of Hansons. If they come around you call Cain here. Not Derrick anymore." Joey nodded to Cain who pulled out another card and handed it over to Eddie.

"Now, about the Daughter situation," Joey continued, "for now, I don't want you selling that truck to his girl. I want you to steer clear of him and his Family. Kids make things more complicated, and from what I hear, that girl of his is a handful."

"She's a good kid," Eddie shot back instantly. "She's smart and works hard. Derrick takes all her money and drinks it away. She has been doing it since she got a job at fifteen; she's been showing up to school with bruises and a busted-up face for years, Joey. He beats her badly, but she still smiles and takes care of the other two kids of his. His wife does the same, those kids are terrorized.

The teachers who called CPS got Derrick all over them, they got no one to protect them." Joey stood up straight in surprise. Eddie looked angry and defensive, his tone implied that Joey should have known what was happening to the girl.

Cain was shocked that no one had reported this to them or even the police. If it's bad enough Eddie knew about it then others had to. He pictured the redhead, bloody and beaten and his blood heated. She was a woman and had been a child. He knew there were two younger children, also trouble makers according to Derrick. Cain remembered days of being young and beaten and was sure Joey was also reliving his own childhood trauma in this area. They never would have let a child beater be involved with the Family.

"Why didn't we know about this?" He asked, turning to Cain. Cain knew that Joey tried to maintain contact with all the families and that Carol, Joey's wife, had relationships with most of the wives.

"You all never care about the families of your men or your clients. Your bottom line guys" Eddie said bitterly. Yea, he was definitely angry at Joey and blaming him for all the misfortune in this situation, Cain thought with a hint of admiration for the old man.

"I care," Joey said evenly to Eddie "I just need to be told, so Eddie thank you for telling me" Eddie stood up straight but looked a little shaky. Yelling at Joey Bonetti was never a good idea but this kind of information would be put to great use. Derrick had just crossed a line that almost no one knew Joey had. Cain knew because Joey was his closest friend and a father figure. Joey had grown up in a similar situation so he knew this would not be let go easily. It would also have to be verified.

"Derrick never brings the kids to the get-togethers. He has always kept his Family distant and when he does mention them it's always to complain. I know he's got three kids. Two girls and a boy and his oldest turned eighteen last year and he was complaining that she wasn't able to go away to college." Eddie grunted his disagreement at that statement.

"She's smart, she stays for those kids. She's all they got that's good." Eddie said after Joey just stared at him. "She's a good kid, never says a bad word, she mentioned you today Joey."

"What about me?" Joey asked and his tone changed, like he was trying to end on a good note.

"She asked," Eddie hesitated trying to remember then he paled slightly. "She asked if I enjoyed working with you. I told her I did that you took care of your people."

"Well, that was nice. She's old enough she may be looking for better work." Joey glanced at Cain who nodded. Cain was good at recruitment so he would take the lead to connect with her at some point.

"I doubt it, Joey, she's skittish around men and I asked if she wanted to work for you and she said no." Joey smiled lightly.

"With what's been going on I don't blame her." Joey said, "Thank you, Eddie, for updating me, we will do everything we can to help, you said her name was Erin?"

"Yes sir, thank you, Joey. If you could keep me updated on what happens with her. She was my favorite student." Joey nodded as he turned to leave.

Joey looked at Cain sharply. "I want you to get some guys together today and brief them on this gang situation. Find these guys and shut them down. We need to know how far this thing goes. I want you to run this, pick your team, and get the details before doing more and stop them from harassing our people. You're responsible." The message was clear, Cain would be reporting on this daily until it was resolved. The follow-up on Derrick would have to wait but that also seemed a high priority.

"What about Derrick?" Cain asked.

"I got some leg work to do on that. I will handle it myself." Joey said evenly. "I'll drop you at the office, you're gonna need the SUV for the guys" Cain nodded, getting into the Bugatti Mistral and took off.

JOEY

Joey pulled up to the high school that Erin Caruso should be attending. From what he knew she was a Senior this year. He walked into the office and saw familiar faces everywhere. He walked around the counter smiling at the receptionist Kelly, the wife of one of his newer recruits. She was young and pretty with large eyes that looked both excited and anxious.

"Hey Kelly, how is it going?" She swept a hand over her flat stomach and he grinned at the movement.

"Good Mr. Bonetti. How is your day going?" She stood as the principal came rushing from his office at the sound of the name.

"Doing fine myself, hey Charles" Joey said with a nod. The man looked panicked that Joey was there and that made him grin. He didn't have much to do with the man but reputation was everything. "I am here on a bit of an investigation. What can you tell me about Erin Caruso?"

"Erin? She's great, though she turned in her GED this morning and removed herself from classes. She had good grades and never missed a day without an excuse. Did something happen to her?" Charles asked as Kelly sat back down. Joey noted the unconscious stroke of her belly again, as he focused again on Charles. He made a mental note to have his wife Carol send flowers to congratulate them on their new addition.

"As far as I know she's fine. Her Dad got a bit mad at the auto shop and from what he's told me she's a hard kid to raise." Kelly made a sound of disgust and Joey refocused on her. "Yes Kelly?" he asked and watched her squirm. He had to admit, people had a view of him that he felt was unjustified, but he allowed it.

"I know Erin. Cleaned her up several times over the years, what with her parents issues." Kelly said "She's a good girl. Smart too. She has a photographic memory so she gets good grades like Mr. Lewsky said. Her parents are vile. They hit her at homecoming football game last year in full view of everyone. Her sister was complaining and they snapped at her and Erin stuck up for her like big sisters do. Next thing you know Derrick smacks her so hard she fell down three steps on the bleachers. Popped right back up and made a smart remark again. Next week she was walking slowly and wearing lots of makeup. We reported it several times but the woman at

CPS is married to Marino's cousin and knows Derrick and Mary"

"From the school's standpoint," Charles burst in, putting himself between Joey and Kelly who was looking heated. Joey gave Charles a few points for chivalry. "Erin Caruso is a gifted bright young woman with a bright future. She got her GED to get away from her parents and missed out on a four-point-oh and her pick of colleges. Now what else would you like for your investigation?" Joey stared at him for a moment and debated the merit of pissing off Charles more or intimidating him. He opted for light intimidation.

"I want to talk to her teachers, was she in any clubs? Also, her friends."

"The teachers are in class right now, I'll get you a list of class numbers and Steve can escort you." Charles nodded to the school security officer who had appeared in the doorway. Steve smiled at Joey, they played poker together once a month. "Kelly look up the clubs. The only friend I ever saw her with graduated last year. Billy O'Reilly. Kelly can you get you the address of his parents but he may be away at college."

"Mr. Bonetti Erin was not in any clubs this year but in her freshman year, she was in Future Business Leaders of America as well as the student government as the treasurer. She ran cross country for the first few races in her freshman year as well. She quit all of those halfway through after someone called CPS on her parents." Kelly said and handed him a slip of paper with the class schedule for Erin Caruso and Billy O'Reilly's home address.

Joey spent the rest of the afternoon meeting with teachers and talking with the limited friends she seemed to have. His last stop was the O'Reilly house where he was greeted by William Senior. The man was about his age with a healthy gut and graying brown hair. He used to be affiliated with Marino and had gotten out when they had reorganized claiming retirement.

"Billy, I got into a weird situation. I was hoping to talk to your son Billy Junior." Billy filled the doorway instantly, and the unwelcome feeling washed over Joey.

"Why?"

"Not to recruit." Joey said raising his hands "It's about the Carusos. I heard several claims now that the oldest is abused. I wanted to talk to some of Erin's friends, and the only friend anyone could point to is your boy."

"Billy's in college, he will be home late tonight as he's got work." Billy Senior looked cautious and slightly taunting. "I know Erin, she's been coming here for years black and blue and bloody. I had it out with Derrick once and he took it out on her. I told Marino about it but he didn't care. Derrick is bottom of the barrel and brings your name down to nothing. You should have been rid of him when you took over."

"Why didn't you come to me?" Joey asked but he knew the answer. Billy had never respected him, never given him the chance. Just got out and was bitter that he hadn't been one of the selected to be made Dons'. Prick, he thought to himself as he waited.

"What would you have done?" Billy shot back.

"Handled it," Joey said, his voice deathly level. Billy looked defiant.

"It will be handled," Billy Senior said back just as evenly. Joey studied the man in front of him. Was Billy Senior challenging him? "At least I assume that you will handle it now," Billy added and Joey relaxed a bit.

"If you hear of any other families in this situation, you tell me. You don't have to like me or work for me, but you will damn well respect me. I have cleaned the area up, I don't need to be undermined by someone like you." Joey was pissed, he had never liked Billy Senior pompous jerk.

"If Erin is hurt, call me." Billy Senior said his voice was firm and inflexible.

"Last anyone saw her, her father was dragging her down Main Street looking pretty pissed off." Billy nodded and put his hand in his pocket to pull out his phone.

"Take care of it, Joey, like you should have already." With that, Billy slammed the door in Joey's face. Joey would be indeed taking care of it but at the moment he had to deal with some business. He would have Derrick report to him first thing in the morning, to deal with him right away.

CHAPTER THREE

ERIN

*I*t was almost four in the morning when Erin drove her dad's crappy Camry up to the apartment complex. She stumbled into the shower and just sat in there until the hot water was gone and finally cleaned herself off under a harsh cold spray. She was covered in bruises and her face looked like it had been a punching bag but that was pretty normal for her. Everyone knew who her father worked for so no one would say anything about it. This has been the case forever so why change now?

She got dressed slowly and tied her long red hair into a bun on top of her head. After, she applied what makeup she had to cover as much as she could. Now at least you could only see the darkest of the bruises and scratches.

She pulled out her phone and saw the massive number of calls from the Billy's O'Reily as she liked to think of them. Her best friend Billy Junior was her top Lieutenant and her face in the organization. Billy Senior was her second in command, he advised her and directed her. He had helped her build everything she had. She had the drive, and finances needed to lead and he had the legacy knowledge, smarts, and just enough burning hatred to join her. She called Billy Senior back.

"Boss," his voice was groggy with sleep "You alive?"

"Oh just barely. It was a long day. I am going to catch up with you and Billy Junior later today but since I had about eighty calls between the two of you I wanted to check in."

"Bonetti came by asking about you today." The skin on the back of her neck stood up.

"Why?" How had he found out about her already? She had been careful, no one knew the end goal of her organization yet. Panic blinded her momentarily as she sat in her Dad's recliner leaning forward from her still aching back.

"Word has gotten out that you're abused." She laughed out loud at this. "I would expect a visit from him sometime soon. From what Billy and I found, people painted you in the light of a hero. Protecting the kids and all that." Billy sounded more awake now and she could hear him moving about.

"Eddie, I was pulled out of his place by Derrick. As long as Bonetti's only coming to find poor abused girl we will be fine. He will get his money's worth if he comes soon." She said, thinking of her face.

"You hurt?" Billy sounded concerned and she sighed lightly.

"It will never happen again," she said softly "Listen I want us laying low for the next day or so. Until Joey pops up, I don't want him to see me with you or Billy Junior."

"Say the word and your old man's gone," Billy said, he had said it before but she felt it would draw too much attention to herself. Too late for that now.

"You don't need to worry about that, it will never happen again.." She rose from the chair and sucked in a breath from the pain. "I gotta go get the kids ready for school. I will touch base later. Let Billy Junior know. When he complains I didn't call him first, tell him it's because he never wakes up for his phone."

"Will do Boss" he said as she hung up. She needed time to think and that wouldn't happen until her siblings were at school and she was alone. Then she would allow herself to think.

She moved to the kitchen slowly, her back aching, her shoulder burning at the touch of her t-shirt and started packing the kids' lunches. Cut the crust off Josie's sandwiches and make cheese quesadillas for Theo. They got up right at seven AM as usual and didn't flinch when they saw her face.

"I'll drive you to school, they aren't going to be up in time," Erin said softly as they moved quietly through the apartment avoiding the closed door that was their parent's room. Her younger siblings moved around almost soundlessly out of fear, so as to not upset them. "Theo, did you study for your pre-algebra test?" she asked softly over a breakfast of toaster waffles.

"Yea" he said with a shrug "it'll be a breeze" She smiled warmly at him. He was so smart and tough. He wanted so badly to protect her, and she caught him scanning her up and down more than a few times, checking how bad it was. She looked like hell, even with makeup on.

"Good. Josie, it's Thursday. Do you want to go through your spelling on the way to school?" Erin asked and Josie nodded, chewing slowly. "Do you both have the doctor's notes for yesterday?" She asked as they had both had their annual check-ups which is why they were home to hear the battle that took place.

Erin stared at her baby sister's face and sighed softly. She had a small bruise on her chin from yesterday which made Erin's heart break. Erin came around and undid her hair to let it fall over the bruise. "Keep your hair over your shoulder on this side to hide the bruise. If anyone asks about it just tell them you fell."

"I know Erin. I've seen you do it too many times to count," Josie said with a hint of temper in her voice.

"That won't be your life." Erin said softly "Your life changes today I promise." Erin said softly looking between her siblings. Erin patted Josie's head and they got up to go to school in the 2021 Toyota Camry SE her father drove.

When Erin got back home, she went into her parent's room and started pulling out the paperwork from the filing cabinet again. She booted up her mom's laptop and checked the calendar that hung on their wall. It was the day both of her parents had to submit their unemployment benefits claims. She logged in using the passwords written on a sticky note and applied for the benefits for them. She wanted to make it seem like they were still around somewhere.

Her father had taught her how to make someone disappear, or had lectured her on the 'art' of his work. He had brought her to some of his interrogations when

Bonetti needed information. He had taught her how to make someone bend to your will thinking one day she would work for the Bonetti's as well and take after him. He had taught her the clean up skills as well which had helped her with her impulsive decision the night before.

She went about packing up a bunch of their clothes and loaded them into the car. As she was finishing up an email to her siblings' schools, letting them know both her parents would be gone for the next few months on family business, there was a knock at the door. She hit send and shut everything down before going to answer it.

Bonetti stood on her step, shaded lenses covering his eyes and the black hair had some silver at the temples. She had seen him once before when she waited in her dad's car when he had to run an errand. This was his boss. Crap, she thought looking up at the man.

"Can I help you?" she asked half hiding behind the door. He didn't look armed but looks could be deceiving. He was twice her size easily and he didn't look out of shape. Her broken ribs and back wounds would hamper her from running away or struggling much. Had he found them already?

"Hey, I'm Joey Bonetti, a friend of your father's," he said, studying her face. She knew it looked bad and there was nothing she could say to that.

"He's not home Mr. Bonetti," she said softly, trying to sound compliant, but her nerves twitched. He was a big presence and she was injured already. He glanced over her shoulder into the room and she closed her eyes as if in pain. She knew what he saw. The apartment was gross. The kitchen area where the front door opened was covered in empty food containers, crumbs everywhere, and a sink full of dishes. The place looked like a hoarder lived in it with all the cleaning her parents had done.

"Do you mind if I come in and take a look?" he asked softly, his voice full of concern. Of course, he was concerned about her father. According to her Dad, he was his best earner, though the scraps he got in return didn't show it. Erin hated having to let him into the place. She hated that she was so close to this man and didn't have a weapon. She hated that with him this close her natural reflex is to flinch away.

"I don't think I have a choice do I?" she shot back anger in her voice. He looked taken aback at this. The anger burning in her felt like it was going to rip out of her. This man was the reason no one had ever stood up for her or her siblings. Fear of this man had stopped anyone from caring how badly they were hurt. He studied her for a long moment before she stepped back and opened the door. He wouldn't find them here, but eventually, he would figure it out. He was smart, everyone knew that. He stepped in watching her closely.

"Are you ok?" he asked, gesturing toward her face, she flinched back and hit a wall gasping at the pain that shot through her back and ribs. Her knees wobbled and she braced a hand on the wall to hold her back away. A reminder of her faults and fears. She needed to find help for this, she thought bitterly. She focused on breathing and saw stars as Joey braced the door she was leaning on so it wouldn't wobble out of her grip and cause her to fall. Well, that was polite, she thought bitterly.

"Please don't," she said fear laced through her voice. Her pain showed clearly on her face. "I'm fine really" He moved away from her and quickly walked the whole apartment. She stood by the door waiting. She felt ashamed and embarrassed, this was her enemy and she flinched like a helpless child. She felt her cheeks heat and she looked down at the floor.

"Come in here Erin," he said, raising his voice lightly enough to be heard. He didn't sound angry, Erin thought trying to push down her anxiety.

She followed him into the living room. The couch sagged and the coffee table with the broken leg that was sitting on a box to hold it up made him cringe lightly, or maybe it was at the sight of her walking into the room. She sat in her Dad's chair across from him. "Did Derrick do this to you?" She looked up into his eyes defiantly but did not say anything. "What about your Mom? Did she help him?" again no response. He sat staring at her making her squirm as he just stared at her hard.

"That's family business" she finally replied. He was going to be trouble, digging into this and wanting to know details. Billy had warned her that Bonetti would come but she hadn't believed he would. She still held a suspicion that he somehow knew about her Organization. She kept herself so far apart from it. Managing everything through Billy Senior and Billy Junior. To all her other people she was just a voice on a phone. An authoritative and empathetic leader protecting a way of life and her people.

"Where are they?" He asked, there was definitely anger now. Erin felt a quick relief, he hadn't found them.

She may be able to get out of this alive. They would eventually be found but hopefully, by then she was somewhere she couldn't be found.

"I don't know, it's Thursday, try the unemployment office getting their checks." She said with a shrug. Just be calm and confident, you can pull this off, she thought to herself calmly. She was fine as long as he was still looking for her parents and that seemed to be his only concern. A little part of her relaxed slightly. This would be a good opportunity to study her enemy.

JOEY

Joey studied the girl sitting - back straight breathing shallowly because of obvious pain in her ribs or back. Her face was covered in a thick layer of makeup covering what he was sure was more than a swollen lip and eyes that almost didn't open. She sat there defiant with a mixture of pain, anger, and fear in her eyes. He recognized this look. She was a survivor. One day she would be a warrior, and she hated him with every fiber of her being. He could feel the hate radiating off of her like a furnace. It puzzled him and he wondered what Derrick had said to cause this.

"Where are your siblings?" he asked, glancing around the apartment. There was blood in the hall, probably hers from the looks of her face.

"School," she said with suspicion "why?" He got up and wandered to the stain and stared at it. She followed him with her eyes. She said nothing.

"Curious," he said, splaying his hands in what he had been told was supposed to be comforting, He didn't see how it was comforting but his wife told him it was so he tried.

"Your parents won't hurt you anymore," he said slowly. She snorted and cringed in pain. Dammit, she needs a doctor, Joey thought his blood was boiling. "Come on I'm taking you to a doctor"

"No offense, but no thank you," she said, jumping up and dodging back, keeping a healthy five feet between them. Now he was starting to get pissed, he needed to help her but she obviously had a huge fear of men, or was it just him? From what everyone said the kids were jumpy with sudden movements.

"As you said earlier, you don't really have a choice now do you?" he said firmly in a gentle tone. "You know who I am?" he walked over and took her arm, her whole body went rigid for a moment, hate shot from her eyes as he led her towards the door. He felt her try to shift away then gasp and growled low in his throat. He knew he was scaring her and she obviously hated him but she needed help and if she was too hard-headed to let him help, she would force his hand.

He knew this was a sticky situation as it was an internal family matter. The amount of abuse in this case forced his hand. He had decided the moment he saw Erin's face what needed to be done. Derrick and Mary Caruso would be found and unless he found any redeeming qualities they would both disappear. He would find a local family to take the kids in or talk to Carol, his wife, and take them in himself. He should have known about this sooner. Derrick obviously hadn't been hiding what he was doing to these kids. This was Joey's fault for not stopping it sooner.

"Yes sir" she ground out after a long staring contest. Joey grabbed the keys he saw on the counter and locked the door behind them, handed her the keys, and ushered her into the Bugatti. She let her fingers travel over the door and then the dash. When he started the engine he noticed her quick inhale. He didn't know if it was from pain or the thrill of the car which she obviously appreciated. He did note that she sat as far over in her seat as possible, almost pressing against the door. He mentally cursed at this.

"You know I talked to Eddie yesterday," he said casually as he pulled the car away from the apartment complex. "He had a lot of great things to say about you." Silence "He said you were his best student and still came to visit him." he was being ignored. He had two college-aged daughters, he'd seen the silent treatment before. They had never been able to hold out long but he may have met his match. "I talked to some of your other teachers as well" She had stopped caressing his car now and was listening it seemed but still not looking at him or responding. "I also talked to some of the other kids that are affiliated with our work"

"You mean kids of your employees" she snapped.

"Yes," he said evenly, ok that got a response and not a good one. "They said you don't hang around with them" She was back to ignoring him "They said you don't have any friends. All you do is school, work, and stay home. Is that true?" he asked a direct question. Can't ignore that!

"Sure," She said with a hint of sarcasm though, her eyes got slightly more guarded like she didn't answer truthfully. Why would she hide who her friends were? She closed her eyes and took small shallow breaths. She was in pain, a lot more pain than he thought and he hit the accelerator.

"Your school said you withdrew yesterday, got your GED" a grunt response. Joey considered himself a charming person but this girl must hate him, he wondered idly if she blamed him for the abuse. "What's your plan now that you're not in school?"

"Community college. Stay here until the kids are old enough to go to college" she said evenly "Work and help them" Her eyes remained closed and he wanted to reach out and take her pulse but he knew that would make her jump and possibly hurt herself worse. She was getting paler by the minute.

"Why did you want the truck?" he asked and noted the look of annoyance on her face.

"I was going to leave and take the kids with me," she said bristling at him "Since he took my money now I have to stay" Erin was angry again but he didn't quite believe her.

"How did you get that much money saved?" he asked, now time for the hard questions. He had done his due diligence before arriving this morning. He had spoken to her boss at the bowling alley and he said she always seemed distracted and had brief conversations with people who would leave immediately. "You work at the bowling alley right?" a nod, he drove the car into the urgent care driveway. "You've only been there about a year right? Part-time, that's not enough time to save up five grand if Derrick has been taking your money" Yea she was tense now.

"You have your business and I have mine," she said, her voice more mature and slightly taunting. "I stay out of yours and you stay out of mine," she said evenly. Joey had to grin as he hopped out of the car and walked around to open the door for her. He helped her out of the low car and walked inside. Now, Joey thought smiling, this is the interesting stuff. What has she been doing behind her old man's back and how was she going to protect them from their parents when they got back from wherever the hell they were? He walked with her to the desk and the nurse jumped up and ran over to him.

"Mr. Bonetti! Everything ok?" Stacy the nurse who was one of the wives of his guys came racing over. She was a tall thin woman with a high ponytail and lots of pens in the pocket of her scrubs top.

"Stacy thank the Lord you're on duty," he said warmly kissing her cheek. "This is Erin Caruso, Derricks girl" Stacy looked over Erin's face and arms and stepped back looking at Joey with confusion and anger. *She thinks I did this*, Joey thought "She needs to be looked over, clean that makeup off her, and see how bad it is. I need to see how badly we will be responding." Both women stared up at Joey in shock.

"You wouldn't," Erin said, slowly stepping away from both of them. She seemed to be considering him, her eyes going hard. He could almost see her mind racing. Yea, he thought, I'm not as bad a guy as you think. Maybe you shouldn't hate me.

"Yes, I would," Joey says evenly. This was his in with her. She's already prepared to take care of the other two but she won't have to now.

ERIN

Was he serious? How funny that the man she was going to take down as a pawn to draw out Marino was trying to help her and would even claim to defend her. Erin gave him a more appraising review. Letting this play out was dangerous. Her crew was too small. She was not in fighting form currently thanks to a little two-on-one action she had with her parents. She had only just gotten to the point where she had enough infrastructure she could finally start living off of her profits. It had been a long three years of building her empire and getting Joey right where she wanted him. As far as she knew he had no idea her organization existed. Billy Senior and Billy Junior were her face. They kept her the mysterious boss and she was sure they enjoyed it.

She decided she would continue on her path of building and strengthening her crew. The complication of her parents would be the downfall of this entire thing. She hadn't planned on her parents dying but it had become too hard to just take it. When they hit Josie and took away what little innocence she had left. This was her breaking point. She pictured them whipping and branding Josie and she had snapped. She thought back to those decision-making moments of the evening.

When they had come home she had retrieved her father's gun from under his bed and when they entered their room the look on their faces made it all worth it. "We need to talk" Erin had said, motioning them to sit on the bed. "Mom, Dad, you have both been terrible parents."

"Now Erin, we are your parents and you will put that gun down now." Her father started to raise his voice.

"Dad, I learned from you, that whoever has the upper hand is the one that's in charge. In this situation, who has the upper hand?" She wanted to hear him say it.

"You bitch." At that, she pulled the slide back on the nine-millimeter chambering the round and he fell silent.

"Now we are going to make some changes. I want to show you something I bought. Let's take a trip and know that if you try anything I will kill you first Dad." She was calm in her voice but her mind was racing. There was no actual plan at this point and she was a person that needed a plan. She was hurt badly but had a gun and that was a great equalizer as long as they stayed a distance away. "Mom go tell Theo and Josie to go to bed and stay in their room and meet us in the kitchen." Mary had gotten up silently and done as she was told.

Mary was the real tragedy, she used to be a halfway decent mother and she still put in effort with Theo and Josie, but her father had broken her down and she had complied with whatever he wanted. Erin never understood why she was the one they both hated. Like she was a reminder of when they actually felt love for each other, and now they just hated her. Mary had her own anger problems and though she was weaker, her abuse still hurt. She had followed her parents out to the car and sat in the backseat with the gun pressed to the back of her father's neck. She had him drive to the docks and loaded them on a boat.

"Who's boat is this?" Mary asked as she zip-tied Derrick's hands together. Her mother looked more curious than scared.

"Mine, see I stole from you Dad. I took some money you needed for work. You remember when that bag that you were carrying for Joey and you had gotten blackout drunk before delivering it. I took it, enjoyed the time you had a broken arm from your punishment though. I invested in it. You know what an investment is?" He cursed at her as she pulled the boat away from the dock.

"I'll tell you, you see yourself as a sophisticated wise guy. This boat is an investment that has your work family doing my bidding and paying me weekly. You always told me to be smarter than your enemy. You thought you were the smartest guy in the room but you're just a drunk." he cursed at her again when she turned the motor off the boat and let it float on the tide.

"You little bitch, you're not going to get away with this. Joey will kill you."

"Not if I kill him first," she said, shooting her father in the head. He fell back and off the boat into the cold deep ocean. Her mother screamed and the second shot killed her. She slumped onto the deck and Erin felt a mixture of emotions in that moment. Fear, terror, excitement, relief. She got her mother, after a lot of cursing, off the boat and into the ocean. She cleaned the blood as best as she could in the dark night and brought the boat back to her space at the dock. She had driven home with blood on her hands and arms and had added a huge wrinkle to her plan. Part of her revenge was going to be to show her parents what they had created and she *mused, she had done that in a way. They would never know the lengths she had gone to hurt them, to hurt Marino. But what was done was done and now they would never hurt Theo or Josie again. She felt free and like a superhero coming home from a big battle.*

Erin refocused on the current situation of the Urgent Care facility they were at. The Nurse looked anxious as she kept scanning Erin up and down. She took Erin's hand and they moved one step away from Joey. He wanted to protect her and exact revenge, well that would be a little hard now wouldn't it? Joey looked at her as if he was excited for some kind of reaction from her.

"We will see," she said softly, each breath hurting both her back and ribs. She let herself be whisked away by the Nurse and was very soon given a slight sedative. Joey remained outside during her examination as the chart was compiled. Three broken ribs, hairline fracture on her zygomatic, aka cheek, her back whipped and possibly infected, and the brand. Concussion to top it off. After she was dressed again they went out but instead of Joey, a beautiful woman in her late forties with dark chestnut hair, brown eyes, and a firm handshake, she introduced herself as Carol, Joey's wife. The nurse updated Carol on all of the injuries covering Erin's body, old and new. Carol brought Erin back to their home and they sat and talked about music and TV shows.

Carol snuck in casual questions about Erin's Family. Erin gave vague answers and texted Billy Junior that she had to push her meeting with him to later that evening. This looked like it was going to take a while as Carol showed no sign of letting her leave without Joey coming home first. She had already said she was making up the spare rooms for her siblings.

"I'm sorry, no. I can take them with me. I am Eighteen and I will get a place." True there wasn't a solid place yet but that was what she was supposed to be setting up. Plus with her parents gone, she could stay in the apartment for a few weeks until she found a better place. Erin watched the woman's face shut down.

"We can talk about it when Joey gets back. We are responsible for you all now that we know what's been going on." Carol's voice was filled with empathy and a firmness that said she was in charge. They were going to keep her siblings. Maybe they knew about her and this was their vengeance. His crew was stronger and she could not take them out yet. She did not sense any anger or negativity from this woman, but she didn't know Joey and Carol, how could she trust her siblings were safe? This was spinning rapidly out of control.

CAIN

Cain hated early mornings but he had prep work to do before going to the Hansons coffee shop. He got up made some coffee and scratched his cat's ear while filling her food dish. He looked around his flat went over to the bed and kicked the end of it lightly. Jarring the blonde from her sleep on his bed.

"I gotta go to work," he said softly. He hated when they slept over but he never wanted to push them out after a night of fun because that felt rude. He watched her shyly get dressed and fix her hair before saying the words they all say "So call me sometime this was fun" he grinned and shut the door after her.

Yea, it was fun but that's all it would ever be. He went to his wardrobe and put his holster over his white t-shirt. He checked his 40 caliber before sliding it in place and pulling on a black and white plaid button-up. He rolled the sleeves up to just below the elbow and pulled on his shit kicker boots. He slipped his backup piece, a twenty-two handgun in his boot holster and added a nine-millimeter

Glock to his lower back. He checked his reflection before draining his coffee and rinsing the cup. He pet the kitten on the head and she purred up at him. "Later Lady," he said, smiling down at the kitten.

Cain drove to the Hamilton Beach private docks to the dead drop that he checked once a week. There on an old cabin cruiser that never moved, was a bag that had ten bricks of cocaine, seventy bottles of various prescription pills, and a typed note with the bank account number to transfer payment into. He noted what looked like blood on the seat of the cabin and did not want to think of whose it could be. He turned to glance at the camera pointing directly at him with a remote-controlled bomb facing him. He pulled out his phone and turned to the camera "Calling for payment approval" he said to it and saw the light flash on the wall to show they were listening.

He had been doing this for a year now. *A letter had been delivered to him by some kid on the street with instructions for a discounted deal exclusively for the Italians. After debating with Joey on the validity of a deal, Cain went alone as instructed with a few guys waiting in the car. That first trip he had been shocked at the bomb and stood still for ten minutes trying to decide if it would go off before a voice that had definitely been altered scared the life out of him. "If you try and take the bag without payment, you will die. If payment is received the light will flash and you can take the bag. If the price is not to your liking you can leave the bag and this offer will be given to another." He sighed with relief and sat on the bench seat that ran along the edges of the boat, putting his head in his hands.*

Now he drives out there every Monday to do this trade. A different bank account every week, which would be emptied the same day most likely. They had tried to trace it but whoever this was had someone at the bank on their payroll. They always provided a great product that sold fast. Though they always included antibiotics, diabetes meds, and birth control which was indicated as free for those in the community. Once the payment was transferred to the account the light flashed and he waved at the camera before lifting the bag and walking out.

After dropping the sellables at the warehouse they set up four blocks away he took the free medications to a local pharmacy that had been designated as a drop point by the mystery supplier. The pharmacist thanked him and for the first time, revealed something new.. "If you talk to your boss let her know that we need some antipsychotics. We have an underprivileged family whose son has schizophrenia, and those meds are expensive."

"She?" Cain asked, raising an eyebrow. The man paled, realizing his mistake. Cain felt a thrill at finding out any detail about their mystery supplier. It made sense that a woman would be taking care of the community like this. He was sure it cut into her profits but they had been consistent. "Have you met her?"

"No," he said, "It, it, it was a phone call. The girl sounded young but I could be wrong. I'm terrible with that kind of thing." The pharmacist started babbling about his wife always telling him he was terrible at estimating age.

"I'll let her know, " Cain said with a smile. Now this was interesting, she called the pharmacist and she is a woman. He would find her one day. He and Joey had been so curious about this person that having even this small detail would have them discussing options and people for months.

Out of curiosity he drove back to the drop spot and got back on the boat. He saw the camera follow him as he sat on the bench. The light flashes once. "The pharmacist has a request. Got a family with a schizo kid. You may want to give him a call to find out what meds they need." There was a long pause then the light flashed again dismissing him. He nodded his head and got up to leave but paused. "Why are we doing this?" he asked.

"Because I can" the voice responded "Leave"

"Yes Ma'am," He said with a smile as he left.

Getting in the SUV he went to the office to pick up the guys for day five at the coffee shop. Over the weekend nothing happened, they sat watching the street with no visitors. If they didn't get any action today he would be installing panic buttons in all the shops they work with, to get immediate help there. They all got in, tired and complaining about the early time. The gang of guys were known to arrive early in the mornings during the coffee rush or when people were running errands before work. This made him think they had day jobs or were in school. They pulled up to the coffee shop and got out, wandering inside. Henderson was stammering in front of four black men with tight pants and leather jackets. They looked like greaser mobsters with similar buzzed haircuts and matching outfits. Definitely organized if their look was aligned like this.

"Hey guys," Cain said to his crew "It's our lucky day" He pulled out his forty caliber and pointed it at the lead jerkoff. The men whirled around to face them and his crew burst into laughter. High school kids. They were causing all these issues.

"Alright, who's in charge of the greasers here?" Cain asked, waving his gun at them as Hanson excused himself to the back of the shop.

"We work for Anton," the tallest of the boys said boldly. Anton the leader of a local gang that had been very strong up until five years ago when the Italians had forced them out. Anton was the reason Cain had caught his assault charge and done two years in prison. "He wants his corners back."

"No," Cain said evenly. "You tell Anton if he sends kids to our territory again they won't be leaving with a few bruises." He lowered his gun and the guys went after the boys, teaching them why you didn't mess with the Italians. After the morning workout of whipping the boys the kids ran back to their Lancer and peeled out Cain called Joey.

"Morning boss, we got a problem," he said before Joey could complain about the time. Cain felt rage coursing through him at the thought of Anton. He had used the police against them last time hadn't he. Even took that stand against Cain as a witness to the alleged assault which had been at most, mutual combat that Cain had prevailed in. He hated Anton. "Anton is making a move to come back."

"Shit," Joey said evenly. "Ok, I'll make a call and get more guys out there for now."

"Yea I'm thinking two crews out here and panic buttons in all the shops," Cain replied. He remembered when they had expanded five years ago and Anton had been strong but disorganized. He rallied his guys and they followed him because he inspired loyalty and high rewards. He was a charismatic guy and that always led to problems when you had a charismatic leader with high aspirations.

"Maybe it's a good time to lean on the boys in blue again."

"Agreed. Anything else?" Joey asked, sounding gruff.

"Dead drop is a woman," he said "She made a call to the pharmacist and Derrick didn't show up this morning with the guys. I left him a voicemail yesterday telling him where to meet."

"Interesting," Joey replied, Cain could almost feel Joey's mind clicking awake. "A Woman? Ok, have you called Derrick this morning?"

"No" Cain was sure Derrick wouldn't answer his call as they detested each other.

"Leave your guys at the coffee shop and meet me at the office, you're with me today," Joey said gruffly before hanging up.

Thirty minutes later, Cain sat in Joey's office as he made a few calls. He knew this was going to mean a war between Anton's crew and the Bonettis', and that wouldn't end well for either crew. It would open the door for the Irish to come in and sweep them both out. He didn't blame Anton for making the move though. They had gotten complacent and weren't pushing forward like they used to. Joey said if you got too big then you would crumble so they should be content with their area. Cain didn't agree with this, they needed to expand but they needed to grow as well.

"Thoughts?" Joey asked, after hanging up his last call.

"If we go to war with Anton the Irish are waiting in the wings to clean us both out," he explained evenly. Joey nodded "Peace isn't an option and we are undermanned. We need to recruit as Anton has been."

"We have never actively recruited," Joey said evenly "That's dangerous. Inviting outsiders into a family like ours." Cain and Joey had been down this road before, Joey was a purist when it came to the family but pure Italians were harder to come by, so there was always something else in the mix. Cain himself was one-fourth German thanks to his grandfather on his mother's side.

"I'm not saying go outside the Italians, I am saying get the Italians who aren't involved, to protect our community and grow it. Maybe calling in some reinforcements. Arizona, Nevada, maybe even Miami" Cain said, mentioning the offshoots that had moved to other locations. Joey looked at him hard for a full minute before moving back to pacing the room.

"If we call them in, you are not going to be my second anymore. Out of respect, I would have to choose Nevada," Joey said with a hint of bitterness in his voice. No one liked Marino in Queens. He was violent and fought dirty. He had almost been pinched by the feds the last time he had been there and he left Joey in charge thinking Joey would get pinched instead. Joey was smarter than that and Cain learned that Joey was a master manipulator, and while Marino played Chess Bonetti played Monopoly and he owned Boardwalk and the feds.

"What I am to everyone else does not change what I am to you," Cain said "I am your right hand and will always be your right hand. They only need to know so much about what we do. The dead drop, for instance, they don't need to know about that." They both knew the dead drop was what made them the most money. "They will want their crews to earn a cut out here, that drop needs to stay private. Select men that can be trusted; Freddy, Lorenzo, Gus, Tilly, those four can move that much on their own and can be invisible."

"Agreed," Joey said, throwing himself in his chair. "I'll make the calls. You look into the dead drop woman" Joey's cell rang and he smiled which meant it could only be one person. "Yes?" he said softly, "What do you mean she left? What about the kids?" he frowned "I'll find her, no I'll send Jenny. She may need a gentle touch with all that she's been through, are they ok?" he paused, opening a folder that was sitting on his desk. "I'll have Cain on it, why don't you bake a cake? All kids love cake, she told me the younger two like Chocolate. I love you too" he said before hanging up.

"How's Carol?" Cain liked Joey's wife, she was smart and submissive and yet couldn't be pushed around. She not only knew her place in this lifestyle, she thrived in it, ruling over the wives with an iron fist.

"She's good," Joey said "We got the Caruso kids staying with us now- well the younger two." Joey rubbed his forehead "It seems the oldest took off while Carol was dropping the other two at school and she didn't show up at work. There's something this girl has going on that's making her money but she's so hostile to anyone in the organization that I have no idea what she's up to."

"Want me to tail her?" Cain offered knowing Joey wouldn't want that.

"Nah, I am going to put Jenny on her, they are closer in age and Jenny wants to be more involved." Jenny Luco was the daughter of Gus Luco, one of their oldest guys who was ruthless and unshakably loyal. Cain nodded as Joey picked up his phone to make the call to Nevada.

"What do you need me to do for Carol?" Cain asked.

"She was supposed to try to find Mary Caruso today but with the amount of violence that we can see Erin went through I don't want my wife near that. You swing by their apartment today to see if you can find them. Take a few guys to Derrick's if he's home bring them. I want them both in front of me." Cain nodded and rose to leave as Joey made calls.

Cain picked the lock at the Caruso apartment and cringed at the clutter and dirty kitchen. Three kids made for a mess but they were older kids. The oldest was a woman herself now which was probably why she was giving Joey so much trouble. He saw the family crests and noted the Irish one looked like it had something on it, he took a closer look and cringed. Blood. He saw the blood stains in the hall on the wall and floor.

He poked his head into the rooms and noted the pulled-out drawers from where Joey had come back to pack up the kids' clothes. He picked up a small diary from what he assumed was the youngest girl's bed and slipped it into his pocket. He also grabbed the Nintendo

Switch and games he saw on the boy's bed. He would swing them by the house for the kids to have at the Bonetti's. He knew being in a new home was scary even if the people were nice. Having their things would help. He checked the parent's room and didn't find anything out of place but they definitely hadn't been there in a few days. He went back outside and motioned for the guys to leave.

CHAPTER FIVE

ERIN

*E*rin knew she had to disappear, she would find a way to get to her siblings later but it was only a matter of time before the Bonetti family would find out everything about her. Joey had picked up her siblings from school that day while she was in the hospital. He had made them pack a few bags of their things and moved them into his home with his wife. His children were all in college so their rooms were empty. She had stayed the weekend with them making sure they were well taken care of. Carol was kind and secure, she didn't act like her own mother, beaten down and vindictive.

Carol had brought her home from the Urgent Care facility and had a calm authority when she said, "You will be staying with us until we locate your parents" Her voice was light and soft and she didn't try to get her talking. They rode back to the house in silence with soft jazz playing from the speakers.

"What's the verdict?" Joey had asked over dinner of pizza and cheesy breadsticks ordered from a local pizza place. Josie had wasted no time in telling the Bonetti's that pizza was their favorite.

"Three broken ribs, fractured cheek, a concussion. Her back Joey, they whipped her and branded her with something" Carol said softly close to her husband as if trying to shield the two younger children at the end of the table who were immersed in a conversation about how cool the house was.

"Whip marks? A Brand?" Joey asked his wife concern and something else simmering in his voice as he glanced at Erin. Erin met his gaze from across the room where she stood near the table eating while standing because her back hurt worse when she sat.

"From the lamp cord Dad ripped out of the wall two years ago" Theo supplied easily "He called it the Erin tamer" Erin shot him a look and Theo looked down at his pizza, a flush creeping across his face. She couldn't believe her siblings chatting about the whipping as if these people could be trusted. They did not need to know how badly she had been hurt. They were her enemies. But then again, the kids didn't know that. They were just kids, she reminded herself, she had kept her hatred and anger to herself around them and always had. It was her burden, and though Theo knew about her organization to an extent, he didn't know much.

"He only used it on Erin, she's our protector" Josie put in her small voice scared "He tried to hit Theo with it once and Erin jumped in the way and started shoving him. That was a bad one, remember Erin?" Josie sounded like she was trying to sound supportive. She was so young and had seen way too much, yet she was so naive to the world.

"Yes I remember Josie. But that's family business, and these people are employers, not family. Where do we discuss family business?" Erin's voice was harsher than she meant it to be. "In our room," Josie said, looking at her hands.

"You can trust us," Carol said softly, looking at Josie who glanced up and smiled "We won't let them hurt you anymore" Could these people really want to save them? Had it been that easy all along, just tell Joey Bonetti what her father was doing? She looked at her siblings at the light shining in Josie's eyes. How hopeful she was and the small smile on Theo's face. They both looked hopeful, how could she take them away from this? She had to reevaluate her plans. She needed time away to think. She also needed to get to know Joey better. Her father had always described him as a hard man to please, and one who didn't care about his people.

Joey reached for a slice of pizza and Erin and Theo flinched back. Erin took two steps away from the table and Theo pushed his chair back. Joey and Carol exchanged a look with each other before he sat back without grabbing the pizza. Carol came over and served him a slice laying a hand on Theo's head softly. Erin watched Theo relax into the touch and hated that they had so few soft touches in their childhoods.

She watched Carol's eyes fill and she looked up at the lights. Tears? For her siblings. She felt warmth spread in her chest watching Carol not taking her hand away from

Theo who also looked hopefully at Erin. Erin smiled lightly and nodded at Theo and Josie.

"Erin, we each get our own rooms," Theo said changing the subject. Erin knew this was the best place for her siblings at least until Joey found out who she was. What she had done. Would he use them as leverage against her? She sighed resigned to know that she would have to leave them here because it would be the best thing for them.

"That's great," Erin said, smiling down the table. "Josie, what does your room look like?" she asked, and let her sister launch into the epic tale of her new room.

Monday morning after managing her side business in the morning and being coddled by Carol, she waited for Carol to leave to drive the kids to school before climbing out her bedroom window, and leaving with her clothes and cash. She wouldn't be able to take her parent's car but in New York, you never really needed a car did you? She swung by the bowling alley and picked up her last check. She needed a plan and to talk things out. She arrived at Billy's house and knocked on the back door. Billy Junior answered and ushered her in calling his dad. She sat with both of them in the living room of their two-story walk-up. Both men sat across from her as she sat on a couch as far away as she could be, in the recliner she was sure was usually reserved for Billy Senior.

She gave them a rundown of the situation with her siblings. "What happened to your parents?" Billy Senior asked.

"They are gone." She said simply.

"What happens when they come back?" Billy Junior asked.

"They won't" She saw the recognition in Billy Senior's eyes and he nodded. He shook his head at his son who was still blustering questions.

"You ok with that?" Billy Senior asked.

"Oh yea, it was always the plan, it just happened sooner than anticipated," Erin said, smiling darkly. "My problem is Theo and Josie are living with the Bonetti's and they don't seem willing to let them go."

"I could offer to take them?" Billy Senior offered "We don't have much room but they can have the office, we could turn it into a bedroom."

"No, for right now they are happier than they have ever been. Bonetti's wife, Carol, is kind and the kind of Mom figure they never had. I am going to use it to get close to Bonetti. He's not like my Dad described, he's not like you said." Billy Senior looked slightly uncomfortable. She knew that being in charge meant that she must be feared. Up until now, she had never needed Billy Senior to be afraid of her but she could tell he was uncomfortable and that was enough.

"I didn't know Joey well, he was always quiet and controlled. Smart for sure and he was a planner, like you. His plans always worked, that's why he got so high up so quickly. He took control of the planning for Marino and even helped plan the move to Nevada which I think was his end goal the whole time. Get rid of Marino without a fight and take over Queens."

"Why didn't you work for him?" Billy Junior just watched as his father became more uncomfortable with each question.

"Pride," he said simply. Erin just bet that Billy was burned he didn't get promoted. Joey had not promoted any of the old-school guys. His second was only twenty-three which was unheard of. Joey didn't seem to have shared his logic regarding his choice, but if what Billy was saying was true he had a plan. She couldn't fault him for that.

"So you work for me instead." It wasn't a question. She leaned forward and stared at her second in command "An eighteen-year-old woman" he was squirming "Why? I was sixteen when we started this, you were my first recruit even before Billy Junior, my best friend."

"You have a good plan, and revenge is something we both want. Marino is the true enemy, Joey is just in the way." Billy Senior said, and she could see his temper rising.

"What if I change my mind now that Joey has my siblings, will you walk? Or try to take over?" He looked shocked and blustered before anything coherent came out of his mouth.

"Are you saying you don't want to go after Marino?" Billy Junior asked.

"No, I still want that but knocking off Joey may not be the best way to make that happen." Billy Senior relaxed a bit leaning back on the couch.

"Then it sounds like we may need a new plan." He said and Erin grinned at him. "I'm with you, I have watched you grow and learn and plan. I trust your instincts and you are smart enough to know when to ask advice which I will always be here to give you." With that empowered speech Billy Senior looked like he had passed a test that he had been dreading.

"Good, now we need to lay low until my parents are found. They will be found there's a storm coming in this weekend that will likely bring them in." She saw the illumination in Billy Junior's eyes that he finally got where her parents were. "Billy Senior, I need you to go down to West Virginia and do a spot check on operations. Float the idea of expansion to Jose, Hector, and Gabriel to see if they can work up some numbers. Billy Junior gets with the LTs and reviews areas. I want you all to work up a schedule for your crews at the gun range. We need to be prepared because if they trace my parents back to me then it will cause problems. We also need to do a check on how big they are. Billy Junior, I want you to do that with Benji."

"Yes boss. Are you going to come out in the open?" Billy Junior was excited, he loved these meetings.

"Not yet, I think the mystery of who I am will keep our organization safe. Mystery can be intimidating right Billy?" She asked Billy Senior who nodded.

"Yea, you're terrifying to most that know about you. We have worked hard on that reputation, if word got out about your parents it would add to it. Just saying. We wouldn't have to say they were your parents."

"That would also spark a war with Joey which would put my siblings in the line of fire." Billy Senior nodded at this and backed off. He had aspirations of his own and she knew that. "We are going to grow and our area will expand. With that comes the need for more product, Billy Senior, when can you get out to West Virginia?"

"Today, I'll leave as soon as we break here." She nodded.

"I need a legit business to 'work for' to keep Joey off my back. What would be useful to our organization?"

"Cleaning service," Billy Senior said immediately. She could tell he had been thinking of this for a while. "Get some legit cleaners and customers and then have some who would clean up after our business. I can get a few names for you for that."

"Ok, let's do that. Billy Junior get someone to start recruiting for that. Moms, sisters' of our people if possible. I'll need a manager that can handle the day-to-day and give me alibis." She stood then "In the meantime, I need to handle some personal stuff today. I'll call you later." she said to both men and left through the backdoor.

Erin then headed for an abandoned boat on the water. She climbed aboard the old rusted cabin cruiser and spotted the blood she had missed that night. She scowled and went into the cabin.

Pulling out her laptop she set about setting up the website for her new cleaning business. She shouldn't make it look like it was hers, because if one weekend with the Bonetti's taught her anything it was that they were not going to let the Caruso kids out of their sight or protection, as Joey put it. She would be under a microscope whenever she went over there.

Thankfully, she had worked hard in school and was decent with computers. She also needed to set out a normal path for someone her age so the next step after

GED was college or in her case community college. Virtual classes only, or Joey and his men would find her and force her to go back, or worse, confront her on the location of her parents.

Erin leaned back and her ribs protested. She grabbed the pain pills that the hospital had given her and took two. There were so many things she needed to do now that she was all on her own to create a life that could protect and sustain her and her responsibilities. Erin laid back on the bed that had fresh sheets never slept in and closed her eyes. Later, she thought as the pills kicked in. Her mind wandered to the past.

"You little bitch" Her father spat at her as he ripped the lamp from the wall and pulled the cord off it. "How dare you dump our liquor. I worked my ass off for that money.

"You said you were quitting drinking" Sixteen-year-old Erin stood her ground with the empty bottles next to the sink "You said your boss got pissed that you were always drinking so you were going to quit at the new year and we would be a better family" She had known this was a lie but she had dumped the booze out of anger. She eyed the cord he was holding, fear gripping her gut as she backed away.

"I am in charge and it looks like you need a reminder. Need to tame you out." He said, whipping the cord across her face. She crumpled and hid her face which left her back open for the whipping to continue. He hadn't stopped until she was bleeding badly. Her entire back was wet with blood before he kicked her hard in the side and told her to clean up the blood on the kitchen floor.

He had kept the cord though and pulled it out when he had felt especially brutal.

Flash forward six months *Theo had broken the coffee table leg while goofing around. The cord had come out and Erin watched as her father had gone after Theo. The boy was terrified and huddled in a corner until Erin put herself in his path. She shoved him hard and started cursing at him. Saying every little thing she knew would set him off. She told Theo to go to his room and lock the door, which thankfully he had. That beating had lasted a long time. Her mother had joined in on that one when her father had gotten tired. Her mother had blamed her for driving a wedge in her marriage. Erin had taken her time and energy so she didn't look as good so Derrick cheated. So Mary cheated and Theo came along. Anger begets anger, Erin always thought when she dwelled on the root cause of their hatred of her.*

"You're lucky we don't kill your dumb ass" her father had whispered in her ear before leaving her laying in front of the bedroom door where the kids hid. She had laid there thinking of all the plans that she had been putting into motion. She had decided then to escalate the escape plan but it had still taken another eighteen months before the breaking point of a few days ago.

The next morning Erin got up and dressed slowly before heading to a local gym and purchasing a membership. She ignored the concerned looks she got because her face was still black and blue. The gym was close enough to the docks that she could go there to shower and work out when she was healed enough. She purchased a wifi booster from a local big box store and a new laptop that was clean. She signed up for college classes at the local community college for an IT program and Accounting. The counselor she spoke to informed her that taking on two degrees at once was not advised, but she had her reasons for needing all the classes so early. She left the boat once more that day to go purchase her books as the classes were due to start within two weeks. When she got to the school she spotted a tail at the college. She saw Jenny Luco trying to be inconspicuous with her bright bleach blonde hair and overblown outfit for a bookstore, standing by a shelf near the automotive section. She found all the books required, made her purchase, and with a major effort lifted the heavy books into her backpack which she carried in front of her to not touch her back. Her ribs were killing her and her back ached with the weight of the bag.

"Hey Jenny," Erin said walking by her she led the blonde out of the bookstore and into the cafe on campus. "Coffee?" she asked when Jenny appeared beside her.

"Sure, Joey is looking for you" Jenny was one of those girls that wanted to marry a working man but they didn't seem to be picking her up so she had obviously volunteered to work for the family.

"Of course he is," Erin said, ordering her coffee and moving to a table. Jenny followed quickly. "You can tell him that I'm enrolled in classes here and he can even monitor my grades if he likes. I will be sending money for the kids monthly and I will come by on Sundays for family dinner with the kids." Jenny looked shocked at how calm Erin was "Here is my cell number you can give this to him, it's a burner untraceable so he shouldn't try. He can call or text me anytime regarding the kids and

I'll drop everything, but I will not be going back." The barista brought over Erin's coffee and Erin rose slowly. "Jenny, next time try looking less conspicuous. Enjoy the coffee on me today." Jenny glared at her as she strode out of the cafe trying not to buckle under the pressure of the books on her ribs. She may not be friends with all the other families but she knew who they all were. She had been studying the families for a long time now.

On her walk back to the pier she thought back three years ago when she had intercepted a package meant for her father. It contained a large payment for what they called merchandise that her father kept complaining was "bunk shit". She knew the family sold drugs as well as accepted protection money from local businesses. They never sold in the neighborhood though, so she wasn't sure where they did that. She had taken the money without a thought of what would happen to the man when he was accused of not paying.

Her father had gotten his arm broken and was beaten badly. She had laughed at this because he deserved it. They had searched the house and ripped the entire house apart. That had been the first time she had seen her father look weak to others. He had begged Bonetti to forgive him, saying it must have been stolen out of the car where he had left it. He hadn't thought anyone would have the nerve to rob him. They had taken him out of the apartment to handle the beating. Then he was demoted, again, to low-level collections and assured the only reason he wasn't dead was because of how long he had been with them, and because Marino had heard about it, and called to vouch for him.

It had meant months with no beatings and that had left her strong to start her organization. Erin had immediately started researching how Cocaine was made and what made it "pure" as they always talked about. She learned a high altitude was needed with warm temperatures for the Cocoa tree to thrive and produce the highest quality plants. She had formed a plan that would take a full year to put into motion.

The first step, being fifteen meant she needed a different identity that would be able to make purchases as an adult. Using her school's computers she had logged into the dark web and organized an ID and that was the only transaction she had been stupid enough to do in person. She had met the forty-year-old man in the back of an arcade in Queens and he had laughed when he handed over her ID packet.

"This is an expensive packet to get you into the club's sweetheart" he had commented, making her smile lightly.

"Gotta be prepared" she had replied, shoving the packet in her backpack and handing him the ten grand requested. He didn't ask where she had gotten the money, just took it and left quickly. She had quickly made her next purchase of the cabin cruiser and paid for ten years of membership at this marena. She had told the man over the phone it was a surprise for her old man so he wouldn't have to worry about the dues for as long as he wanted.

Setting up the land in West Virginia had been the hardest part as she couldn't actually go to look at it so it was all handled via Google images and encrypted emails. She had always had a knack for computers and was a quick study. Having a photographic memory helped in these matters. She had bought three hundred acres in the mountains of West Virginia and immediately carved out the middle of that area for Coco trees. Because West Virginia did tend to get cold in the winter, she built a massive greenhouse there as well.

The most dangerous part had been approaching the Mexicans that ran the east Queens area with a job opportunity. This is when she approached Billy Senior. She recognized the need for an older man with experience. He had sat patiently listening to her plans.

"What's the point?" He had asked, "Why build all this when you could join Bonetti and work for him?"

"Because to take down Marino we need to go through Joey. Marino won't come back unless Joey is taken out. If we can make Joey rely on us for the product, we can control his wallet. We can pull it out from under him and cripple him, forcing him to call Marino for help. Then we come out in force and take him down." Billy Senior had studied her, and all the paperwork she had brought.

"First thing, don't bring official paperwork to anyone, even me. That's dangerous. Use a journal or planner for details you may not remember, not your phone, it's too easily hacked or bugged. No meetings with smartphones or devices. If there is a smart TV, Echo, Alexa, or Google device, don't talk until you're somewhere safe. Feds can turn on the microphone to hear what you're saying in any of those things."He had coached her and helped her refine her plan. He had met with the Hispanics for her.

They were a close-knit group that only wanted to be left alone so they had brokered a deal they had sent their best arborists to West Virginia and they now worked for her and fell under her umbrella of protection. They live on the property full time and though she was unsure at the time if she could trust him, Gabriel Cantu had worked out well. He grew the trees and managed her legitimate cocoa seed business of selling the beans to an American-made Coffee and Hot Chocolate company that was veteran-owned.

As well as a licensed Marijuana grower with distribution to two different states. He also packaged all the cocoa leaves and shipped them as compost to Brooklyn. Here she had a warehouse with five employees all who lived in the community of Queens that she served. They processed the leaves exactly as instructed and packaged them. She had them drop the bags off at the boat once a week and she dropped the note with the bank account number herself.

Another hard part for her had been figuring out how to maintain product year-round which was why the greenhouses had come about. The bank was easy as one of the employees from her warehouse, had a husband who worked at the bank, and for a modest fee, he would transfer the money to a cashier's check that she would deposit into a Caymans Island account within an hour of receiving the funds.

It had taken a year to set everything up, and then she had decided to approach the newly out-of-jail Cain. He had been out for two weeks when they approached him. He was cute and ripped, and she admitted her hormones had picked him. He was twenty-two and seemed important to Joey so she knew he would listen to him.

The bomb on board was fake but looked real enough and scared the crap out of anyone who got on board. We couldn't thank the world enough for Ring doorbells though because those were amazing. A voice changer from a joke shop, and she was all set.

Now here she was a year later with a little empire, and though she spent a good chunk of her money on the medications the people in her community needed, she had enough to pay for herself and the kids for the rest of their lives. Recently she had been thinking of expanding but a lot had changed over the last week.

With her parents 'disappearance', the kids now living with the Bonetti family. She felt like they were being held hostage. One thing was for sure, she couldn't live on this boat for long. The cabin was tiny and on Sunday evening her employees would be dropping off product and Cain would arrive Monday to pick up the bags.

She got back on board and unloaded her books in the cabin. She was going to be taking six classes starting in two weeks so it was going to be a lot to manage, so expansion right now wasn't a good plan. Plus it wasn't like Marino needed to come down right now so she had time to get to know Joey and decide which way her plans would go.

Getting her own place would be a smart idea but she didn't want to rent, and landlords were nosy. She booted the laptop up and started looking for flats to buy. She found an old repossessed townhouse on a block that was less than stellar but for her it was perfect. She sent the real estate agent a cash offer without looking at it. She knew the area was right, four blocks from the marina, a mile from the pharmacy, and five miles to the Bonetti house. Living in a big city had perks, she thought as she pulled out the old planner she was using to keep track of her time. Technology was great but everything could be hacked and fire could kill paper. Billy Senior told her that.

Planning was her strong suit and she was going to plan how to achieve becoming stronger than Joey and the Bonetti family without them even knowing.

CHAPTER SIX

CAIN LUCA

"Cain Brescia I would like to introduce you to Luca Morone, from Arizona. Georgie Lanza from Miami and Greg Marino from Nevada, the Dons have all come to offer assistance with the Anton matter." Joey sat at the head of the table in his dining room. His wife Carol brought in drinks for the men and quietly left the room. Cain noticed the slip of paper she had placed in front of Joey and smiled. His wife was a wise woman and knew how to inform her husband of things discreetly.

The Dons had not been assembled like this since Cain was nine years old and they all had dispersed to their corners of the country. Joey had once had to fly to Miami to help with a turf issue when Cain had been seventeen but he had left Cain back to work with the rest of the guys.

He knew that Greg Marino used to run New York and though the stories varied he left when the FBI started sniffing too close. He sent people to Arizona and Miami as well which had weakened New York significantly. Joey had been rebuilding what Marino had destroyed. There was not a lot of love for Marino but since he had the strongest and most profitable branch they all knew they could not complain. Or if they did he had the power to remove them. He had taken all of the toughest guys with him, all the hardcore killers. He was the most dangerous and ruthless.

"Gentlemen," Cain said, nodding at each in turn.

"Brescia, your old man died the year after we all left didn't he?" Luca said as if that wasn't a big issue. Luca was short and fat with a dark mustache and bald spot in the middle of his head.

"Yea, he was locked up doing work for the Marino family. Got into a fight he couldn't win." Cain said nodding to Greg, who nodded back.

"He was a good worker, from what I hear he was a crap father and husband. He was loyal though, and that you cannot buy" Greg Marino acknowledged the widely known fact that his father was abusive to his family. "We regret both his loss and his actions towards his family" he added nodding to both Cain and Joey. "I did not think you would work for any family with affiliation." there was a bit of reprimand in his voice. Cain realized he was upset that Cain did not work for Marino or offer his services. That was the way things were done. All those who worked for Marino here generally offered their services to him before going to any other Don. Cain hadn't done that, he had met Joey and stayed with him.

"I didn't intend to, but Joey is different, he is family." Joey smiled at Cain with pride in his eyes. "I would lay down my life for him any day" Cain finished, this was something that had been said before and it would be said again but he needed to make himself clear, he was Bonetti's man, and no one else's.

"Thank you, Cain, I wanted to introduce you as you have been running point on the Anton situation." Joey shifted when he heard the door open and they saw a kid stop dead. "Theo, Carol is in the kitchen. Can you go see her for me?" Theo nodded and backed out of the room pale and wide-eyed. "That is Theo Caruso, his parents have gone missing. We are attributing this to the Anton situation. Derrick was my collector for the area that has been under siege and he went missing the day we found out about all of this." Luca sat up studying the boy as he retreated.

"You taking in his kids?" Marino asked with respect in his voice.

"The younger two, his oldest, has been reluctant, but she comes to Sunday dinners to spend time with the kids, and hear about their school week." Joey said, "It's nice, she tries to leave me money for the kids, the girl works at a bowling alley" he laughed but Cain knew he was worried for the girl. "Girls got a good head on her though started college classes and is supporting herself at eighteen."

"Sounds like it," Marino agreed. "It's good to see a family that still cares for their people" The jab was a knock at Lanza who had lost a lot of support due to not caring for the families of his men when locked up or dead. Lanza ignored the comment.

"Yes, the families of our men are their support system so we need to be theirs. Speaking of, Cain, why don't you bring us up to date on the Anton situation." Cain stood from his chair and gave the men a run down.

Cain and his men had left one crew behind to guard the shops and went to explore other areas. To the east all the way to the river there was no one. That area had belonged to a Hispanic crew that minded their own business but it looked like they had vacated the area. To the west, Anton's crew was encroaching. They would come out and steal loot and rob people. They had started attacking anyone they suspected may be Italian which meant a lot of undeserving people were being injured. They even went after cops and their families. They had taken to a brute force mentality and they had the numbers. It was shocking what once was a small-time gang was now a well-organized crew of men and teens with one focus, getting more power. They all had the same look. Like an army. Which lent to the intimidation factor.

"Sounds like they grew up a bit since we last met," Joey said softly. He looked calm but the anger in his eyes made them flare and he was tense. "Thank you Cain please let us discuss this" Cain was being dismissed. He knew it was out of respect for the other Dons so it didn't bother him but he wouldn't be far. Cain went to the kitchen to find Carol sitting at the kitchen bar with Theo and a little girl, homework spread out. Carol was bouncing between them looking a bit frazzled.

"Hey Carol," Cain said, grabbing water from the fridge. "Need any help?"

"Are you good at pre-algebra?" she asked, glancing up from Theo's homework.

"I aced it" Cain casually moved over to the boy "I'm Cain" he said sitting next to the boy. He saw the boy tense and grip his pencil.

"I know," Theo said softly, his head never coming up.

"I know you're Theo Caruso too," Cain said in an equally soft voice "What kind of pre-algebra are we talking here?"

"Fractions but it's not due till next week. Erin can help me when she comes, she likes to help me" Theo said. Shut down, Cain thought to himself. He didn't miss how Theo angled his body away from Cain and leaned slightly away from him to give him more room.

"What did she say last Sunday?" Carol asked Theo, making the boy blush. He stayed silent. "I think she said that you need to try and get your work done during the week so on Sundays she can quiz you to prepare for the tests." Theo nodded and grumbled something.

"Well hey I can help during the week!" Cain said trying to sound excited "It would give me an excuse to come eat Mrs. Bonetti's cooking" Carol laughed out loud. "What do you think Theo, can I help you? It would ensure I'm well fed" Theo looked up at him and nodded slowly. This kid was terrified of men, Cain thought to himself. He could help with that, he was a big guy and imposing, but he was going to win this kid over. One math problem at a time.

"I guess," Theo finally said.

"Awesome, so what are we looking at here?" The kid pushed his book over so Cain could take a look and they dug in.

JOEY

Two hours later Joey came out of the dining room and escorted the Dons to the door. Luca lagged behind and looked at Joey with skepticism. "How is the boy Caruso doing? Was he hurt when you brought them in?"

"No he was fine, why do you ask?" Joey leaned against the door still wide open waiting for Luca to leave.

"He's mine. I had a thing with Mary on the side before we left and I found out she was pregnant the week we were leaving. Told Derrick to treat the kid right and I sent monthly support for him. I know Derrick hated Theo, Mary told me in a letter when she sent pictures once." Joey's eyebrows were so far up his forehead he thought they might leave his head. His head was going to explode and he tried to keep his face blank.

"He's scared of men and from the stories I have been told Derrick took out his anger mostly on the oldest girl. She protected Theo and Josie as much as possible. We are keeping them safe now." Luca looked put upon with this information.

"You find Derrick, you let me see him before you handle your business." It wasn't a question and Joey knew that. He could see the rage on the man's face and watched him smooth it out. Joey couldn't help but agree that the thought of all the kids went through made his blood boil.

"Of course. What are your designs on the boy now?" Joey asked, lowering his voice.

"I can't take him, Courtney would kill me and my kids would stop talking to me. I'll send my support to you from now on." Joey shook his head. He didn't need support from another Don, that would not happen. It did give him another reason to keep the boy safe.

"We don't need it, put it in a college fund for him. When you're ready, after Theo is settled we can talk to him together and introduce you." Luca nodded his appreciation and left slowly down the stairs. Joey shut the door and headed for the kitchen where he heard small voices.

Joey stood in the doorway watching Cain build a Lego set with Theo and Josie. Carol was packing their lunches for the next day. "...you have no idea she can handle anything, best person I know" Theo was telling Cain.

"She is, you would like her," Josie told Cain.

"Who?" Joey asked all three heads jerked up to look up at him. One with a smile and two looking scared.

"I am hearing the epic adventures of Erin, the sister who knows no fear and is the smartest girl in the world. She has a photographic memory, you know?" Cain said, smiling easily. "She is their hero, even better than you Uncle Joey" he laughed, making Joey clutch his heart.

"Well, we can't win them all and Erin sounds epic," Joey said, making Josie smile. "I look forward to getting to know her on Sundays when she comes to dinner," he said softly, ensuring the kids knew it would be on her terms. He had learned over the past few weeks that ensuring he moved slowly and spoke softly was important with these two. Theo still flinched if he got too close but he let Carol hug him that morning when he left for school.

"She's healing fast too," Josie said quickly "Did you see her face was mostly normal last week and I bet she looks fine this week when she comes." Josie looked at Carol.

"We still need to be gentle with her. Her left eye will still be bruised but the swelling should be gone. Those ribs are still going to be tender for a few months. Her back, I don't know how she's on her feet as it is. I wish she would at least stay here to heal." Carol sounded worried. Joey wished that too. The girl was a mystery, she kept herself away from everyone as much as possible. She sat across from her siblings at the table next to Carol's end of the table. After the kids went to bed she kept the kitchen island between herself and Joey at all times.

"Yea me too." Joey nodded to Cain to follow him. "Gotta steal Cain for a bit kids" They didn't protest but Theo looked a bit disappointed.

"I'll be back for homework tomorrow" Cain promised Theo and Carol smiled. Cain followed Joey out and to his study.

"Are you going to be a daily presence in my house?" Joey asked, sitting in his chair and rubbing his hands over his face.

"I am on homework duty, plus it looks like they need to get used to men in a non-incharge style so I can be that for them" Joey eyed Cain "You were that for me," he said the words that hung between them.

"I appreciate that," Joey said, it warmed him to know Cain thought so highly of him. He considered Cain the son he never had. He was strong and smart and sarcastic and just enough of a nerd to catch the details most people missed. Like when he brought over the diary and the nintendo switch for the kids. Details mattered to him.

"The Dons find it odd that there is no one operating in the East blocks, I know it's not much area but what happened to the Hispanics?" Joey asked outright, Cain shrugged.

"I have Gabriels number somewhere I can call him and see what's up. I know they were a small crew, only a handful, but for such a small area it's all they needed." Joey nodded his approval on this. "Picked up the shipment this morning and she got the meds the pharmacist requested already. Must have gotten in contact but damned if I know how, we tapped their phones back when we started this arrangement. Boat was a little odd this morning, like someone had been staying there. It didn't smell as musty and looked like it had been cleaned. I went a few weeks back and there had been blood on it. My guess whatever happened occurred at night and the clean up was missed until they went back."

"I want you to ask a question for me next time you go." Joey said looking grave "I want to know where this powder is coming from and if there was an option for expansion in the near future." Cain looked surprised, he had been pestering Joey about expanding for awhile now and it was past time he did. He didn't like Marino being the strongest of the families.

Joey hated Greg Marino with every fiber of his being. He had been set up to take the fall. He had watched Marino set him up and heard from his FBI contacts that it was coming. They had blocked it of course as they were on the case. Marino loved Joey's plans but he knew Joey could and would outplan him at some point. So he had crippled New York and taken the best with him to

Nevada and farmed out the rest to Nevada and Miami. Spreading them to thin and making deals that tied his hands. He had left liabilities like Derrick Caruso and Gerald Branzi who had both cost him millions of dollars. Gerald was dead and the only reason Derrick wasn't was because he had young kids, and Marino had already been pissed that Branzi had been killed. He shook himself back to the present as Cain responded.

"Yes boss," he said without question. Expansion had to happen if he wanted to take on Marino at some point. He needed to move forward with plans himself. He admitted he had gotten comfortable and complacent which is why Anton could get a foothold.

"In the meantime I want our guys moving East and securing the ocean. I don't want the Irish moving in that direction. We are getting twelve new crews of four men each from the Dons. Nevada is staying but Miami and Arizona have small turf issues of their own so they are going back to oversee their affairs. It's time we expanded as you suggested so I am going to have you running the dead drop and recruitment. Marino and I will coordinate the Anton issue and those crews. I need you behind the scenes to build up our ranks and handle the sales aspect. Take Freddy, Lorenzo, Gus, and Tilly like you suggested." Joey laid all this out. "Dinner is usually at six and homework happens around five but that may change. Carol is already talking about putting Theo in martial arts and Josie in gymnastics."

"Once a Mom always a Mom" Cain said "I will make myself available for homework whatever time it is needed" Cain smiled "They are good kids, no luck with the sister? How did Jenny do?"

"Jenny was spotted, had a coffee bought for her and then was told to do better at blending in. She's been caught four times which are the only times she's bothered to try. Erin sounds like a smart and tough cookie." Joey sounded proud yet distracted. He worried about the girl but she was an adult so he couldn't control her. "She's not staying in their apartment, I have no idea where she went but she's registered for six classes that started this week so I'm thinking she's going to be super stressed out with the homework load. All her classes are online though so we can't find her to follow her."

"Did anyone else try?" Cain asked "I could…" Joey shook his head. The girl was smart and fast. It was starting to feel like she was taunting him when it came to these tails.

"She caught skinny Pete and Tilly too" Joey laughed "She's good and for someone that Derrick kept away from us, she knows all our faces. She just walked straight up to the guys and told them to try again next time. Then she disappears into thin air. She's got three broken ribs and whip marks on her back and a brand! She should be slower."

"She's used to it," Cain said softly "From the sounds of it this isn't even the worst she's gotten." The anger that filled his chest was for any child abused by their parents. Both men had experience with it and both men hurt at the idea of the girl that stood in front of her siblings to protect them. Most kids would just be happy it wasn't them being beaten but to bring it on herself as much as she had, she was going to be a beast as an adult. Joey pitied the man she settled down with, he wouldn't get away with anything.

"From what little we have gotten out of those kids, she took it for them most of the time. The youngest Josie, only got a couple of smacks once in a while. Theo, he's a little trouble maker but even he has never broken anything. They would start on the kids and Erin would body-check them. She would take on Derrick and Mary knowing she was going to lose." Joey sighed "Those two are loosening up some at least, they are afraid of men mostly but even with Carol they flinch."

"Josie is your best bet" Cain said "She's a sweetheart and the way to her brother and sisters heart and she wants to be liked" Joey nodded. Josie was somehow a bucket of sunshine even if she was timid. She wanted so badly to have a family and be a kid, and Joey wanted that for her. She was already making more friends at school and had a playdate set for this weekend.

"You know Derrick told his kids that because they are half Irish they shouldn't associate with the other kids. That they were unworthy of being Italian." Joey spat with disgust. "That's terrible," Cain said with disgust in his voice. "They will be ok, so will Erin, you just need to give them time. Still no sign of Derrick and Mary?"

"No not yet and I don't know if it was Anton or not. They may have run off since he wasn't doing his job." Cain nodded and Joey silently wished that they wouldn't come back for the sake of the kids. He and Carol had already decided they would keep them. He knew other families would volunteer but he had missed this and he felt he needed to make this up to them. Josie reminded him of his own daughters and it broke his heart. As Cain left he picked up the phone to call his oldest daughter Maria.

CAIN

A few days later Cain got a call from their NYPD contact informing them of two bodies discovered in the water. Tilly had been sent to confirm the identity of Derrick and Mary Caruso. The pictures he brought back had told a story. Their hands had put up a fight, or been used to hit a lot. Derrick had been shot in the face while Mary was shot in the chest. They had no damage to their bodies apart from the hands. The bullets didn't match anything in the system so the gun was not registered.

Cain delivered the news to Joey who cursed and rubbed his face. As Cain left the house Joey was calling Luca for some reason to inform him. Cain felt that this was good news

for the kids but bad news for the family. You couldn't take the murder of one of your guys laying down, and they needed to find out who was responsible for that.

Craig Dillard was put on the case for the NYPD and as he also worked for the family he shared his reporting with Cain. They had been taken there in their car with Derrick driving. Whoever had shot them rode in the back seat and wore a black hoodie and jeans. He watched the footage of Derrick and Mary getting out of the car in the parking lot of a local marina. The marina itself had no cameras but the bar across the street had cameras that caught the car entering and three figures got out of the car and walked down to the docks. They couldn't see anything below past the cars. Two hours later the figure in dark clothes got back in the car and drove back the way it had come.

Searching traffic cameras the Detective said the car went back to the apartment complex that Derrick lived at. This made sense as their car was still outside the apartment in his assigned spot. Person was hunched the entire time so size would be difficult to estimate. No defining features could be seen in the grainy picture. This was going to be a tough one. Cain told Craig to keep him informed as they dug in and he would have his men ask around.

The tight jeans may be a member of Anton's gang. The hoodie wasn't the standard leather jacket but it did serve to disguise whoever wore it. This would be first blood with Anton if that were the case. Derrick was well known and his reputation preceded him everywhere. He would likely be a great first target, take out the most vile to show you're not afraid. Cain could see the logic in this but the wife too? That's crossing a line, even if she tried to defend her husband. Why were there no marks on them? No fight back to whoever they beat, likely their daughter. Derrick never tried to make a move, maybe doubted it would come to this in the end, waiting for his perfect time.

Cain thought that no matter the person it meant that they were ramping up for something big.

CHAPTER SEVEN

ERIN

*E*rin changed into a pair of thrift store jeans and
a thermal shirt that was tight but warm. Pulling
on her a new baggy white zip-up sweater she was
ready to go. Her face was completely healed and her back
no longer hurt and only mildly itched where the scabs
lingered. The pain in her ribs was still there and it would
be for a few more months. She arrived after a brisk five-
mile walk to the Bonetti household. Over the past two
weeks, he had tried to have someone tail her back to the
boat but she had caught them easily.

Over the week she had completed her first week
of school attending classes virtually and turning in
assignments. She had also been informed that the Italians
had moved into the east territory. She had been recruiting
more for her crew to protect the area and gave them strict
orders to not engage or piss off the Italians. Her crew
was more diverse not just taking pure-blooded Italians
but any percentage was welcome. She did not meet them
in person, but sent Billy her second in command but they

all thought she was older and more mysterious than any of the other crime bosses. Her crew once standing at Thirty people now was well over a hundred. She was creating a nice little family that would eventually help her rule over all the other families.

Billy Senior and Billy Junior were the only ones who knew she was in charge. Everyone else referred to her as "The Woman" and she liked it. It kept her distant and scary to not only her crew but to outsiders where her reputation was slowly growing. Billy Junior had been her only friend all through childhood. He had hidden her from her father and cleaned her up on multiple occasions. He was mostly Irish but what little Italian he had in him made him loyal to her.

She had three rules: follow simple instructions, go to target practice once a week to ensure improvements and lastly do not get in the way of the Italians until told to do so. Truthfully she didn't want to go against the Italians, she just wanted to take over the organization. They were scattered families spread across multiple states, all not answering to one boss just relying on the old ways to ensure they all prosper. That wasn't going to be the way. Eventually, she would unite them all.

She jogged up Bonetti's front walk and rang the bell. Carol opened the door with a smile ushering her in. "Erin the kids just finished their homework and can't wait to see you"

"Thank you, how have they been?" she asked and both women knew it wasn't just a pleasantry. Erin was concerned about the transition for them and how they had been treated.

"Good I think, I want to talk to you about them after they go to bed tonight. We have some ideas to help them integrate and be more protected. Also Joey would like a word in his office before you see the kids. It's important." She showed Erin the way to the stylish wood desk, she wondered what type of wood was that dark and shined like it was polished daily. He had a desktop computer on one side leaving the vast majority of the desk available for him to look across at you and give lectures.

Joey Bonetti was not alone. A man sat across from him and stared at her. She searched his face and racked her mind for the name to match the face. She froze immediately and glanced between the two men. She felt herself going pale. It was too soon for him to be there, her heart ached as rage filled her at the sight of him. She was nowhere near ready to face him. Panic clutched at her throat and she took a breath and made her face smooth out. Control, she thought to herself, Control!

"Greg Marino," she said in a small voice. They knew! They were going to kill her and keep her siblings. They found the bodies or even worse they knew about her people and this would be an execution. She knew it had been too soon, she moved too quickly, she should have waited.

"Yes," Marino said, surprised, scanning her up and down, obviously trying to place her in his memory. "Most young people don't know who I am," he murmured to Joey. "I saw your picture once, my Dad told me who you were." her eyes were locked with Joey's searching for an indication of the type of meeting this was going to be.

"Sit down Erin" Joey said, his voice soft and coaxing, like he was talking to a scared animal or tiny child. She did as she was told her skin was getting tighter on her body. Her entire body screamed "RUN" but she sat, still searching Joey's expression. He paused glancing at Marino then back to her. She would wait, no matter what happened she would face it.

"I wanted to talk to you alone before we told the kids. This is going to come as a shock but your parents," *I knew it*! She thought, closing her eyes as if pained. "We found their bodies. We believe this was a retaliation from some rivals in our area, and we will handle the funeral when the police release their remains. I know you kids had a difficult relationship with them but with this finalized I would like to give you a moment before we discuss the kids."

She kept her eyes closed for a moment trying to hide the relief she felt. She knew her body had relaxed the moment he said it was being blamed on a rival. Though it probably appeared to be after hearing they were dead. She sat for a full minute in silence as she worked through the emotions running through her. She stood and walked around a small couch that ran sideways through the room off the desk. She walked to the window and looked out, the distance from them helped.

Anxiety still high, she felt her eyes fill and willed the tears away. She would not be weak in front of her enemy and Marino was definitely her enemy. She would be strong and be as stoic as any Don would be.

"Thank you for telling me privately." She took a deep breath preparing the request she knew would be denied but she had to ask, beg if needed. She placed her hands on the back of the couch and leaned for the first time ever toward Joey. "I would like to take custody of my siblings when I turn Nineteen. In the time in between I will find us proper accommodations and ensure my work schedule is consistent to be available after school times."

She felt Marino jump at her request and look between them confused. Joey looked both surprised and a hint of awe if she wasn't mistaken. Marino kept his eyes on Erin and she struggled to decide if she should be trying to look more sad.

"May I give Mr. Marino some context into why you would respond like that?" Bonetti asked kindly. She nodded and looked down at her shoes as she listened to Joey list her injuries currently. He stressed the brand and whip lashes. Marino took a sharp inhale when he took the photos the hospital had taken of her back. "Yes, Erin was in a very bad situation that no one thought to tell me about. I have had discussions with all of my men and my wife has spoken with all of the wives'. If anyone is being abused like this I need to know." There was a grunt of approval.

"My request sir?" she asked, trying to sound like she was not embarrassed that Marino of all people got to see her in a weak position like this.

"When do you turn nineteen?" he asked, sitting back in his chair and considering her.

"In ten months" she said evenly. That was almost a full year that they would have with Joey and Carol and she could see how they looked as a family and learn how to provide that for them herself. Her original plan did not have her calling Marino out here for another two years. If she could find out why he was here maybe she could help him to go home. Why was Marino here? Was Joey in trouble? Erin felt a fresh wave of fear and glanced down at the couch.

"We can discuss it in ten months then. For now we need to let your siblings know and I think you should be the one to tell them. If you want I can do it for you but I thought you would want the choice." Of course he wasn't going to give her the answer. She looked around this grand room with bookshelves covering two solid walls and a giant window with thick bullet proof glass showed the brisk fall evening. He would do this for her if she let him, she could feel the need from him to lean on him at this moment. She would deny him it again, she felt odd that she felt bad about not giving Joey Bonetti what he wanted.

"Can I use your office?" she asked, her voice soft and defeated. She knew in ten months he would have a reason, probably a sound reasonable one that kept her siblings with them. She couldn't say they were being treated badly. They were thriving. He nodded and rose with Marino who looked at her and attempted to pat her shoulder, she leapt out of the way and she hit the window frame and cursed low and long. Her ribs shot pain threw her body causing her string of profanity to be choppy and gasping.

He stared at her with concern in his eyes and Joey gripped his shoulder and murmured something too low for her to hear. Jumping like a scared sheep in front of Marino galled her. She huffed and paced away putting her hands on her hips, if it had been anyone but Marino it wouldn't have galled her this much. She needed to find a way to stop doing that. Thankfully the only people she didn't flinch around was Billy Junior and Senior. She had known them so long, and trusted them completely. She tried to tone down her glare at Marino as he stood with what looked like surprise and concern.

"Even the family we hate is family. I am sorry for whatever part of them you will miss, girl." With that he left, striding from the room with confidence. She pondered what part of them did she miss? A flash of pre-drinking days came to mind. Mom happy and laughing and Dad still stern and overbearing but strong and watching with contentment. Then Dad lost his job and Mom had cheated. Theo came along and then Josie and they had never known the happy Mom or the sober Dad. She alone got those moments, which made it ten times worse that they had turned on her.

Theo and Josie were ushered in by Carol and both were thrilled to see her. "You look all better!" Josie said, bounding into her arms. She gasped and Carol rushed forward. "Josie gently, remember her ribs" Carol's soothing voice was reminding her sister. Carol helped Erin sit and the pain started to subside.

"I'm sorry" Josie gripped her hand and she smiled at her.

"All good kid, don't worry about me," Josie smiled back. "I got some news I need to tell you.

"You're leaving?" Theo said the accusation in his tone. Theo knew about her crew and knew that one day she would likely have to disappear at least for a little while. "You can…"

"No! Never, why would I ever leave you?" She asked "We are Family, I am your family and you will never lose me when it's my decision." She hoped that conveyed enough. She knew this office had to be bugged and didn't want a utterance of her organization to come out.

"Then move in here" Josie demanded. Erin sighed and laid her head against Josies. Carol made a discreet exit now that she was sure Erin was ok. Josie was still in the dark, she was too young and hung onto her childlike naivety.

"I can't. I have some issues that I'm working out and I can't do that here. I will be here every Sunday rain or shine for dinner and updates. Hopefully one day you can come live with me, but in the meantime, you two need to go to school, do good and do what the Bonetti's tell you. They are nice people who seem to care, if you're lucky you can have a real family with them." Erin had to tell them and she wasn't sure how they would react. "Let's sit down."

After they were all seated she took a deep breath, her ribs smarting as she did so. "They found Mom and Dad, they were killed in the line of duty." she rushed to the finish, eyeing Theo.

"Did you kill them?" Theo asked, his voice harsh. Erin didn't flinch at this or act surprised. It was no secret she wanted them dead. She was annoyed he had asked here, but in reality where else could he ask?

"They died in the line of duty according to Joey Bonetti" She had to be clear on this, one day she could tell the truth to her siblings, but this room was probably bugged. Theo's eyes shone with various emotions.

"That's the story then huh?" His voice was kinder now thick with emotion. Josie sat quietly looking at her hands. Erin let the weight of it sink in. Their parents were gone, they were free of the pain and stress. The anxiety of what will set them off, washed away.

"Yes, that is what Mr. Bonetti just told me." Theo scoffed and looked at Josie

"How are you feeling Jose?" Erin asked, crouching down in front of her.

"This means they can't hurt us anymore right?" The hope in her voice brought tears to Erin's eyes.

"No baby, they can't hurt us anymore, we are safe." Erin hugged her sister and felt the crush of her brother joining the hug. Her ribs hurt and her back ached but she clung to them. These two had gotten her through and made the pain worth it. Their constant love for her made her feel like the superhero she wanted to be for them.

"Thank you" Theo whispered in her ear. The terror was over, the fear for them of having to go back to the apartment. They all clung to the hug for a long time just holding each other.

The kids weren't in a cheerful mood but they weren't depressed either. They ate their dinner with a quiet conversation about school and the week they had. Theo had a new math tutor, Mr. Cain Brescia, Joey's second in command. He came over every weekday night to assist with homework for both kids and stayed for dinner. Theo and Josie were smitten and kept saying they should introduce him. Erin smiled thinking about her current business relationship with Cain. She had to admit when she started the business relationship it had been because he was close to Joey. Now she enjoyed looking at him through the camera. He was always dressed well but not flashy. His five o'clock shadow was perfectly trimmed. Plus he was tall and she definitely had a thing for tall guys. Not that she had dated anyone, hard to explain to your boyfriend where your bruises kept coming from. Plus she flinched way too much when men were around.

"He sounds nice," she said for the eighth time, glancing up with a smile for Carol and Joey. "So did you join the cross country team?" she asked her brother sitting back in her chair and wiping her mouth with her napkin. This was the only real meal she had eaten all week.

"I went to the lunch meeting but Mrs. Bonetti is already doing enough. The race schedule is crazy and practice every night after school for an hour, it would be out of the way." These were all the excuses her father had said to refute any of them joining any team.

"I think cross country is a great idea," Joey said easily "We can swing after-practice pickups. What time do they end?" Joey was trying to sound offhand but Erin worried it would be asking too much as well.

"Five PM daily," he said looking up "This is just the prep team, the serious team is high school though, so I don't have to..."

"Nonsense," Joey said "I will pick you up myself on my way home from work, that way Carol won't have to go out twice and I would love a schedule for the races so we can go to some of them" Theo flushed. Erin beamed at Joey and he looked like she had slapped him.

"Ok I'll talk to the coach tomorrow," Theo said "Thank you," he said to Joey looking the man in the eyes. Joey lit up like he won the lottery. Yea, Erin thought, Theo wasn't big on eye contact with authority figures.

"Anytime Theo, any club or activity you want to do let's do it, school is the time for you to learn and grow and find what you want to do with your life," Joey said joy pouring out of him. Theo just made this man's night by looking him in the eyes. Theo flushed and nodded. "I wish I had clubs to join" Josie pouted "fifth grade blows"

"I'm sure we can think of something," Carol said conspiratorially to Josie who lit up like a Christmas tree. They were being so kind, that Erin blinked rapidly for a moment. Her heart swelled to see her siblings shining with Joey and Carol.

"Erin, Carol helped me bake cookies yesterday. Do you want to try one?" Josie bounced up from the table, clearing her and Theo's plates.

"I would love some cookies," Erin said smiling at Josie who was pure joy. You wouldn't think losing your parents would relax them as much as it did but both Theo and Josie were so much more relaxed now than they had been in their entire lives.

After Theo and Josie were off to their rooms Carol poured Erin a cup of coffee and they sat at the bar in the kitchen like old friends. "I wanted to talk to you about extracurriculars for the kids, I know Theo will be doing the racing but I have ideas."

"I love that idea. What options are you thinking of?" Josie loved horses and dancing. "With my twins I wanted them to know an instrument, learn Italian, and do a sport or something active." Carol said "I'm not saying start all that with them both as that's a lot and this time has been a big adjustment." she added quickly "I was thinking for Josie we could do gymnastics. And Theo I was thinking of some form of martial arts to build his confidence and help him be more comfortable with men."

"I like both of those ideas although I know Josie likes to dance as well. I would be willing to pay for both depending on how often it is. I don't want to put you out running all over the place. You already are taking on so much and I wish you would accept this." She passed an envelope with four hundred dollars in it across the counter. She could afford more but she noted both her siblings wore designed clothes today so Carol had obviously been spending money on them apart from groceries and gas.

Joey came out of nowhere and grabbed it counting the bills before adding some cash to it and handing it back to her. She flinched at his quick movements but kept her seat, so that was progress. Her ribs ached from all the flinching earlier.

"I wish you would stay here and tell me how you are making this money?" he sounded annoyed, Erin's whole body clenched "I know you quit the bowling alley and I don't want you out there hustling the street for money. You're better than that and we can provide for you. We owe you that."

"You owe me nothing," she said, a hint of the anger that still burned inside her, sparking her voice. Erin cursed herself and put effort into calming her tone down. "I owe you and trust me, Joey, I'm not doing what you think I am to get this money." She pulled out a brand new business card with a cleaning service on it. "I got a job at a cleaning service. I volunteer for the hoarder houses to get paid extra. It's a really good gig"

"You can do that around your classes?" Carol asked concerned, "How was your first week?"

"Good, a lot, but it was good. I think I have a schedule down to handle the coursework and my new job. I'm getting in the groove of things." Erin liked Carol. She was nice, but she wasn't a push over.

"Where are you staying?" Joey asked, sipping his coffee. He had asked the question each time she had come for dinner. She smiled at him but didn't respond. "Come on Erin, how can I protect you if you don't let me"

"I don't need your protection," she said, standing easily. "Have you given up on sending your guys to follow me? It looks cold out and I don't want to have to walk to the Bronx to lose them tonight." Carol looked shocked.

"Joey, you tell them to leave the girl alone," she said, swatting his arm.

"No," Oh this was his Don voice. Erin took a hesitant step back at this tone. "She is our family's responsibility, I don't care if you don't trust me. I will try to protect you."

"And I will evade you and your goons," She said, pulling her jacket over her thermal.

"Alright you two, stop" Carol's voice was sharp and both stopped looking at each other and slid their gazes to hers. "Erin, we are deeply saddened by the life you and your siblings have led. Joey had a similar but not quite as horrific childhood which is why he is so passionate about this. Joey the girl is you twenty-five years ago. You didn't trust anyone either. Give her time and make the guys stand down."

Erin appreciated Joey's position but it was highly inconvenient for her plans to overthrow him if he wanted to have oversight of her all the time. She needed this relationship to be a positive one for Theo and Josie's sake. Be kind, she told herself, eventually he would regard her not as a child to be protected but as a rival to be handled.

"I appreciate all you are doing for Theo and Josie but that is already more than I can ever pay you back for. These extra activities, and getting them a tutor. You have gone above all expectations. They are less broken than I am." Her voice was soft as she said it. She needed him to be ok with leaving her alone and give her space to operate. "I need to be alone right now to set myself up for taking them when I turn nineteen."

"Ok Erin, if you do need something will you let us know?" Carol asked in the most motherly voice she had ever heard. She imagined that Carol was a good Mom and wondered what it would have been like if she had been raised by someone like her and Joey, rather than her own parents. "And if you need to talk to someone we know of a great therapist that has a private clientele"

"Text me his contact information" she said, maybe she could find help to stop flinching around men. She needed to break that cycle fast if she wanted to come out into the open. "If it is acceptable, I will see you next Sunday, you have my number if you need me."

"Can I get you a real phone?" Carol asked after a pause "One you can listen to music on? Or download apps?"

"I have one," Erin smiled. "I just don't carry it most of the time. I like my nice untraceable phone. It serves its purpose." with that she smiled and instead of walking out the front door she went out through the kitchen and wandered off through the backyard jumping their fence, hopefully the tail wouldn't see her leave this time. She saw the shadow of her tail moving quickly to catch up. After three blocks she rounded a corner and waited, Jesse Giampa rounded the corner and jumped when he saw her waiting for him.

Jesse Giampa was her age, still in high school. He was tall and attractive and if she recalled, very popular. His dark chestnut hair was styled in the hair swoop that was popular today and his dark eyes shined with surprise. "Running errands for your Dad?" she asked softly. He blushed and stepped back, "Go tell him, I said your tailing skills are worse than his."

"I just wanted to talk to you" the boy stammered looking upset.

"No" She said, smiling before turning and blending into a crowd crossing the street. She heard him call her name but she moved quickly and blended well. She lost him completely ten minutes later and doubled back. She walked in the shadows past the Boretti house and saw her siblings' windows turned out for the night. She could see Joey in his office with another man she didn't recognize. They seemed relaxed, smoking cigars. She put her head down and kept walking all the way to her new brownstone. She walked in and turned on her alarm system after locking up. The place was a foreclosure that had been trashed out and needed a lot of work but it was an opportunity for her to add things she wanted to it. She unrolled her sleeping bag on the first floor living room floor and opened her planner for the next week.

Her life was highly compartmentalized at this point and she knew it was not going to be easy to maintain. She figured she could spend Monday splitting her day between school for the week and cleaning out the trash in the house. She would manage her business as needed and take each day as it was.

Erin grabbed her phone and dialed the Billy O'Riely's to debrief.

"Yes Boss," Billy Senior said

"Hey, where are we?" she asked laying on her stomach and doodling on her planner tasks that needed to get done.

"Shipment is on. The boat night guard is there as usual, waiting for Brescia's arrival in the morning. Got some new, old faces around our area, not sure who they belong to."

"Marino is in town." She supplied helpfully.

"What do you mean in town? He didn't just send men?" Billy Senior sounded more alarmed than she had been.

"Yea I saw him tonight at the Bonetti's. They found my parents bodies as well, they are blaming someone for it. A rival they said, I can't remember the name, I was too relieved they weren't blaming me." Erin thought about that for a moment. If Marino was here with men then there must be a threat too big for Joey to handle. Could the kids be in danger?

"Must be something big going on." Billy Senior confirmed.

"Want me to find out?" Billy Junior volunteered.

"Yes," Erin said softly. "We need to know what it is."

"May be a good way for us to be introduced, if we want Bonetti to trust us. We already work with them, solve their problems for them. Bolster your reputation. Bonetti is recruiting too and taking some good people. He's going to know about us soon as some of our people are being approached." Billy Senior put in.

"Anyone taking up the offer?" she asked with a stab of fear in her gut.

"No, they all report when it happens." Billy Junior said easily. Thankfully her people were loyal.

"That would officially mean we would be removing Bonetti from the line of fire," Erin said thoughtfully. Get him on her side and they could take down Marino together. "Find out what the problem is first."

"Will do," Billy Junior said happily.

"Get some rest tonight guys," she said and hung up on them.

Marino being here meant that there was a war brewing and that couldn't be good. If there was a war that meant her siblings would be in danger and it also meant that she needed to find out what was going on and ensure it was handled quickly and safely.

Erin also now had to plan to open a legit business, a dispensary she was opening for Marijuana that would be in Brooklyn. She would get Billy Junior to work on the staffing for the dispensary as Senior was working on the cleaning service. She firmly believed having legit businesses that did not touch her illegal ones would keep her off people's radar for the most part. This was the problem with most criminals; they only relied on their criminal enterprises to support them. She grabbed her keys and headed to drop the account number at the boat before calling it a night.

War would mean her siblings could be in danger. Was it worth befriending Joey in hopes that he won't stop her from hurting Marino. It would all depend on how he responded to making contact with her on her terms. With how often she flinched at sudden movements when not on high alert she couldn't handle a sit down.

Tomorrow would be a day of wonders, she was going to extend the olive branch and the Italians would know about her. Excitement and anxiety rushed through her at the thought. She needed to stay distant but also have an on-call point of contact.

Erin drummed her fingers on the notepad she was writing notes out on. Cain was already so involved with her and her family that it was only fitting that she pulled him a bit closer. He was a strong attractive man so making him jump through hoops for a bit could be fun. She spent the rest of the evening planning how to be mysterious while introducing yourself.

CHAPTER EIGHT

CAIN

Cain woke Monday morning with a groan. He didn't like having unfamiliar crews working their area. Recruiting was going ok but a lot of the Italians or part Italians he was approaching were declining and one had slipped up and said they were working for someone already which was troubling. Were the other Dons recruiting in their area? An internal war would be catastrophic for all of them. He dressed and got ready to pick up the dead drop.

When he arrived he saw the flash of the camera light acknowledging him and grabbed the paper with the transfer orders. He handled the transfer then turned and sat down on the bench looking at the camera.

"Are you listening?" he asked and the light flashed. "We are looking to expand and wondered what you could do for us?"

"By how much?" the garbled voice came through the speaker if he had to guess it sounded tired.

"A third more?" Cain asked, pulling the number out of his ass. He hadn't thought to ask Joey that question. That would have been a good question to know the answer to.

"Yes, starting next week." Agreed the voice.

"Thank you, Ma'am," he said with a smirk. He knew she was a woman and he wouldn't let her forget it.

"Leave Cain" the voice responded reminding him that she knew who he was which topped knowing one small detail about her. He nodded and grabbed the bag leaving the boat. He dropped the prescriptions at the pharmacy after handing off the bag to the warehouse. The pharmacist now didn't meet his eye and was very short with him.

He went out to meet with his crew of Freddy, Lorenzo, Gus, and Tilly to discuss recruitment. They had been approaching people from the area and needed to branch out. East was full of decliners and mystery crew. He had a meeting with a group of younger guys from the east today that would hopefully bring light to this new crew when his cell phone rang.

"Cain, your meeting has been canceled" the garbled voice from the boat was on his cell.

"How did you manage that?" Oh, now he was pissed. This intrusive woman who thought she could issue orders was canceling his meetings.

"My people are off limits, recruit to the west." the voice responded "We do not want conflict with the Italians."

"You're taking Italians," he said, this was a revelation. The woman was recruiting and they were his people. "What right do you have to Italians? They are our people."

"I will not argue with you," the voice said back to him. "You will meet with Billy today and he will give you the respect owed as an Italian branch but you will bring Bonetti and Marino. We want peace and will assist when needed." This was news. An unexpected ally amid all this tension.

"When?" he asked as Tilly got on the phone with Joey quickly.

"Five PM" the voice responded.

"Family obligation," Cain said without thinking "Earlier or later?" a small laugh came back to him.

"Tomorrow then ten AM at Mr. Hansons. Billy will come to you and if he is harmed our deal is gone." the line ended. She was issuing orders from the shadows like some mob queen. Who did she think she was ordering two Dons to a meeting. She had said the words of giving respect but this was the opposite. Tilly handed over his phone with Joey on the line.

He relayed the new information to Joey in what he was sure was a bitter-sounding voice. Joey was silent for a moment. "She wants her guy to meet you and Marino, how the hell does she know he's in town?" Cain was paranoid that Marino was pulling something with this, it was all a little convenient

"She won't be there?" Joey asked, the tense voice told him that Joey wasn't alone which was par for the course these days. Marino was breathing down Joey's neck acting like he was in charge again. It pissed Cain off that Marino was acting like that, Joey had rebuilt everything they had from the ashes of what Marino had left.

"I assume not." Cain could feel the tension through the phone. He didn't like this being over a barrel to an unknown voice. This deal that was making them all their money was now holding them hostage. "She agreed to a third more starting next week," he added as a reminder of the deal.

"Fine we will be there but our guys will be all over that street," Joey said evenly.

JOEY

Joey stood in his office with Marino who was browsing his books while he took the call. "I should tell you about this" Joey motioned for Marino to join him. Greg sat down looking casual and light as if they were old friends. The relationships between the families were always polite with an undertone of condensation from Marino to any other Don. He had been the boss and given all of them the capital to run their areas. They had paid him back ten fold but that never mattered. "I have a business relationship with someone that supplies us with products at a discount. We recently learned that she is a woman and has a crew to the east. She is calling a sit down between her top guy and us. She knows you're in town." Marino took all this in and didn't look upset.

"I had heard that your product was great stuff and selling like crazy." This intrigued Joey. Of course Marino had heard Joey was doing well, he had spies everywhere. "Have you ever met this Woman?"

"No, she sent a courier to Cain with instructions. She's got a dead drop that we utilize and she is very well insulated. Honestly it was too good a deal to pass up but it seems she's been expanding her reach. She has us at a disadvantage but Cain is on it." Marino stayed silent for a moment measuring what he wanted to say. He took Joey by surprise by changing the subject completely.

"Cain, he is your second?" Joey nodded to this obvious question. "He's young for a second," Marino said evenly.

"He is, but I wouldn't change it. Cain is the best." Joey said, leaning back in his chair.

"I want to get to know Cain a bit more myself, can you have him at the meeting as well?" Marino looked positively excited for some action. "I like all the excitement out here. Nevada is great but nothing beats New York for the intrigue." Joey nodded at this, the big city was always where the action was.

CAIN

There was never more of a tense time than having a cold meeting with another crew. Joey and Greg sat at the outside table of Hanson's cafe sipping coffee and waiting for someone to show up. Cain stood behind the table stoic and tense. There were three crews on the street outside of every shop tense and waiting. They all saw the kid, couldn't be more than eighteen riding up on a bike, and disregarded him instantly. When he stopped in front of Joey and tossed a backpack on the table they all jerked and looked at him.

"Mr. Bonetti and Mr. Marino, can I say that it is a pleasure to meet you." Billy got off his bike and sat across from them, all ease and grace. "I'm Billy" His blonde hair was curly and his green eyes shone with confidence. He was the picture of a high school kid. "My employer wanted me to give you this as a sign of respect and support in these troubled times. She was very clear that we are all Italians even if not pure. We will stay out of your way and would request that you stay out of ours."

"How long have you been operating?" Joey asked "And where did the Hispanics go?" This little prick was pissing Joey off and Cain knew he wasn't going to get any answers when the boy smiled sly and confident. Cocky little shit, he's toying with grown men and if he wasn't careful he would get himself killed and his boss would become an enemy.

"I am not permitted to answer any questions about our organization sir. I came as my employer respects you both and wanted to show that. She also respectfully asks that you keep your crews and dealers out of the east side. We have worked hard to clean up the area and have succeeded. Also," the kid pulled out a business card and handed it to Joey who passed it to Cain. A phone number and a B. They were making fun of them. "Please call me if you need our assistance with anything. I have been chosen to be your point of contact."

"I want to meet your boss," Joey said "If she wants to show respect she will show herself to the Dons"

"No," Billy said easily "No one knows my boss, not even our crews." This shocked Cain, working for someone they never got to see. Trust that they have the organization's best interest at heart. That was insane.

"How can you work for someone you don't know?" Marino asked casually.

"I didn't say that I don't know her," Billy said then paused. He wasn't supposed to say that. Kid was cocky. "My men don't know her. She works better in the shadows. Besides she has, what did you say yesterday Cain? Family Obligations, why risk her identity and her family when she has control where she is." Silence followed this statement as the two older men exchanged a look. It had never been done that way but it made sense. Cain wondered why hadn't any of the Dons operated from the shadows like this? It would insulate them from the FBI or any other alphabet organization that wanted to take them down. She probably had kids to protect of her own. Smart for a woman to use mystery and shadows for cover.

"What kind of support is she offering?" Joey asked.

"Soldiers if needed." Cain was getting nervous. This kid seemed cocky but he was nervous, his tapping foot showed that. The kid glanced around the street and his eye caught on

something down the street a bit, before he sat up, stopped moving his foot and became more professional in his demeanor. He's not alone, Cain scanned the street and saw a few pedestrians walking on the sidewalk by some shops. He saw a UPS truck pulling up outside the liquor store and a cleaning van by the auto shop. Nothing screamed 'Mob Boss'.

"We will take that under advisement," Joey said "I don't like working with people I can't talk to in person."

Billy rose and bowed his head to both men. He got on his bike and before he rode off he looked at Joey. "You have talked to her in person sir, you have proven to be trustworthy." Billy was pointedly talking to Joey here before shooting a slight glare at Marino. Billy looked back at Joey pointedly. "What you need to know about her is she respects you," Billy's face showed a bit of surprise at this as if this hadn't always been the case. "So much that when you started moving in she told us to pull back. We have strict orders, hands off all Italians and to render aid if needed. She's a guardian angel, Mr. Bonetti, she protects her people and one day will unite us all under one family. The way it should be." with that Billy pedaled away. Not the most dramatic exit, but his words hit home.

"She wants to take over," Marino said. "We need to know more about her."

"First we need to deal with Anton and his crew then we need to find the Woman and deal with her," Joey said, glancing up and spotting a girl across the way at the auto shop and waved. She waved back and got into the van with the cleaning company's logo on it. He only caught a glimpse of red hair and assumed it was the Caruso girl.

He signaled Tilly to follow Billy and he did so following the blonde bob at the end of the road in his car. He doubted it would lead anywhere. She was careful and if Billy was high enough to rank meeting the Dons he assumed he wouldn't be going anywhere near her for a while.

"That Billy kid, he's part Italian but mostly Irish right? He's from the neighborhood. Cain, find out who he runs with, we need to start identifying these fools." Cain nodded and followed Tilly's path heading down the path Billy was heading likely to whatever teenage hang out this group was associating with.

Turns out Billy still lived at home but had graduated the previous year. He was attending college at the local university on a Soccer scholarship. Cain met with his old man who was standoffish and deflected. "You work for the Woman too?" Cain had asked him.

"If I did I wouldn't tell you" which was all Cain needed to hear. So she wasn't just recruiting kids. Smart, probably started with the parents and when kids came of age took them on too. Would bolster her numbers and keep whole families loyal.

"Have you ever met her?" The old man smiled and shook his head. It was a taunting smile like he had been waiting to be asked and thought it was a great joke.

"No, my son has, which is all I need to know. So far her decisions have been sound and as long as they stay that way it's alright by me." Cain looked at the old man. "Are you running this with your Son?" He asked. It didn't make sense for the only one to meet her to be Billy. He was too young to be that high in an organization. Cain knew this because he was too young to be a second and Joey was looked at differently because of the choice.

"I advise my son and sometimes attend conference calls as an advisor which is all I am permitted to say. See she knew you would look into Billy and end up here" Mr. O'Reily was smart enough to say just enough to keep himself safe. Well insulated and smart enough to take advice from older men who were wiser than her second.

"Ok Sir, thank you for taking the time." He went back out to his car and sat to wait. When Billy got home two hours later from class with Tilly still following, Tilly got in Cains' car.

"He went to class. I sat in the back of United States History and learned about the real causes of the Civil War today. Then followed him to his History of Rome class." Tilly looked annoyed "He's a history major"

"His Dad says he wants to be a history teacher" Cain supplied helpfully. "They both work for her"

"Figures," Tilly said, they watched several boys and men come and go throughout the next few hours. Some were known to them, others were not. This was obviously the command center. At four thirty Cain said good night to Tilly and left him to head to Joey's for homework and dinner. It was now his favorite part of the day.

Walking into the home without knocking he heard Theo having a melt down in the living room. "I want to call Erin!" Theo was yelling at Carol. Theo had a black eye, and a lip that had been bleeding.

"Whoa," Cain said walking in. "What happened?"

"Theo got in a fight at school," Carol said when Theo closed his mouth. "Joey had to talk to the principal. Apparently, something was said about his parents abandoning him and he hit the other kid."

"Did you hit hard and fast?" Cain asked, sitting on the couch. The boy nodded and Cain shrugged "Did you win?"

"We both came out bloody," Theo replied, anger burning. The kid was obviously not counting that as a victory. Cain could appreciate that, he had been in more than a few fights in school because of things that were said about his father.

"Sounds to me like he won't make that mistake again. You handled it like a man. I would have done the same thing." Carol huffed as Joey came in the room holding a phone out to Theo.

"Your sister" Theo paled a little but took the phone. The boy vanished into another room and Carol floated after him. "Kids got his Dad's temper, but Erin said she can calm him down. I have never seen him so angry."

"Don't matter if your parents were terrible, no one else can talk about them. Plus they died, they didn't abandon him." Cain said looking around for Josie "Where's Josie?"

"In her room, she hides from shouting," Joey said, rubbing his eyebrows. Cain felt for him, he was in the middle of a turf war on all sides, Anton to the west, Marino in his face, The Woman from the east. Then he had internal issues, merging crews, handling sales and recruiting, and the kids that he had inherited with a lot of baggage and damage. He may lose those eyebrows if he didn't stop rubbing them, Cain thought and patted Joey's shoulder.

Ten minutes later Theo came into the room looking sheepish. "I am sorry Mrs. Bonetti for shouting at you, it was disrespectful when you have been so kind to let us stay here." it sounded rehearsed and he looked like he got lectured.

"It's ok Theo," Carol said, smiling kindly at him "How about we get Josie and get started on some homework and I'll make some queso and chips for a snack while I finish up dinner?" Theo smiled and nodded, heading to his sister's room. Cain followed at a distance and watched Theo check the closet and find it empty; he looked surprised and checked the drapes. He spotted a pink shoe under the bed.

"Psst" Cain said to Theo nodding to the bed. Theo nodded and peeked under the bed. "Hey Jose, I shouldn't have yelled," Theo said he didn't apologize but he sounded sorry. "You done?" she asked, ten-year-old anger in her voice.

"Yea come on we are getting Queso and Cain is here." she scooted out from under her bed, her blue jeans and pink sweater rubbing against the carpet. She stoutly ignored her brother and walked straight to Cain. He smiled down at her.

"Hi," she said shyly "I'll get my backpack." she scooted past him out the door and Theo followed. Carol quickly laid the chips and Queso on the counter as kids sat on either side of him and they dug into homework. It warmed his heart that they both leaned towards him now instead of away. Josie didn't flinch at all anymore and Theo only when Cain reacted quickly.

They joked and laughed and learned how to spell words like 'approximately, Conscience, and choreographer' and worked through some physical science homework. After dinner, Cain sat in Joey's office and de-briefed him on the day of staking out Billy O'Neal's and he didn't look surprised.

"I just spoke to Billy O'Reilly a few months ago, his son is friends with Erin Caruso, her only friend. I wonder if that's where she got all her money from, working for the Woman. Let's keep a pair of guys outside conspicuously. If Billy meets The Woman, then I want to know about it. I want a keep list of people who go to the house and pictures of those we don't know. Act like the feds, and see what shakes loose. If you see Erin there let me know." Cain nodded.

"How is the Anton situation coming?" Cain asked, lighting a cigarette as Joey lit a cigar. "Slow"

Joey sighed "It's cat and mouse."

"Anything I can do?" He offered knowing he would decline. Cain said nothing when he declined. It seemed they were being hit on all sides and things were getting complicated. He didn't know how Joey did it, compartmentalizing everything. He had Carol though, he noted her presence as she came and sat on the arm of Joey's chair and whispered something in his ear kissing his temple before leaving. That was a love that you read about. Those two were solid, even when times get rough. Cain had a vague sense of yearning but that wasn't likely to happen. Most Don's wives were vain and controlling of the other wives, but stayed out of the business to look nice and stay happy. Carol gave advice and listened attentively when she was in the room. He would put money down that Joey told Carol a lot of what was going on.

As Cain was leaving the house that night, a gift basket of flowers and cookies showed up for Carol from the mystery sister as an apology for Theo raising his voice. That girl was determined to ensure the kids were taken care of. It was a wonder that she didn't move in to ensure they were protected. Though, from what Joey said, she flinched at any movement that startled her so badly that she was likely to fall off the furniture. Marino had mentioned that she had leaped away from him when he reached out to her like he was going to murder her. She probably felt safest alone right now.

CHAPTER NINE

ERIN

Billy's meeting had gone well and as it could have, he went a bit off script but that was always a possible outcome. It's not like she was perfect; they were both still teenagers. They had met one last time before his meeting where they discussed the next few months. Billy said his house was being monitored now he claimed feds were parked out front but when she passed by it had been two of the Bonetti men. They had a camera and were acting like Feds though. She called Billy on one of her burners and couldn't help the laugh she had in explaining the situation.

"You should have your Mom bring them dinner." she laughed.

"I will, she will get a kick out of that." He said, chuckling. "So what have you been up to?"

"Normal stuff, school and cleaning out this house." she said "You know, typical ruler of the world day in the life, maybe I should start a vlog" she joked pulling into her parking spot. "I am going to do some virtual interviews tomorrow for the cleaning business, do we have anyone that needs this or can be of more value here?" she asked, walking inside. She triggered her alarm and walked into the now empty living room to the kitchen at the back of the house. "Your first two of the day can be alternative cleaners; they work for Joey's crew as well as cleaners but could use the extra income," Billy said and she could hear him flipping through his planner. "Everyone else is for the legit side, do you have customers lined up?" he asked.

"I have a few but I can get more. I am going to use my connection with Joey to get clients. He's always saying he wants to help." She shrugged off her jacket and set her takeout on the counter. "Speaking of asking to help us, they want to increase product volume by a third. I know we have been having a surplus so just pull from that. See if that helps the capacity issue. You know I am annoyed that you told them you're my second in command that was off script." She had been listening to the exchange through the wire Billy had worn.

"We can manage the increase no problem and that was all Dad's idea, Bonetti was just out here asking about you. He figures if he's not seen as the number two they won't assume he's too big in it. He doesn't want them to think he's running anything." He said easily. "What happens if they don't respond to our request?" He asked simply.

"I haven't decided yet. I chose you so you could be unassuming, telling them your second makes me look naive. How is the North looking, are the Irish onto us yet?" she asked. They had been flying under the radar, but word of their product had gotten around and she had offered an olive branch to the Irish to keep them as allies since much of her organization was part Italian and part Irish just like her.

"Not yet, Bonetti's number two is twenty-three. I don't think they judged you because of me." he said "We have some firm commitments and a few possibilities. They want to run our product up North." he made the request casually.

"I'll think about that too," Erin said, sitting on the counter next to her food. She pulled her gun out of the small of her back and set it on the counter. "How's school?" she asked, leaning her back against her fridge.

"Good, I got a couple of papers due already. Dad got approached by Joey today, and said that he wants to meet with you even if it's just a call." Billy liked talking business. He enjoyed being high up in an organization like this.

"Tell him that next time they approach to tell them not yet and be cryptic with it," she said slowly. This was going to be an issue. She hadn't wanted to out herself or declare her hand. "I need to do a pulse check myself but I only go on Sundays so it will have to wait. Nothing drastic will happen in a week; they have bigger issues. Let me know if they call you directly to request help.

"I have rented out the range three days a week for the next six months. I need you to update the list of approved visitors for the days and get it to Francis so he knows."Erin said, Billy agreed. Francis was the owner of the gun range and had taught her how to shoot. He was the first man that she didn't get jumpy with because he had spent so much time at her shoulder. He didn't turn down cash or product as payment which was convenient. "Get the new recruits in there twice a week. Have Benji and Phillip oversee their training. I want them to run like a unit. That's the problem all these other crews have. They just hand their people guns and don't work on the training." She had said it before but it needed to be reiterated.

"Will do" he sighed "when can I see you again?" His voice was flirty. She was pretty sure Billy had feelings for her, or imagined that if they got together he would be running the Family. She had worked too hard to just hand it over to Billy. She should really consider what would happen if she was found out and killed, because she did not want to leave her people, or more importantly her siblings without a path forward.

"Not for a while with them tailing you. They want you to lead them to me and that can't happen. How is Hillary?" she asked, reminding him of his girlfriend rolling her eyes and taking a bite of an egg roll. Simple pleasures, she thought dipping it in the red sauce, good chinese food made her happy.

"She's good, you know, still going to school. She's coming over tomorrow after school. She wants to join us." He brought up the subject, surprising her. Billy may flirt with her but he had been with Hillary for three years since his sophomore year and her freshman. He had always been very protective of her so him wanting her to join was big news.

"Give her something low level, recon of the North on weekends with someone." She said after a short pause. "I don't want her to distract you" she was blunt, this had to be understood. "I don't need you to be distracted right now, times are pivotal and we need to be careful." He sighed in response. "I have to go make a few calls and some homework to do."

"Ok, call you tomorrow," Billy said before she hung up. She needed to do these debriefs with Billy Senior on the calls, those always went faster. Billy Junior was an old friend but he was young and hot headed. Taunting Joey and Marino today was proof of that.

An hour later she was upstairs in one of the bedrooms dismantling some old creaky furniture. She cursed and lugged the furniture downstairs. The first step to this place was to

empty out all the crap that was left behind, and clean it. The kitchen had been tough but was finally as clean as she could get it without tearing it down, and currently she needed it to be functional. Not that she knew how to cook, but she could reheat and make frozen pizza like the best of them. Cooking would come a little later in life, she thought distractedly. As would a love life, the bitterness behind that thought had her throwing the bed frame down the stairs. She would love to be like all the other girls her age, flirting and spending time worrying about if Eric likes her or not. She had to grow up many years ago and had formed her plans a while ago.

She finished bringing the furniture downstairs from the first two rooms and was exhausted. She hadn't brought anything from her parents apartment, hadn't gone back, neither had her siblings as far as she knew. She wanted nothing from that place but to forget it.

Erin logged into her laptop for the telehealth therapy visit with the shrink Carol had given her. She kept her camera off and considered the voice changer. The doctor came on camera, an older man with white hair. This was their second visit together and as she described her issues he was kind and understanding. He did not want to hear her describe her past further than he needed to find root causes. He listened intently to her struggles, and what she wanted and he gave her tangible goals.

She would try finding a man to befriend over the phone to get used to hearing the voice constantly. Exchange pictures fully clothed if she was comfortable and start by just being friends. Billy Junior didn't count, they were her comfort zone so she had to pick someone else.

Crawling into her sleeping bag she thought of who that could be and smiled when she decided to insert herself further into Joey's world. It was time to get to know his second in command.

The next day she started a new routine. She woke up and since her ribs still ached she stretched and did light yoga in her living room. Then she took her laptop to a cafe two blocks over and set it up in a corner booth with her homework and headphones. She had scouted this place the week before and it had good wifi so she could sit for a few hours, drink some coffee, and eat a brunch-type meal. This was another part of her therapy, being in public alone and mostly unapproachable, to get used to a man's presence in a harmless way. She had her air pods in her ears and was listening to the newest Paramore album when her food was delivered. She glanced up and light brown eyes met hers.

The man who smiled down at her was at least two years older and handsome. His auburn hair was curly and down to the nape of his neck. His bright smile caught her off guard and she smiled back. Thank the Lord her face had healed! "I've seen you here before," he said, pulling out napkins from his apron. He laid them down slowly with extra care. She flinched back into the booth away from him and he jerked back. She flushed and avoided his eyes.

"I just moved to the area," she said, shifting some of her books to the booth. Trying to fill the space between Patrick and herself. Calm, breathe, he's being nice and bringing you your order, Erin lectured herself.

"Well make sure you come back, I'm Patrick Miller," He said with a small smile catching her eyes again.

"Erin Caruso," she said immediately and then cursed herself for giving her real name. She had never heard of the Millers so they must be civilians. This was ten steps ahead of where she was supposed to be, trying to get with men, at least she felt that way.

"I'll leave you to study Erin." he said nodding to her books "If you take a break and want to chat I'll be around" With that he swaggered away. She flushed as she pulled her Business Mathematics book onto the table and opened it. That was a distraction she didn't need, but she still watched his butt as he walked away. Looking wasn't getting involved, it was enjoying the scenery.

Over the next few days she focused on school at the cafe, which included small conversations with Patrick and clearing the house in between handling work issues. Joey and his crew kept popping up in Billy Senior's days, and confronting Billy Junior. Erin hired ten women to work for her cleaning service and provide her alibi's for the Bonetti's and if needed the police.

On Sunday afternoon she arrived in the Bronx at her warehouse. She nodded to her employees wearing pocketless pants and tight shirts. It wasn't that she didn't trust her employees but she wasn't stupid either. When you work in this industry being prepared is important. The gas masks protected them but she had no idea if they used the product they processed. She spent the afternoon taking an inventory of what they currently had in overage. They could handle upping the limit now but if they requested another increase she would not be able to manage that.

It was time to expand and she wasn't ready yet. A trip to West Virginia was needed. She was now old enough and had the freedom to do this and she had been a little hands off. Her age was going to be an issue. She needed a change in style, this was going to take some thought. Glancing at her watch she cursed, she needed to get to dinner with the kids. She got in

her new car, an Audi Q8 suv, which in New York wasn't ideal but most people didn't drive in the city and she intended to travel quite a bit and would need the space. The drive wasn't long and she pulled up two blocks away and did a quick jog to the door.

Theo opened the door excitedly and shoved a piece of paper into her hands without even a "Hello". She read the printed-out race schedule and smiled.

"You're on the team! That's great, I can't wait to see you run!" she said, following him to the kitchen. Joey was nowhere to be seen and his office door was closed. Carol was working four pots at once on the stove as Josie watched.

"Yea and I started Jiu Jitsu once a week on Thursdays. My coach says I can miss up to two practices a week, so we are going to start with one to see how good I am" Theo was the most excited she had ever seen him. Erin noted he was wearing more new clothes and looking fresh and clean. No stains or baggy pants. Her heart warmed when she watched him run around the counter to Carol and hug her before snagging a bite of whatever she was throwing together.

"That's exciting I'll have to get the details so I can sit in on your practices sometimes," she said grinning down at him.

"Let's wait until I'm good first," Carol laughed at this comment.

"He's banned us as well. Joey sits in the car working during practice." This made Erin feel terrible but also a little warm that they were willing to do this for them. Why did these people care so much for her siblings? She was mature enough to know that it wasn't Joey's fault her parents were abusive. Why was he not just pawning them off on another family in the organization?

"Hey Erin, maybe you can meet Cain today!" Josie said happily. "He's in with Uncle Joey right now" Uncle Joey? She raised an eyebrow at Carol who shrugged and smiled. She shrugged back, it showed they were getting close if Josie felt that comfortable around Joey. This could complicate things in the future but hopefully Joey was falling in love with her siblings the way they were falling for him. Josie too was in a designer dress with pretty matching shoes.

"Oh, Sorry Jojo," Joey said entering the kitchen and pecking Carol on the cheek "Cain just had to run an errand for me" He smiled at Erin.

"Anything major?" Carol asked, arching an eyebrow.

"No, just legwork on The Woman" he said casually. It took all of Erin's willpower to not stiffen.

"The Woman?" She asked casually "Everything ok?" she glanced at her siblings who seemed oblivious talking to each other about dinner.

"Nothing to worry about just trying to figure out the new game in town. She seems friendly, her people helped out today in a big way to the west. No idea what they were doing there but she likes to leave notes through her people. Woman's a mystery. Speaking of, your friend Billy O'Riely works for her and it got me thinking about all that cash you had to buy that truck." Joey's tone went from mostly positive to openly curious "Do you work for her?"

Erin smiled broadly and laughed out loud at this, taking both Joey and Carol off guard. "No I don't work for her, I've heard of her from Billy though. I don't think I could ever work for someone in that industry." which was completely true, she didn't work for The Woman. "Do you have a problem with the O'Reilly's working for her?"

"No, I am curious how she created an entire organization without anyone knowing." Erin thought about this. If he had been paying attention he would have found out. If he dug into the shipment and tracked her people Billy would have led straight to her.

"I don't know," Erin said softly "I've only heard a casual mention of Billy's boss, he seems to like her." Erin shrugged and snagged a bread roll and started snacking on it.

Erin thought about the trouble his men had run into that day. She had sent one of her crews to follow one of Marinos to determine the war going on. They had engaged a group of men that were attacking civilians and when Marinos men got involved, she had her crew move in to assist. It had been over quickly and in her true fashion they had handed over a note explaining who they were and then left without a word to anyone.

Her guys loved being cryptic and loved even more how mysterious she was. She thought it was both useful and hilarious. She couldn't help the small smile at knowing it was driving Joey and Marino crazy.

"Sounds like someone you should meet," Erin said, leaning back in her chair. The comedy of this situation was both hilarious and troubling. One day Joey would find out and she hoped he found the humor of this exact moment rather than the betrayal of it.

After dinner and the kids were off to their rooms she sat in the kitchen as had become their custom. "I was wondering if I could ask for some referrals?" she said to Carol and Joey. She flushed lightly and they both beamed at her. "I'm new to the business world and getting business is hard work. I have a solid team of cleaners but I need to keep them busy."

"I thought you worked at the company as a cleaner?" Joey said, sipping his coffee.

"I do, well did, I got a slight promotion to running my team and helping with hiring and stuff. It's good experience for my business degree but it also came with a pay raise so I jumped at it." she took a deep breath and over exaggerated her wince for her ribs. "I over promised on the amount of work I could bring in. If you can't help that's fine I will figure it out I just thought I would ask."

"I have some friends that could definitely use some help, and a few businesses as well. Do you all do commercial properties?" Carol asked calmly.

"We will do whatever is needed." she glanced at Joey "we could be of use to the family" this was the moment she had been waiting for. The offer of assistance to see if he would accept help from her face to face. "It would be like working for the family but more accessible to me accessible."

"I can get you some customers and I will think about the family's needs for your business. You focus on school and if work becomes too much let us know." He looked surprised by her offer and he hadn't said no. She slid a stack of business cards for the cleaning service over to him.

"How is school? Have you met any friends?" Carol asked leaning forward and Erin blushed without meaning to. "Oh I know that look, you have met a boy! What's his name?" Erin thought for a moment about not telling them about the coffee shop but she had been meaning to run his info and it would be good to know if he was affiliated with them. Plus it was normal for her age to have crushes on boys.

"Patrick, he works at a cafe on Seventh Street, he's in the Army Reserves and going to school to be a lawyer. He's twenty" she said when Joey raised an eyebrow.

"Twenty? Patrick what?" he asked and she could see Dad mode kicking in.

"Patrick Miller," she said slowly "Why?"

"I don't know him," he said, looking at Carol. "Have you met his family?"

"No, I haven't seen him outside of the cafe. I do homework there every morning, they have really good wifi. That shrink you gave me says I need to practice being in public and being comfortable." Joey and Carol shared a surprised look and Carol smiled warmly.. "Patrick and I just talk, we are friends, he hasn't asked me out or anything just talking." Though he liked flirting with her he had yet to ask her out and she would never make the first move. It would be just another complication, she didn't have time for a relationship. Though the shrink was encouraging it. She had stopped flinching around random men on the street and guests at the coffee shop. The gym was still hard but she was more confident that she could soon meet with her people face to face. That's what she was working toward.

"But you like him?" Carol wanted all the details. Erin blushed again and smiled lightly.

"Yes, but I've never dated anyone before plus it's complicated with my family history and the kids. I am just focusing on school and work right now but I like talking to him "

"Good girl," Joey said grinning "don't let stupid boys distract you! You're going to rule the world with all those majors" Yup total Dad mode. Erin smiled lightly at this, he had no idea whose world she would run. She could just imagine him thinking of how valuable she could be to the family with all these degrees.

"Tell me, how do your daughters handle you while dating?" she asked him and his eyes lost all humor.

"They are careful who they select for dating as you should be," he said "They go to an out-of-state school and have a security detail which I wish you would let me get you one."

"No thank you," Erin said smiling at Joey "I am my own security"

"You armed Erin?" he asked, his eyebrows raising.

"I have what I need to protect me," she said "I know who my father was, though to be honest I always thought he inflated his worth to us to make out like he was better than he was. I know he has enemies which is why I didn't fight you on keeping Theo and Josie. They are thriving here."

"You could too," Carol said, sadness in her voice. Erin hated that Carol wanted to take care of her so badly.

"I am thriving, in my way, we aren't going down that road. I have a house that I'm fixing up," she announced out of nowhere and cursed herself. She hadn't meant to mention that. "I'm doing repairs around work and school so it's slow going but I've learned I love to swing a sledge hammer and I'm learning so much about mold removal." They both looked shocked.

"Do you want me to send some guys to fix it up?" Joey offered and made her smile.

"No thank you. I want to do this on my own. It may take a few years but I'm young and have the time. Plus I don't intend to invite anyone over for a while. I am fixing up the second floor first because bedrooms are cheaper than kitchens. I'll take some pictures and Carol. I would love some decorating advice when I get to that stage. I know nothing about it." Carol looked touched

"I would love that," she said smiling. Erin liked Carol a lot and she enjoyed sparring with Joey. She wanted to believe that after all this time Carol was a friend now.

"I have to say, cleaning the place out is kind of therapeutic. I finished cleaning out the kitchen down to the basics until I'm ready to remodel it and I felt like it was a new start. I know it's weird but the Shrink is into it and says it's a physical embodiment of remaking myself after trauma." These therapy tidbits seemed to be impressing them and giving her the excuse to keep it private. She was remodeling her life to suit herself and this house represented that for her. It looked broken and a mess and worthless much like she had when Joey had found her in the Apartment all alone. Her body was healing and so would this house. Joey and Carol shared a look of interest but Carol gave a small shake of her head before turning back to Erin.

"So what's your favorite class so far?" she asked. They chatted about school and work. She told them about her routine of stretching as her ribs were healing and her back was better. The cafe and school time and then her random work schedule. By the end of the visit they had broken out the cross country schedule, the dance class schedule, and the date of the recital for Josie and she had marked them down on a piece of paper to be added to her planner.

"Why do you help us?" she asked Joey as he sipped a beer in his office that she had wandered into after him. She wanted to pick his brain as she did not understand this man. Her father had painted him as a tyrant and hard boss to get along with. She could see almost everything she had heard was likely wrong and her father was a relic of a past Don's mistakes. All of her agony had been caused by Marino but Joey could have helped if he had known.

"Because I should have noticed what was happening to you, and I failed you," he said without blinking. "I take pride in helping the families that work for me and I knew Derrick had anger issues and Carol knew Mary had a gambling problem but whenever we asked about you kids they said everything was fine or," he looked uncomfortable "he would complain about you acting out. Told me when you rammed into him said he needed to tame you but I didn't look past that. I thought he was joking."

"I can understand feeling guilty but this is above and beyond" she said browsing the books on the shelves. "You could have put Theo and Josie with another family. You're the Don, you took them into your home and you're harassing me to take care of me, someone who doesn't want your help. This is a bit much and I'm not sure what the catch is here?" He looked wounded to say the least. She had her boss voice on and she wanted answers. He was saving her sibling but also complicating things for her. If he found out who she was then he might take it out on her siblings.

"Let's leave it as, I think for the amount of pain you and your siblings went through it's time for you to be lifted up and shine." He looked earnest as he said this while smoking his cigar lightly. She didn't like this response. This was charity and also controlling. He was suspicious of her and she could see his eyes appraising her as she stood in front of him. At worst though based on his questions tonight, he thought she worked for The Woman but she hoped she dissuaded that as much as she could.

"What issues are you having that you need Marino out here?" She asked, her tone sharpening. She needed answers, she needed details so she could intervene and protect him and her siblings. Well, that shifted quickly. She would need to find the right words later on when it came time to take Marino out. If she was lucky this situation would resolve and Marino would go back to Nevada and wait to be called again.

"You don't worry about that" Joey said, stiffening slightly.

"Joey, I do have to worry about that. If you're having problems that put you in danger then they are in danger." He eyed her with a studying and suspicious eye. Had she gone too far? Was this probing going to give her away? Or was she coming off as a concerned sister?

"I can understand your concern," he said after a long pause. "It is a small turf war but Marino is here to help as well as men from Miami and Arizona and The

Woman is offering assistance if we need it." He looked uncomfortable with the last statement. It surprised her that he would even mention it. He had for all intensive purposes been ignoring her attempts to help.

"What do you know about her, can she be trusted?" Erin was now poking the bear and she knew it. If he ever discovered who she was she was going to be in big trouble. Maybe her age was making her act impulsively but she wanted him to trust her as The Woman.

"Not much, she runs the east bay and plays on being mysterious. She has a young crew but they seem well organized and pop up out of nowhere. We have been working with her on a side project for about a year so there is a trust that has formed." Both Carol and Erin raised their eyebrows in surprise. Carol said nothing, she would not question him in front of anyone. Erin was shocked to learn he did have some trust with her organization and his tone was respectful. The complement of well organized made her feel warm inside knowing he did appreciate the hard work she had put in to ensure her people were ghosts.

"Ok, thank you for reassuring me but if you ever need me to take the kids for a few days, if it gets dangerous please let me know." she said softly "And if you really think I am in danger by proxy please tell me. I know you will always be concerned but if there is a true threat just let me know." Joey nodded his head.

"You are a lot more mature than an eighteen year old should be. You know Theo and Josie think you walk on water and know everything." Joey said, trying to steer the conversation away from his business. Erin smiled and rose putting on her jacket.

"Lets not let them know I'm still just an eighteen year old girl then" she said grinning. "I gotta take off. I have my first exam for Java Coding on Tuesday and I need to study. Thank you again for caring so much and I hope your work issues are resolved quickly. Marino makes me nervous, you make me nervous" she laughed when he looked shocked at this honest moment. "but I think you have good intentions." She stressed 'you' in that sentence more than she should have and tried to read if he caught that.

"You still don't trust me do you?" he asked, shocked and if she wasn't mistaken hurt in his voice. She trusted him with her siblings, that would have to be enough, Erin thought watching him.

"No" She replied slowly, "But I trust Carol," she said with a wink at Carol who giggled.

"Well we will work on that" Joey said "If you're carrying a weapon I want to take you to a range and show you how to use it" this took her by surprise and she stopped. This would be very revealing but also may be a good chance to see where and if he trained his people.

"I would like that," she said after a moment. "I can do Tuesdays and Thursdays but not for another three weeks. My ribs probably wouldn't handle the kick back well." She said after a long pause. He nodded and they said their goodnights. Well this would be interesting, she thought as she walked the two blocks to her car. There was no tail for a change and she drove home quickly.

CHAPTER TEN

CAIN

Cain sat in a bar on the east side and had to admit, this area was officially safe. From what the locals said the Hispanics had left suddenly with no cause. Their families had left with them and they had thought someone would come in as that was normal for the area but no one had. When the Irish had attempted they had quickly left. Most of the area was Irish and Italian and the people seemed happy. At least in the few places he had been able to visit, he did this on his own time after recruiting and handling the sales portion of the business. He was taking a risk by coming here after being warned off. He could blow their agreement and lose the shipment if he played her cards wrong. He hoped he was extending an olive branch, even if he wasn't Joey himself. Cain wanted to know more about the Woman that was behind the scenes.

The bartender was a young woman with dyed blonde hair, she was pretty and perky and liked to talk. "You know, I'm pretty sure you're not from around here," she said leaning over the bar and filling his drink.

"I live twenty minutes west," he said. In most areas that wouldn't mean anything in Queens that meant he was an outsider. She straightened slightly and searched his face. "Your Cain Brescia of the Bonetti family" she said with defiance in her voice and fear, he thought, why would she fear him? "You were told to keep your men out of our area." He sat back and assessed the woman in front of him. Interesting, he thought to himself.

"And how would you know that Cherie?" he asked, reading her name tag. She didn't look nervous or scared anymore, the fleeting emotion contained, she was in control of herself and self assured of her safety. Could this be The Woman, he thought to himself.

"That doesn't concern you, why are you here?" she asked casually leaning back against the bar back. He saw her tap her smartwatch twice without looking at it and she extended her arm out to the side so he couldn't see the face of it. She was good, this was definitely The Woman, he thought to himself. In a bar, she was assessing him carefully and he sat still letting her get her fill. He knew what he looked like and the effect he had on women. He gave her a casual flirty smile.

"If I tell you, I came in for a drink and to get to know who I'm working with?" he asked, listening for movement around him. She thought for a moment before responding.

"I would say The Woman is a private person and has loyal supporters. We don't want to get to know you," she said, not giving anything away. "Right now at least." Her eyes traveled up his chest and focused on his lips. His slow smile answered.

"Are you The Woman?" he asked, making her laugh. Her laugh was throaty and seductive. The surprise on her face told him he had caught her off guard.

"If I was, I wouldn't tell you," she said matter of factly. The door swung open and four men walked in following Mr. O'Reilly Senior who moved directly to Cain and sat next to him motioning for a drink. Cherie got him a drink quickly without asking what he wanted. They knew each other. "Mr. O'Reily"

"Mr. Brescia" he replied "Can we help you with something?" he asked in a taunting tone. Cherie scowled at the older man who was looking at him.

"I was just in the neighborhood trying to make some friends. Thinking of asking Cherie here on a date" Cherie laughed softly as she filled drinks for the rest of the men now sitting at the bar.

"Wouldn't Mr. Bonetti think that was a conflict of interests?" O'Reily asked as Cherie's phone rang. She answered it and moved away from them.

"No he doesn't care who I date. I think he will only care when it comes to marriage and besides I thought we were all friends here?" he said, turning to look at O'Reily.

"You can take me to dinner tomorrow night, that's my night off" Cherie said appearing before them. She looked confident and O'Reily"s jaw dropped. "Eight sounds good to you? I know you have obligations until six" this surprised him. How did she know he was on homework duty with the kids?

"What obligations are those?" He asked casually. He felt a pang of fear which was rare. If the Woman knew about the kids then she knew way too many personal things about Joey for comfort. Casual mention was a show of force and veiled threat. He stamped it down and made a note to check security for the kids.

"Obligations you will not be blowing off" she said evenly with no hint at what they were. "Pick me up here at eight tomorrow and it better be a nice place to eat." Cherie poured a drink for him and grinned down at him. Cain trailed his eyes down the blonde and smiled.

"It will be," he said, slapping cash on the counter and downing his drink. "It will be a night to remember Cherie," he said, heading out the door. He got in his car and drove straight to Joey's house for a late night discussion.

Joey sat in his robe at his desk listening to what had unfolded and laughed. "So you think this Cherie is The Woman?" Joey asked contemplation on his face. "She didn't seem to answer to O'Reily, who we think is the real number two in the organization. She wasn't afraid or nervous with me or anyone else. She also didn't deny it, she just said she wouldn't tell me if she was or not." though he thought of her surprised expression "Though she was surprised when I asked her, it may have been from the question or from shock of being confused for her. I couldn't tell."

"Alright well, take her out and see what she's about. It troubles me that she knows about your arrangement with the kids. No one should know about that or them." Joey rubbed his face. "I need to tell Erin they were mentioned by the Womans' people." Cain knew Joey was trying to win the girl's trust and telling her that her siblings were mentioned by a possible enemy was not going to do that. "In the meantime I want them to have security with them at school and everywhere else. Also put some men outside my house and with Carol. I'll call my girl's security and ensure they are covered."

"She was well-informed about my activities. I need to pay closer attention too, if I'm being watched." He bet he was under observation though he knew he was likely a target it didn't usually bother him. The Woman was very interesting, to know all this very private stuff. He had not mentioned to anyone that he was helping the kids. He wondered idly if they had mentioned it to their friends and it was getting around that way. "I'll take her out and see what we can find out"

"Follow her lead a bit though, she has agreed to go somewhere private with you. Use it and see what her attitude is. Maybe take her somewhere inside our territory. Maybe Per Se I'll make a call and get you a table." Joey said easily. Cain nodded, yea that would be a nice place to go, not really his style but he was trying to impress and Cherie was young she would be impressed.

"Thanks Joey, I still don't know where they stand. They came in force but were respectful." Joey stood to go "I'll be by for homework tomorrow and I'll get the security detail organized tonight." Joey nodded and dismissed him with a nod.

Cain picked up Cherie at eight o'clock on the dot. She was in a shift dress with a matching purse slung over her shoulder. Her breasts pulled at the fabric and it hugged her curves. Her hair was falling in soft curls over her shoulders. She looked like she could have any man eating out of her hand in seconds. He hopped out and saw O'Reily at the door of the bar. He nodded and opened the door for Cherie who climbed in without a glance back. She was definitely in charge with this attitude.

"Where are we going?" she asked lightly as he got back in the driver's seat.

"Per Se" he said, pulling away from the drive. She flushed lightly and nodded. "So Cherie, how long have you worked at Finnegans?" he asked casually. She paused as if taken off guard by the question.

"Since I turned twenty one, so just over a year now." she said "How long have you worked for Joey?" she countered. Touche, he thought, smiling broadly.

"Joey took me on when I was sixteen, so seven years now. How about you? How long have you been involved in this lifestyle?" she tilted her head toward him.

"A year" she said evenly. "How is the conflict going?" she was vague, maybe they didn't know what was going on as well as Joey thought they did.

"What conflict?" he asked, raising a brow as he pulled into Per Se.

"The one that brought in the other families" she said, getting out of the car without help. Her heels made her a few inches shorter than him. She was a tall woman to begin with so this was impressive.

"Slow," he said, smirking at her. So this was the game they would be playing, small details but no actual insight. "How did you know about my obligations at night?" She smiled a soft smile as they walked inside. She waited until they were ushered to their table, a discreet booth in the corner. Each step he itched for this answer. It bothered him that anyone would bring the kids up. They had nothing to do with the families.

"It is a good obligation, the kind you should always keep. You're making a huge impact." her eyes didn't show any sarcasm or joking, just pure delight in what she talked about. He shifted uncomfortably with the praise. "You can rest assured they are not in danger from us, we would never hurt children or families."

"You are The Woman" he said sitting back against the booth. She laughed softly.

"I didn't say that," she said watching him "Just know that I am well-informed" She was serious now. She had to be The Woman, she was too confident. "Let's not discuss work anymore I want to get to know you"

"Ok" He said after a moment "What are your dreams and ambitions?" he asked, picking up the wine that had been poured. She laughed and they chatted about nothing important for over an hour. He liked her, Cherie was smart and funny and ate the food like it was a gift. He saw when she turned her head that she had an earpiece in her ear. He ignored it and tried to enjoy his time with her.

Once back in his car he drove her to the bay to watch the waves. They sat chatting for another hour about all the small things you talk about on first dates. Family, friends, college. She was going to school to be a Veterinarian. She had a love for animals and had grown up with nothing but cats. She still lived at home with her parents who also worked in her organization. By the end of the night he was still unsure of if she was The Woman or not but he did know that someone had listened to their date and fed her responses to tricky questions he had peppered in regarding the business. He drove them back to the bar as she didn't want him going to her home yet.

"Can we do this again?" he asked casually as he parked the car. She blushed and nodded softly. He leaned in and kissed her cheek softly, "Next time leave your earpiece at home" This made her laugh. She was a fun woman and interesting. Even if she wasn't the Woman he wanted to spend more time with her.

"You didn't think I wouldn't be connected at all times did you?" she said, leaning back. "I'll talk to my people and next time I think we can be unsupervised." He leaned forward and kissed her full on the mouth. She responded after a moment. Melting into him, she tasted of the wine and cheesecake they had shared at dinner. "Goodnight Cain" she murmured against his lips before getting out of his car. He watched her go into the bar and grinned. He glanced down and saw her earpiece on the seat. He drove down the road and slipped it in his ear pressing the small button on it. There was no ringing, just a pause then a click.

"Hello," he said to no one.

"I think she likes you and from what I heard, you could be good together" The female voice sounded brisk. "I'll be watching, keep this on you, the charger is in your glove box" There was a click. He kept the earpiece in as he drove back to his place. So Cherie was definitely not The Woman but he now had a direct link to her with no voice changer for a change. This was an opportunity. He could now communicate with her when needed but she still had all the control. He didn't have a number to call, just an earpiece. He now had a random black earpiece that would definitely make him look like a cop wherever he went. She was mocking him. He felt both thrilled and galled by how the evening had gone.

Cain got home and kept the earpiece in. He clicked a button on it and heard a tapping sound like a connection was being made but it wasn't quite a ringing sound. "Yes," The Woman's voice said, annoyance in her tone.

"I don't work for you," he said laying back on his bed. May as well be comfortable when chatting with the mysterious Woman that people were so curious about. Lady his cat jumped onto his chest and snuggled in for attention.

"Never said you did," she said easily "You have been hounding my people for weeks now" She sounded like she was doing something laborious on the other end of the connection.

"I didn't know you existed until then," he said easily "When can we meet?"

"Never," she said, sighing as if she set something heavy down for a moment. "You did know I existed, you just didn't know I had power. You thought I only provided drugs. Your eyes have been opened, my organization is bigger and more efficient than yours. Why hasn't Joey asked for my help yet? And why won't you tell us who you are fighting" She sounded annoyed and there was a crash on her end of the line. She cursed and her breath came rapidly for a moment.

"Are you ok?" he asked sitting up, Lady protested, jumping off him. He watched her take two steps on the mattress and give him her back. He was being shunned now. "Where are you?" he grabbed his keys. She laughed softly at him.

"I dropped something, it's fine. I shouldn't be multitasking while talking to you" She sounded like she was lecturing herself. "Answer my questions." Her voice was soft and sweet like honey. She sounded aggravated and he didn't know why but he wanted to flirt with her.

"He is keeping me away from the conflict and he hasn't given me permission to tell you. I'll ask tomorrow when I see him. Why don't you talk directly to him?" She didn't answer for a long moment.

"Joey Bonetti is an honorable man, it is not time for him to speak to me. Not yet." she sounded both distant and fearful when she said this. It was good to know she feared Joey as she should.

"But you will talk to me," he said easily "Should I be offended?" he laid back again on his bed. This was fun, it was like a blind date after the date he just had. Lady ignored him and started cleaning her legs.

"You should feel honored that I'm talking to you directly. Cain, I need to go, as you know I'm a busy Woman" she said easily. He could imagine a bewildered woman staring at the mess of whatever had fallen and it was a picture.

"I like your voice, Woman," he said out of nowhere. He didn't know why he wanted to flirt with her but she laughed. She laughed again and it hit him like whiskey. He laughed as well just because her laugh was infectious.

"I like your voice too Cain, you're off the market though, Cherie would be heartbroken" With that there was another click and she was gone. He plugged the earpiece in and went to bed.

Cain made his report first thing in the morning to both Joey and Marino who both looked surprised. "I have the earpiece in my car, I'll keep it in for most of the day when I am not with you. She wants a way to connect and she is afraid of you," he said nodding to Joey.

"She's smart" Marino said "She should fear Joey, are you going to continue to see Cherie?" Marino looked concerned.

"Yea, I like her and it's a connection to them. If we are seeing each other it could bond our groups at least for a while. She's smart and high up enough to get an actual conversation with the real Woman in charge." Both men nodded. Cain thought of Cherie and smiled. She may not be in charge but she was a fun girl to be around. It had been a long time since he had dated anyone seriously and he had a feeling Cherie was serious.

"Just be careful she can be dangerous to you," Joey said.

"Yea I will be" he assured Joey. No matter how much he may enjoy her company, Cain knew where his loyalty lay. It would always be with Joey.

Cain spent the rest of the day meeting with new recruits and fielding calls from his guys. He kept the earpiece in but didn't hear from the Woman until he was home watching some crap tv.

"Cain" her voice was soft like she was tired.

"Yea" he said back, perking up.

"Cherie wants to see you again, I'm texting you her number," she said sounding exhausted.

"Ok I'll call her, you ok?" he asked, kicking his feet up on his coffee table. Be a friend, he thought, someone she can learn to trust.

"Long day"" she said easily. "How was your day?" she asked, sighing. How normal was this? He thought like they were friends catching up.

"Joey and Marino are not comfortable telling you details of our issues," Cain said and she didn't say anything right away.

"Ok, what are you watching?" she asked out of the blue.

"I'm binge watching the walking dead again" he said, enjoying the casual conversation. They were both silent for a moment before she started talking with him about the show. They spent an hour discussing which shows were the best to watch over and over again. She sounded like she was exhausted. "What can I call you?" he asked as hour number two started.

"I don't know," she said "How about you pick a name" There was humor in her voice. "Alice?" he asked.

"Oh a Resident Evil reference, I like it," she said giggling. She sounded so vital when she giggled like she would bounce up at any moment.

"Ok Alice, you sound exhausted. Go to sleep," he ordered softly.

"Oh I like the bossy, maybe I'll listen. Good night Cain," she said softly.

"Good Night Alice" he said and heard the click from her end. He wondered idly if she was as lonely as she sounded. He would work on building this friendship and see if he could convince her to meet in person. He also knew that he needed to keep this friendship private. He may tell Joey if he could use it to help the family but neither Joey or Marino would like him having a friendship with this mysterious and calculating woman.

She had backed them into a corner and now they had to work with her or lose their best revenue source. She did sound sad and lonely though, he wondered if she had anyone to talk to that didn't work for her. Joey had Carol and he hoped after all these years that Joey counted him as a friend. Cain also knew that Joey still held some things close to the vest and when decisions were made he was not to be argued with. It's hard to have a friend you can vent to in this world. Maybe he could be that for her.

CHAPTER ELEVEN

ERIN

Erin was exhausted, this week had been packed with way too much to do. She had hired a personal shopper who had filled her wardrobe with sophisticated clothes set to make her look older, and more mature. She had gone down to West Virginia and met with Gabriel and his crew. She started another deforestation area to build a large greenhouse to support the ability to expand again. On Gabriels advice she started a side hustle of local organic farming that the wives of the community could sell at the farmers markets throughout the state.

She liked having legitimate businesses on her land so that it wouldn't be misconstrued. She also made an offer on the land next to hers which was another forty acres. That was going to be pushed through and that would bring her land all the way to the highway on one side and a large river on the other.

She had kept her routine of every morning going to the cafe. Even though she now had the internet in her home. Her classes were more difficult than she had anticipated as well. She had always done good in school without trying but college was a bit different. The teachers didn't actually teach, they assigned reading and assignments and graded them. She was six weeks into the classes now and had a solid routine.

Erin had braved the shooting range with Joey that week and was pleased to see he was a good shot. She had aimed off center but was still hitting the paper for most of her shots. She did hit one dead center which made Joey cheer for her and that had warmed her heart, he had looked at her with pride. No one had ever looked at her like that before.

Now that her ribs were healed she got up at five in the morning and went to the gym close to her house. She worked out for forty five minutes and showered there as her bathrooms were still disgusting and she refused to shower there until she could get around to replacing them.

Then she grabbed her books and by six-thirty in the morning she was at the cafe, books spread out on a table for two hours of school and twenty to thirty minutes of Patrick talking to her. She was growing to like Patrick, he was simple in a world gone crazy. He liked to talk about himself which saved her from having to disclose much about herself. Then she went home and made calls and decisions for her crew. In between and around that she was working on her home. All the rooms were now empty of the trash and old furniture. She had started tearing out the walls of the upstairs bedrooms. She was taking them down to the studs and putting in new insulation. She was redoing the upstairs bathroom as well so smashing out tile was both a workout and stress relief.

She needed to gut both the upstairs and downstairs bathrooms so a plumber could come in and do what was needed to move things around. She spent her evenings doing more homework and now having nightly conversations with Cain. It had started as a mocking call to ensure he would answer if she needed. It had turned into a pleasurable almost friendship. He was smart and funny, he liked to talk about tv shows that he enjoyed and seemed to only enjoy older shows. They had debated Star Treks' even though she had never seen any of them. She had actually gone out and bought Next Generation, Deep Space Nine and Voyager so they could discuss. Her therapist was thrilled that she had a phone friend like he wanted and even more thrilled that she was talking to Patrick. She hadn't jumped when approached by a stranger at the coffee shop that morning when he had asked for her sugar caddy so she was pretty impressed with herself.

Her phone rang and she knew it was Billy Junior calling to debrief the day. She was still driving back from West Virginia but pushed her wireless headphones to answer the call. "Billy," She said.

"Erin!" He sounded out of breath "We got trouble"

"What?" she asked, hitting the accelerator and kicking herself back into the seat. She was thirty minutes outside of the city still.

"Benji got taken by a crew that runs under a dude named Anton. They think he's with Bonetti. They called me and said if we didn't schedule a sit down with the boss

Benji was toast. They want to meet tomorrow at noon." she cursed. Well they finally knew who Bonetti was fighting with. She had a quick flash of Joey mentioning the name when he was telling her about the bodies being found. She should have paid closer attention.

"What do we know about Anton and his crew?" she asked, flying past cars on the freeway.

"They operate in Ridgewood mostly but they used to operate where the Bonetti's are now. They were pushed out because they were stretched too thin. Looks like they are trying to reclaim what they feel is theirs." Billy said quickly, she could almost feel him looking at maps on his kitchen table. She could hear Billy Senior on his phone with someone as well.

"Do we know where Anton hangs?" she asked.

"No" Billy sounded scared, he should be. This was the first real danger their people had come across. This is what they had been training for. She needed to be the leader they had grown to respect. This was the first real test of her ability to take care of her people. Plans flitted through her mind as she raced towards home.

"Let me make a call, get the guys ready to go out in force tomorrow. We are taking this personally. Tomorrow we will be entering this little war and wrapping it up quickly. We will show this Anton that he picked up the wrong person and make him regret it. Get the Leutenites to the warehouse tonight. I will be there in" she glanced at the clock on her car "three hours. We have some cells there that were constructed for animals. Bring chains to ensure they close and have someone check them before

I get there. Let me know if they need maintenance." He grunted in response and she hung up.

She quickly dialed the earpiece and the click of it being auto answered clicked on. "...you guys let me know if you find anything. We need to know who was taken if Antons claimed he took someone." Cain's voice was firm and he sounded angry.

"Cain!" She said her voice was full of the anger and hurt she felt when her people were in trouble.

"Alice!" he sounded shocked.

"It's my man that Anton took. Why didn't you tell me you were up against Anton?" she said her car growling even faster up the road. They both knew why he hadn't told her, but she was still pissed about it. She took the exit ramp faster than she should have and slammed on her brakes at the light. "Benji is his name, he's my lieutenant, you didn't tell me that Anton was your enemy and now he has made himself mine. When I remove him from your area and his own I will be claiming his area with my men" She spat at him.

"Alice, I can't speak to that," he said with uncertainty in his voice. "Are you ok?"

"I'm fine I was out of town handling my other part of our joint ventures. I'll be home soon. Tomorrow I am going to make Anton wish he was never born so I need to know who is close to Anton? I want his number two's name and a location."

"His second in command is a man named Shawn Holmes, he hangs at a sports bar called Eddy T's on Cooper Ave." he sounded resigned "Let us help you get

Benji back. Your guys were helping ours and saved lives tonight. We owe you."

"You owe me a lot and trust me I will collect. Anton has made a mistake in taking Benji. He called my man and wants to sit down with Joey tomorrow at noon. He thinks Benji is yours obviously. I will send Billy Senior to introduce us as Billy Junior will be busy, as will I." She pulled into her driveway and closed the garage door behind her.

"Let me come with you." He said, he sounded concerned and aggravated, she heard a lot of movement all around him like people were shuffling. She laughed out loud at this, weeks of them talking about nothing important at night had been due to her therapist's suggestions and her curiosity about him and he now wanted to protect her. She had to admit she liked that someone wanted to protect her that knew what she was up to. She couldn't have him there though, not for what she had planned. Her therapist would be thrilled at this little revelation.

Years of torture from her parents had taught her how to hurt people and hardened her to stone. Tonight she would be handling business and setting the expectation to the world that you do not mess with The Womans' people. She would not flinch away tonight.

"No, not this time Cain," she said her voice was changing, hardening. Though she was sure he was a good fighter she didn't want to out herself just yet. She got into the house and dumped her backpack and went to the gun safe that was in the hall closet. She pulled out two more guns and a thigh holster. Racing up the stairs and ripped off her clothes of jeans and a t-shirt and heard breathing in her ear. "I thought you hung up," she said feeling oddly revealed standing in her bra and panties with Cain on the line.

"What are you planning to do?" he asked as she heard a door opening on his end. "Cain!" Theo's voice came through the door.

"Hey Bud, can you tell Joey I'm out front?" he said and there was a shuffling sound. "Alice, I'm waiting?" he asked.

"There's that bossiness again" she said, putting her thigh holster on and slipping a twenty-two in it. She slid on her shoulder holster and placed her two other guns inside while she slid on a short skirt that almost didn't hide the holster and low cut loose top that covered the guns. It showed the tops of her bra and lots of flesh. She got in front of a mirror and forced her hair into a messy bun with red tendrils spilling out. She turned to check her back and saw the edges of her scars showed and grimaced lightly.

"I am going to take someone important to Anton and inform him exactly who he is messing with. I am going to get my man back and then I am going to remove the threat of future hostility." She pouted her now red lips at her reflection. She slid on a long black trench coat and buttoned it.

"How are you going to do that?" he asked and she could hear Joey climbing into his car.

"The only way I can, by being underestimated." Slipping into tall heels she raced back to her car. "Update your boss Cain, my call might be late tonight or maybe early in the morning"

"Alice you will call me" his voice was demanding and tense. God she liked it when he was bossy. She had no idea why but that voice demanding of her made her insides clench and yearn and calmed her immediately. Like he took the choice out of it and she just had to do what he wanted. It was oddly liberating.

"I will call Cain," her voice was softer than she intended. "If I don't, Billy will be in touch. Take care of your people,"

"Make sure you call, I don't want to talk to Billy" She laughed softly and hung up on him.

In her car she raced for Eddie T's sports bar. She got there at eleven at night. She pulled up social media photos of Shawn Holmes as she dialed Billy Senior. After giving sharp instructions for him and her men. She had him hand the phone to Billy Junior and gave him clipped instructions.

"Do not antagonize Anton until we have Benji back." She saw Shawn Holmes get out of a car at the head of the parking lot with two other men. "I am getting leverage for us and will call you back later tonight. Have Phillip and Cherie meet me at the Foster Ave warehouse tonight with their crews armed." She hung up on his shocked retort, Yes tonight her people would meet her but would they like what they saw?

Erin slid out of her car and moved toward the bar easily. She flashed her fake ID and entered the bar moving two stools down from Shawn who noticed her the moment she walked in. She didn't take her jacket off as she sat, she let it hang down off the stool and ordered a shot of vodka straight. She tossed it back and felt the burn in her throat and chest. She wasn't big on drinking but it had its purposes. Shawn and his men stared at her chest as the flush worked down her pale skin. Vodka put color in her cheeks and always made her look drunk long before she really was.

"Hey girl" Shawn called "You look like a girl on a mission," he said moving one stool down to sit next to her.

"I am," she said easily "Got a lot to forget and only a few hours to do it," she said tossing back another shot.

"Your man do you wrong?" he asked, ordering her another. His leather jacket was shiny like he had polished it or something.

"Good guess." she said sipping this shot "You wanna help me forget about him, Daddy?" she asked looking up at his dark eyes. His black hair was cut tight with a fade going towards his neck. He was an attractive man and he knew it, the cocky smile he gave her said it all. She fought the urge to flinch as he leaned closer to her. She could do this, be strong for tonight, you're in control, she told herself.

"I can make you forget him for more than just a night," he whispered in her ear.

"Then I think you should come with me," she said, standing and stumbling a little to make him think she was already drunk, plus it gave the added bonus of moving away from him. Her chest released a little of the anxiety coursing through her at his closeness.

"You're a lightweight baby," he said, offering a hand. She took his hand and glanced at his guys, who were laughing and joking about a record. He waved them off and followed her to her car. "Oh I think I should drive, baby this car is beautiful like you." his charm fell flat when he turned and saw the gun she leveled at him. She tossed zip tie cuffs to him and he tightened them with his teeth. "Bonetti?" he asked as she popped the trunk. She frisked him quickly and removed three knives, two guns and a razor blade.

"No, you fucked with the wrong crewman, took the wrong person, and pissed off the wrong Woman," she said, shoving him into the trunk and pulling out a hypodermic that she shot into his neck. His eyes fluttered closed as she closed the trunk. She peeled out of the parking lot and took a quick drive to her warehouse. It took thirty minutes, she wanted to ensure she wasn't followed. She pulled into the open truck door and it slid shut after she drove in. Phillip ran up his brown hair buzzed close to his skull. She didn't roll down the window, just sat for a moment to give herself a moment to be strong. No flinching in front of your people, she told herself. She got out and looked at Phillip and motioned to the back of the car.

"Get him out and put him in a cell," she said, Neither Phillip nor Cherie had ever met her in person but both recognized her voice instantly. "Cherie, get me some tools and if possible some dental equipment." Shawn was hefted into a makeshift jail cell that was meant for zoo animals "Phillip put the crews on security, they don't need to see me" he nodded, getting the groups of people at the far end of the building moving outside. With fewer people around her, she felt herself relax. She needed to be relaxed and she wished Billy Junior was here already. She glanced around for him. Billy Junior knew he was supposed to stand between her and everyone else, he was her buffer.

Cherie appeared with a small bundle of tools that unfolded quickly.

"Billy Senior said you would need these." she smiled at the Woman.

"How's everything going with Cain?" she asked as she spread the tools out on a table outside the cell. She needed to keep things light. She had no idea how she would get through this, but knew she had to. She was, after all, her father's daughter. She had seen him handle this type of stuff for Bonetti from time to time. Her father had been a pro at tearing people apart, and now it was her turn. She shoved the guilt at what she was doing away and focused on her purpose. She would get Benji back because you don't take her people and get away with it.

CHERIE

Cherie watched as The Woman organized the tools in some sort of order that only she knew on the table and then moved to the cell. This was the Woman that they all worked for. She was young but very efficient. The Woman turned to Billy Junior who came running in after Phillip took the guys out. Billy hugged her and looked her up and down quickly as if checking for injury. "You look different," he said to her, not letting go of her hands.

"I am the same," The Woman said sharply, "I have to do this, we need Benji back." She said her voice was firm and in charge. Billy looked nervous but after a moment of reading the Woman's face, he stood taller and was more sure of himself. He placed himself between the Woman and everyone else and glanced around.

"What do you need?" he asked.

"I will take care of Shawn here, we need some information. You and the others rally the men, get some maps of the area that Antons crew runs and we will be ready to hit it tomorrow at noon when he meets with Billy Senior and Bonetti." Billy Senior who had appeared next to Cherie looked a little surprised but nodded, moving away to get the maps. The Woman glanced over at Cherie and Phillip who had just returned and nodded for them to approach.

"Get him out and tie him to the chair. Make sure he's secure." The Woman's dark blue eyes showed with excitement as they did as they were told. The Woman pulled a small packet out of her purse and popped it under Shawn's nose, rousing him almost immediately. The large factory was isolated and mostly empty, they had not started using it for the intended purpose yet. Cherie and Phillip backed away as the Woman slowly circled the man, her high heels clicking aminosly, until he finally cracked and screamed at her.

The Woman casually leaned over and started talking in his ear low for no one to hear but them. When he started screaming at her again she calmly went and retrieved a set of dental instruments and leaned over the man. Cherie winced and turned her face into Billy Junior's shoulder and he patted her back gently. Billy Senior was looking on with pride as the Woman handled business.She could hear the sounds of the instruments being used around screams and something wet hitting the ground.

"You need to be able to handle this" Billy Junior whispered "or she will demote you, this is the price for being under a boss, we see the dirty sides of things." Cherie nodded and turned back. She watched as slowly methodically The Woman worked her way through tools. With each scream she felt her skin crawl and the fear of the woman she worked for got higher. She realized now that she was in over her head but had no idea what to do about it. Her cell phone rang and she forwarded Cain to voicemail. This was going to be a long night.

CHAPTER TWELVE

CAIN

Cain had called both Alice and Cherie, but neither was answering. He had updated Joey on everything going on, and he was pissed. They were mobilizing to be ready to deploy their men wherever Alice's men appeared. It had been five hours since he had been hung up on, with her laughing at his order to call. Five hours, and neither woman had answered. He had appeared at the bar Cherie worked at to see it closed for the night, even though it was only one in the morning.

He sat in Joey's office as he called Cherie again and finally, she answered. "What?" she demanded.

"Where are you?" he demanded, Joey sat up at his desk looking more alert.

"Yea, I'm not answering that." He heard a man scream in the background and fast footsteps of her hurrying away. "I only answered because you are harassing us. Why do you have her direct line?" she demanded jealousy in her voice.

"I don't. I have that earpiece you left me and I just hit a button and it calls her if we need assistance." He felt defensive of the earpiece and Joey grinned at him lightly.

"Do you need assistance?" she demanded Cherie was pouting. Cain put his phone on speaker so Joey could hear the conversation.

"No, we would like to offer assistance." Another scream but this one was muted by walls. "What is she doing?"

"She is finding out where they have Benji," she said evenly. "I've never met her before, she is intense. All in four inch heels, she is The Woman" she sounded awed and breathless.

"How did she get Holmes?" Cain asked and Joey leaned forward listening intently to the background noises.

"It looks like she picked him up at a club the way she's dressed. She had on this little skirt and really gorgeous sequin top that was flaunting her assets. She's gotten a location on Benji and is working on Antons location now." Another scream came through the phone. "She is ruthless," Cherie sounded both afraid and amazed. "I wouldn't have the stomach for this."

"She's torturing him?" Cain asked with shock in his voice, Joey sat back and cringed.

"It's effective." there was a soft clicking sound and then Cherie got silent. There was a mumbled conversation and the phone was disconnected. Almost instantly his earpiece clicked and heavy breathing followed.

"I have the information I need, Cherie is cleaning up our guest, we will hold him while Joey and Billy Senior meet with Anton tomorrow. We will be moving then to get Benji out." she said "You let Joey know that I put this on his feet. If you had told me I would have taken additional steps. You say you don't know if you can trust me well tonight was a preview of how far I will go for my people. Can you say you would do the same?" she spat into the phone.

"We have our men waiting, tell me where you need them," he said quickly.

"I need them protecting Joey and Billy Senior. I need you to act as strong as possible during that meeting. I need a distraction away from South Queens. Go at them towards the west once we recover our man. I will be sending my men to retrieve Anton from your lunch." Cain could feel his heart clench. Both women he had grown to care about were going to be in harm's way. He also had a moment of pause as he noted Joey went from Bonetti to Joey which was odd. "I will keep Cherie out of it. She will be monitoring our guest, with her crew." she sighed deeply. "I need a shower. This counts as our call tonight"

"It's morning Alice." Cain pointed out "almost five in the morning." she cursed. "I expect a call tonight after everything shakes out." she sighed again.

"Fine, tonight I may fall asleep on you though," she said with exasperation heavy in her voice "Get some sleep Cain, today will be a busy day." she hung up and he leaned back.

"She's bringing war on Anton. She knows where her guy is and where Anton stays. She tortured the guy and is sitting on him. She is mad at us for not telling her who we were dealing with. Oh, and you're Joey now, not Bonetti." Joey raised an eyebrow at this.

"We didn't ask for her help," Joey said with petulance in his voice. "I would have done the same, though I have someone to do that for me," he said with a shrug.

"Cherie sounded awed, she saw her in person. Girl in four-inch heels and a club outfit taking care of business." Cain had to smile. He would pay anything to see that because the picture he had in his head was of a bombshell brunette with green eyes in a short skirt and sheer top blood-covered hands.

"Think we will get to meet her after all this?" Joey asked, "Now that some of her people have seen her face."

"Doubt it," Cain said "She's consistent though, she will call tonight" Cain knew he sounded worried and he was. He liked Alice even though she could be an enemy and eventually would be if she followed through on overthrowing the current regime. Joey would have to bend the knee and he didn't think he would.

"She needs a favor from us. She needs a distraction in West Queens. They are holding her guy in South Queens. I say we split our forces half with us at lunch and half in West Queens on the offensive pushing their guys out of the area. From the sounds of it, she is going after Anton. We can banter over who runs what area with her after. She seems to consider us cousin organizations." Cain reflected on all of their conversations "She doesn't like Marino, she has this tone when she mentions his name like he's something to detest." Joey nodded.

"A lot of people feel that way, hell, the kids are the same way, they act carefully, are polite, and shoot him dirty looks whenever he's around." Joey replied "Marino makes people uncomfortable because he's the most powerful Don and everyone knows it. Does she know we know that she wants to take over?"

"I'm not sure she does. She has mentioned that when Marino leaves it will be business as usual." Cain said, "Seems to me she's only helping to get the guy gone" Cain didn't mention that she had mentioned Marino had been an idol to her father. A slip she had made late one night after two hours of talking about anything and everything. "I call her Alice now, she let me pick the name."

"How does Cherie feel about you talking to her boss like this?" Joey asked, raising an eyebrow and tossing a throw blanket at him.

"She doesn't know, Alice doesn't tell her and neither do I," Cain said grinning "Alice and I are an epic game of cat and mouse. We talk about nothing important and try to slip in important questions." he shook his head "she asked me the other day if you had planned to move west or south next. This was in between discussing the slipping standards of public school and Star Trek Next Generation episodes." Joey laughed, getting a pillow from a cabinet and tossing it over. "Cat and Mouse"

"Don't get eaten, she sounds harsh. How often are you talking to her?" Joey paused and smiled "Star Trek? You got her to watch it didn't you?"

"Yes I did, We have been talking every night. She is interesting. She won't let us get close enough for her to eat me, don't worry." Cain said, laying back.

"Good morning Cain" Alice's voice was in his ear and he jerked awake. He was still in Joey's office. It was seven in the morning and he could hear the kids bustling around the kitchen with Carol.

"Morning sunshine" he groaned as he stretched "How are you awake already?" he grumbled as he stood.

"I haven't been to sleep, lots to put into place today." She paused as she heard the kids bust into the office and yell his name. Josie bounded over and hugged him, knocking the earpiece out of his ear. Theo picked it up and smiled.

"What are you listening to Cain? He asked, putting the earpiece in his own ear. "It's quiet," he said, handing it to Cain.

"It's not on dude," Cain said putting it back in his ear "Give me five minutes to wake up and I'll join you for breakfast" he promised. Both kids lit up and bounded from the room. "Alice?"

"I left donuts on the steps for you and the kids, Just wanted to say good morning." The click that ended calls with her sounded in his ear. He got up and ran to the front door throwing it open and there on the steps were two dozen donuts. An entire box of sprinkles and he had to laugh. He brought them in the kitchen and Joey and Carol raised eyebrows.

"Alice," he said to Joey who moved to the box quickly. A smiley face on top in black marker. Josie squealed with delight, apparently, sprinkles were her favorite. He frowned knowing he had been so close to meeting her, she had woken him up as she dropped them off he was sure of it. Joey went to his computer to look at the security camera on the front door. A door dash delivery driver pulled up and dropped the donuts and Cain cursed once again from getting a look at her.

"She's good," Joey sighed, sitting back in his chair. "She called?"

"She woke me up yea" Cain shook his head. The Woman was crazy, doordashing donuts to Joey Bonetti's place the day of sit-downs. She was definitely brave and felt like she was untouchable. "What's the plan for today?" he asked Joey.

"We will do as requested. I heard from Billy Senior this morning he will be at the cafe at eleven and we will all go together to Forest Hill Golf Course, we are going golfing" Cain groaned, he hated golfing. He was going to sit and watch Joey, Marino, Billy, and Anton golf, this was hell on earth.

CHAPTER THIRTEEN

ERIN

Erin hung up on Cain and was thankful she heard her siblings' voices at least once more before the day began. Today would be risky for her, she wasn't like other leaders, and she didn't hang back. She had to be sure things were moving forward. Anton had been blowing up Shawn's phone with calls and texts, he was still under the impression Shawn got lucky last night. Likely reported by the guys that were left at the bar.

She had changed into jeans and a gray tank top. Her shoulder holster was strapped with two guns. Her thigh holster over the jeans and an ankle holster. She had knives attached to her belt, and one that held her hair in a tight bun. She looked like a fiery GI Jane doll. Her lush red hair pulled into a tight bun on the top of her head. She had two computers in front of her and two cell phones. It was a two-pronged attack and she was having her men clear the areas of civilians now. It was eleven thirty and she pressed her earpiece to connect to Cain.

She had no idea why she needed to call him but she was nervous about today.

She couldn't confide that in anyone in her organization. She glanced over at her people across the room talking quietly. No one came close to her but the LTs and even they were all terrified of her after the night they spent together. She slid her wireless headphones on her left ear only.

"Don't jump and don't speak" she said softly. She caught his intake of breath and heard Joey ask him if he was ok.

"Yea, I almost sneezed," he said easily. "Damn pine trees," She laughed in his ear.

"I don't want anyone to know we are talking. You can hang up anytime you like. I just wanted to call. I'm not sure why." Her therapist would have a field day she was sure. She was growing dependent on Cain's quiet strength. His bossy quips and right now she needed the calm he caused inside of her. He remained silent but he didn't hang up. She had never felt this calmness with anyone. She wondered idly what it would feel like to see him in person and banished the thought. He was off limits, he was a Bonetti.

"I'm nervous. Billy has orders if something goes sideways he is to deliver a package to you, it will tell you who I am, and when you know that you will understand why I have acted the way I have."

"Don't say that" he whispered softly.

"Bossy," she said, relaxing a little more. She rolled her shoulders and watched her people giving her a wide berth. Billy Junior had told them off for staring at her and ordered a ten-foot minimum unless they needed to speak directly to her. "I hope one day you can boss me in person," she said suggestively. Oh, she would like that, she thought, she could see him standing over her with a sexy smirk on his face as he dominated her in the best way. The thought terrified and thrilled her, that she could even consider giving over control to someone else.

He chuckled lightly. "One day" he murmured, making her smile.

"I shouldn't say this because I am the boss but it's just you and me," she said sitting in her chair "I'm scared and I need you to boss me right now." His sharp exhale caught her off guard. She heard the men in the car talking amongst each other.

"You will call me tonight as soon as you are alone and safe. If something happens you will call me when you're in need, with a location, say yes" he demanded in a deep voice ringing over the phone. He had stepped away from the men.

"Yes" she sighed and it clicked into place. She was calm again, the fear of what would happen was off her shoulders because she now had to call Cain and that was her goal. "Why does that work?"

"When we meet in person I will show you why," he said, his voice deep and dominant. "Our next conversation is going to be a lot more flirty." He said quickly.

"Don't tell Cherie" she said standing up as Billy Junior, Phillip, and Cherie headed toward her. "It's time for my debut, don't let Anton beat you in golf." She said,

"Leave the line open so I can hear you," Cain demanded.

"For now" was her only reply. "Billy, have you located the building where Benji is being held?" Billy nodded, taking a swig of Redbull. "Phillip, you have your orders, take your half and head West to distract them, if I'm right Bonetti men will be waiting to assist and do not move until Noon." Phillip saluted her and raced out of the building. "Cherie, I made a promise, you're staying put with your crew. Watch over our guest, I am leaving ten additional men for protection. Your father was concerned as was Cain." Cherie flushed, Yea the Dad and Boyfriend combo could be embarrassing, Erin thought smiling.

"I should be at your side," she said her voice wavered but she did not back down. She did not want to be seen as weak and Erin could appreciate that.

"I need you and Billy safe, Billy will be monitoring our perimeter with his guys. We are open for attack today. I will take the rest of Benji's crew to get Benji." She looked at Billy, Benji was his cousin and they were very close. "I will get him back," She looked over at Shawn. "When that is taken care of I will move on Anton; and Shawn here has already agreed to take whatever men are left and leave the state. I hear Florida is nice and warm right Shawn?" she called to the bound man in the cell who nodded vigorously since his mouth was gagged. "See we can all be reasonable," she said, her voice light. She heard the soft chuckle in her ear. "Let's go," she said, moving to the cars. She got in a box van filled with ten of her men and drove. She was calm, she would not flinch away today.

When they arrived at the house that they were holding Benji in she saw two men out front as described by Shawn and there would be three men inside. They had orders to not kill Benji no matter what. She turned to the men in the van and looked at the one beside hers. She could hear muted conversation of the game of golf that had ensued on Cains' end. "Who's winning?" she asked lightly.

"Billy," he said softly and she laughed out loud. Her men looked at her with apprehensive smiles of their own. They likely thought she was a little crazy.

"Ok, guys let's show them why you don't mess with the Italians!" The cheer that rose was loud and caught the attention of the two men outside. They rushed them. She pulled her first handgun in a two-hand grip and shot the knees out of the first man at the door and he crumpled to the ground. She heard Cain curse lightly and could almost feel his tension but she pushed that away. She wouldn't worry about him right now. Half her men rushed the door while the others ran around the back of the house. She entered before her men and slid along the hall wall. She entered the first room while her men broke off to hit the other rooms. Hers was empty of people but held a long table filled with rolling papers and high-grade marijuana. As that was legal she put money on this being laced with something.

Moving to the next room she found her men shouting at Anton's men. Guns on both sides drawn. "Silence" she yelled and heard Cain curse and some conversation in her ear. "Now I have this house surrounded. We can all shoot and I may lose some guys but you two will die. Put your guns down or die now." They both dropped their guns. She heard a door burst from behind and turned and shot three times killing two more men.

Benji was slightly injured from a few bare-knuckle punches, but safe, and in the van within five minutes. Both vans peeled out and headed in opposite directions. The one with Benji to the warehouse to drop him off with Cherie and hers was heading for the golf course. She got there and saw in the tree line above the golf course a spattering of men belonging to Anton, Bonetti, and Marino.

"Ok Cain, I am going to try and do this quietly. I need you to get Joey, Billy, and Marino down and out as soon as the first shot is heard." She saw Cain casually scanning the perimeter. He spotted the van but she knew he wouldn't be able to see her. She already had blood splattered on her from the damage she had caused. "Don't look for me, that's cheating and takes the surprise out of it" she said and he chuckled.

"Curious" he muttered and she laughed.

"Ok guys use stealth, surprise is our friend. The longer they don't see us the better. Anton's men only try to take them out quietly. Once the first shot is heard we move with precision, whoever captures Anton alive gets a bonus" she said to her team as the men slowly one by one left the van looking like golf club employees. She was the only one who had not changed. She watched Cain line up his shot and get out of the van. She moved low in the trees and came upon a tall man with black leather and pulled him back into the trees pulling her knife from her hair, losing the bun, and slicing the man's throat. She brought him to the ground slowly as quietly as she could.

She had a black surgical mask over her mouth and sunglasses on just in case anyone did see her. The man crumbled to the ground and she moved on. One by one Anton's men were collapsing. After the last one fell her men came out of the trees and bushes like a well-rehearsed army. She stood back at the top of a hill and fired her gun into the air.

"Move Cain," she said and he grabbed Joey and Marino and shouted for Billy to follow. They were surrounded and Anton, though cursing and swearing retribution was cuffed, gagged, and thrown in her van. She saw Marino, Joey, and Cain standing in the middle of the golf course looking up at her. As the last of her men loaded in she grinned. "Thank you for bossing me," she said before hanging up on Cain. He took off at a run toward her van as she peeled out. She saw him hit the street as she rounded a corner.

An hour later she was standing back in her warehouse with all her lieutenants and Anton on his knees in front of her. "Who the fuck are you?" he demanded his voice horse from screaming through his gag for an hour.

"I am the Woman you took from." She said slowly in a low voice. "I am the Woman whose employee you took and injured." she motioned to Benji. "You mistook my employee for a Bonetti and thought you could treat him like garbage." She moved back and allowed Benji to hit Anton in the face. "I am the one who has painstakingly taken the area that you are trespassing on. I am the Woman that is going to end you." vicious curse words and threats came out at her and she smiled.

"My second will kill you bitch and he will make you hurt" he shouted out at her.

"Do you mean Shawn?" she asked and stepped aside so he could see Shawn, beaten, bloody and shaking. "He's agreed to take your men and relocate to Florida, personally I think that's a smart move don't you Billy?" She asked Billy Junior who grinned.

"Have to say I agree" Billy said in a passable southern drawl, he was being funny. "But before he goes he is going to spread the word that when you mess with the Woman not only will she kill you but she will tear down everything you have built, won't you Shawn?" Billy asked Shawn who nodded tears trailing down his face.

"It's always satisfying to know you have broken someone so completely that they will heal like the worthless dogs they are," Erin said smiling at Anton, her father had said that to her when he had broken her mother into complying with his every demand.

"More important than the outside world you know, My people will now know that if someone messes with them I will rain down hell to get them back. Loyalty Anton, it's something I prize above all else. Goodbye Anton" she said and raised her gun shooting the man in the head. He collapsed and Shawn cried out once. "Billy, call the cleaners" she said moving to Benji "are you ok?"

"Yes thank you, what can we call you?" he asked, staring at the body as blood moved across the floor.

"Alice," she said without thinking. Cain was going to have a field day when he heard this. She thought with an inward sigh but there were too many things to keep track of and her real name would be the end for her.

"Thank you Alice," Benji said quickly. Cherie looked shocked at her giving a name. Billy Junior looked taken aback but just shook his head grinning.

"Alice in Wonderland huh?" He said, pulling her into a quick hug. She leaned against him, her only true friend. She should put distance between them for the sake of the organization but Billy Junior was her friend. "They are on the way I need to go check on Dad he sounded shaken up"

"He was winning, just remind him of that" Erin said watching Billy jog out of the door.

By seven o'clock that night she was on her new couch and was watching Star Trek Next Generation and eating pizza. She had waited as Anton had been dealt with and then with a black bag over Shawn's face drove him to his home and let him go. Word was already spreading that The Woman named Alice was a threat and not to be messed with. Her teams were setting up shop in the west area and Bonetti didn't know it yet but she was splitting the area with him. She glanced at the bottle of Champaign Joey had sent to the bar and Cherie had delivered to the warehouse for her. She popped the top and poured a small glass as she watched a black blob of goo kill Lieutenant Yar.

She was showered and her homework was not happening tonight. She glanced at her planner it was Thursday so tomorrow was Theo's first cross-country race. She had agreed to drive out with Joey, Carol, and Josie. She dialed Cain's earpiece and it clicked on.

"When you have an 'x' on one side you can solve for it by dividing the six from both sides. So if you divide six by six you get?"

"One" Theo's voice was small.

"Good, and six from thirty-six?"

"Six" the response sounded more confident. "X equals six?" Theo said.

"You got it, man!" Cain said smiling. "I need a quick break guys keep going and if needed Carol can help out" she heard the kids reply and a door closed. "Alice?" he asked, his voice deep.

"I thought you would be done by now," she said apologetically. "I can call later."

"Thursdays are extra curricular days for them so we get started later. Tell me, how did you know sprinkles were the little girls favorite?" His voice was both concerned and curious. Erin kicked herself for interrupting school time, she forgot about Thursday's. She was a bad sister, she stopped herself before she went down the self guilt route.

"All little girls like sprinkles on their donuts" she sighed "Personally I like Maple bars"

"I'll remember that," he said with a grunt, must be sitting down. "I hear a Woman named Alice should be feared," he said with a chuckle. "If only your crew knew I named you"

"Oh the power of knowledge Mr. Brescia" she said softly "If your crew knew you spoke to me daily what would they think?" He paused and chuckled.

"They would think I was both brave and lucky. Joey knows I told him." he replied "You're fast by the way. The image of you standing, gun in the air, hair blowing in the wind will be in my mind forever."

"If only my face wasn't covered" she said the words she knew he didn't say. Their relationship had changed and she knew it was her fault. She had feelings for someone that was so far off limits to her that it was crazy to continue. Sitting here in her solitude with no one to talk to, she clung to these calls. She couldn't look weak to her people, and that included Billy Junior. Cain was distant enough to be safer and close enough to not turn her into the cops.

"I like your style though leaving Shawn on his front step, I'm assuming Anton is gone?" The question didn't bother her.

"Not sure we will have to see what turns up" she said easily "This was more for my crew than it was against Anton. My people need to know they are valued. I have a message for Joey, is he around?" there was a pause.

"You want me to pass you over?" he asked.

"No, just tell him we are splitting the area down the middle. He can have the Southern half of Antons area. I'll take the North with the understanding that we are allies, not competition. If there is ever a conflict with the footmen I expect you to bring it to me" he relayed the message letting her know Joey was in the room. She heard Joeys' response of assent. "Is Marino leaving?" she asked quickly and waited for Cain to relay the question.

"In a few days, why do you hate him?" Cain asked and she sighed. She wasn't going to tell him that he had left her father and abandoned him, knowing Bonetti would not protect him when he had violent outbursts. When he left her fathers job security also left. Bonetti had taken a different approach and tried to tamp down on her fathers violence in favor of outsmarting his enemies to brute force. Marino abandoned his people without a care for what would happen to them. That was not how a leader should operate.

"I just feel like he will encourage conflict between Bonetti and I," she said after a long pause. "You're busy, call me when you're home later though I may be asleep."

"You should be celebrating tonight, a great victory and your debut was more than successful. Joey says you should come over for a drink." Cain said his deep voice filled with pride. This warmed her and she pictured how she would like to celebrate laying on the couch in Cain's arms falling asleep to Star Trek. She laughed at Joey's suggestion and smiled when Cain told Joey she was laughing at him.

"I hurt a lot of people today" Erin said slowly, she hated that she had been capable of torturing a man to get information but she had seen and been through worse and fear for Benji had pushed her to cross lines. "I permanently disabled at least two people and three will never see their families again." she sighed deeply "I crossed a lot of lines yesterday and today and lost a bit of myself."

"Do you want me to come over?" Cain offered his voice low. "We can watch star trek and just talk."

"Nice try Cain" she laughed, oh she would love for him to come over and snuggle and boss her around. She needed to be able to cope with these things. Her parents had more than deserved what she had done to them, and her scars would forever remind her of that night.

Today it was like she had given the last of her innocence away in trade for her organization.

"What if I boss you?" he asked, the smirk in his voice transparent.

"We both know that's the one thing you can't boss me on" She said "Thank you for staying on the line today" she realized she needed someone like him for her second in command. Someone who could temper her and build her up. Maybe he could be that from afar. Give advice but not actually see her. "Go finish Math homework Cain, I am going to crash."

"Good night Alice" he said as she hung up. She passed out almost immediately with the TV still on, her cell on her chest.

CHAPTER FOURTEEN

CAIN

Cain sat back on the couch in Joey's office and he smiled lightly as Alice hung up on him. "Are you still dating Cherie, or are you starting a thing with Alice?" Joey asked, leaning back in his desk chair.

"I'm dating Cherie, Alice and I are, I think, friends." Cain said "today was rough on her" he sighed. He wished she would let him come over. He would like to at least sit with her while she worked through her emotions from the past few days. "She said she crossed a line with some of the stuff she did."

"You need to remind her of how many lives she saved by doing what she did. Anton was jerking us around on that golf course talking shit and not giving any ground." Joey said "This was going to be drawn out and she swept it by taking out the top and scared the life out of anyone who wanted to mess with her and by proxy us." Joey's voice showed his pride was hurt by this. "I should have thought of that plan."

"We both should have," Cain acknowledged. "She is smart but she sounds sad. Cherie says that Alice is younger than her and she's twenty-two" Joey's eyebrows rose up to his hairline. Cain shrugged, if she was younger it couldn't be by much. Cain would put her at twenty maybe twenty-one.

"So you're still with Cherie, did Cherie give you any more description of what she looks like today?" Joey asked and Cain shook his head, he hadn't spoken to her since that morning after donuts with the kids. "see if you can butter her up and get a description. Or any details. Maybe we can find out more." Cain nodded but didn't like it.

He was probably too close to Alice at this point but it felt underhanded. She had been nothing but honest with them and she had proven to be ruthless. He questioned if he could be with someone as ruthless as her. He remembered the screams coming from the other end of the phone. One thing was for sure, if she wanted to protect you then she would stop at nothing.

"I'll see what I can find but we saw her today so not much more we could get," Cain said. Dark hair and lots of it, short for a woman and thin. Pale skin at least what he could see of her arms had been pale.

"Accurate height, eye color, name, address, phone number. Any detail will be something we don't have. I couldn't tell what color her hair was, just dark and long." Joey said evenly.

Rising, Cain nodded again "I need to finish up with the kids and take off. What do you need me to do tomorrow?"

"Get with Alice and discuss boundaries and let the guys know. Get a team working on recruitment and sales in those areas." Joey sighed "You coming to Theo's race tomorrow?" Cain shook his head.

"Cherie needs some attention. Today was rough on her too, I told her I would take her out to dinner and a movie. She has her heart on some chick flick." Cain said heading for the door. "I'll make the next one," he said, heading out. He rescued Carol from the rest of the Math homework and listened to Josies Poem memorization before a quick dinner of Fettuccine Alfredo with Chicken and Broccoli. He kissed Carol's cheek then Josies' and gave Theo a high five before Joey walked him to the door. The kids no longer flinched when he was around, their grades were up and they both had friends that were frequenting the Bonetti household now.

"Cain, you'll tell me if you're getting too close to Alice. She is not one of us, she's distant and doesn't trust anyone including you." Joey said "We don't know the damage she can do to us if we cross her. We need to try and convince her to come under our umbrella, under me." Cain raised an eyebrow.

"When do you want me to broach that subject?" Cain had a feeling Alice would not see things this way. This would be the straw that broke this very fragile friendship.

"Not until she tells you her real name or you see her face." Joey said "this will be a long game" Joey said and Cain agreed. This was not a game they would likely win. Alice had more men and was more organized. The only hope they had was that she was young and ill prepared for this lifestyle long term.

When Cain arrived home he couldn't help but press the earpiece and heard the clicking of the connection. "Yea?" she said half asleep.

"Sleepy head," he said softly "It's only nine o'clock," he said as she groaned.

"You're evil" she said into the phone but didn't hang up. He heard the Star Trek Next Generation theme in the background and he grinned.

"I'm home and wanted to check in, you ok?" she sighed heavily and he could hear her TV volume go lower.

"I will be," she said after a moment's thought. "Cain, if I was a different person and not responsible for everything that I am, I would have taken you up on your offer. I would snuggle into your arms and let you hold me until their faces go away." He could picture the image he had of her in his mind on his couch watching Star Trek.

"I would like that," he sighed. He hated to admit he was falling for a woman that he didn't even know the name of.

"Unfortunately we are who we are. Plus you have Cherie and I might have someone. Can we settle for flirty friends?" she asked. This perked his interest, she might have someone? Who was it? And why did it bother him so much to think of her resting her head on someone else's shoulder.

"As long as I can boss you," he said, his voice almost growling.

"Of course, you're the only one I have ever wanted to boss me." She laughed as Cain laid out on his couch.

"I like to boss you Alice. I really hope one day you will learn to trust me" she sighed deeply into the phone.

He imagined her stretching, raising her breasts into the air.

"One day. I trust you more than anyone else if that makes you feel better. I couldn't tell anyone else I was scared or nervous like I did with you today. You made me stable and I don't know why" she sounded concerned "your dangerous for me, you will be my undoing" she sounded both concerned and excited.

"I don't want to be your undoing," he said easily the more he spoke to her the more he wanted to get to know her.

"I know, but we will cross that bridge at a later date." She sounded exhausted.

"How about we focus on one day at a time, Start your episode of Star Trek over and go back to sleep. I'll call you tomorrow to discuss work stuff."

"Yes Sir" she mocked. She hung up and he took the earpiece off to charge. He called Cherie on a whim to check on her.

"Cher, how are you doing?" he asked when she answered the call.

"I'm good, you know, steady." she sounded like she had been crying.

"Rough day, I know," He said, sighing. She was a headstrong woman for sure. "Want to come over?" he asked. She had been to his place once before on their third date.

"Yes," She said softly.

"Then come over baby," he said easily. "I'll make you breakfast in the morning." he heard her smile as she agreed. Within thirty minutes she was at his door and they were in bed ten minutes later.

JOEY

Joey Bonetti was a patient man who planned things well. He had gotten comfortable and hadn't realized Alice was growing her organization. He had gotten comfortable and hadn't realized Marino had sent spies to report back. Now he sat in his office in his damn house with the Caruso kids in the dining room, eating with Carol and staring at Marino who was grinning like the Cheshire cat.

"I have been thinking about moving back here, there seems to be a lot of chaos right now. This Alice is strong and organized, driven, it would seem. Been a long time since I have had a challenge like that."

"Alice helped us today" Joey pointed out, he hated Greg Marino. Smug bastard ruled by brute force and fear.

"Yes she did, but at what costs?" Marino asked "What will she want in return. You are in her debt now so she can call in that marker whenever she wants."

"She's earned the marker," Joey said again, patiently waiting.

"I think a man like you needs to take a step back. You have little kids around again, that beautiful wife you want to keep happy. Your girls Maria and Lisa in college. Got a lot going on in general. Plus your prodigy is regularly talking with the enemy and dating one of her top people. I think Joey unless you want things to get unpleasant it would be best for you to take a step back and let me return." Joey saw red, he inhaled his cigar slowly as he worked through the raw anger and hatred he felt for the man across from him. He was threatening his wife and his kids both biological and adopted. He was known for attacking families of traitors or snitches. That's how he deterred people from snitching or leaving the Family. It was underhanded and dishonorable, which summed up Greg Marino completely.

"Do you think the men will follow you over me?" Joey asked, spinning his cigar in his fingers. Marino had more men at his disposal. Joey knew it, he could fly in hired killers to anywhere in the states and Italy. Plus he could call in Arizona and Miami to help him.

"I think that if you tell them to, they will follow me. I think if you're my number two they will stay in line. Then we can focus on finding Alice."

"Me and my men can't help you with that." Joey said "It would be dishonorable after she just saved us."

"I need assurances Joey" Marino said in what he thought was a godfatherly way, Joey was sure. The guy was a cliche among cliches with the theatrics. Joey would wait, and Joey would plan. It wouldn't be as easy to get rid of Marino this time. Excitement coursed through his veins as he nodded to Marino.

"What assurances?" Joey asked, he just bet the man was worried about him. Joey was smarter than Marino and they both knew it.

"That you won't turn on me and try to kill me at some point," Marino said with a slow smile turning up his old face.

"Can you assure me that you won't kill me at some point?" Joey asked, bad timing as Carol walked in and almost dropped the drinks she brought them. Joey gave her a look and she left the room quickly.

"Ok so neither can assure that" Marino agreed "How about that if you won't help me find Alice you won't help her hide from me. Just stay out of it."

"I can do that." Joey agreed. He had no idea if he was lying or not as an idea had just popped in his head. Have Alice kill Marino. He smiled broadly at Marino. "I will tell my men we do not help either side in this witch hunt of yours which for the record, I do not condone and I protest as your second."

"You were always the smart one," Marino said, standing to shake Joey's hand. Joey wanted to shoot him between the eyes at this moment.

"One last thing Greg, if you ever mention my wife again, you won't have to worry about Alice. I'll kill you myself." Joey stood shaking his hand wearing a grin when he said it. Marino frowned and thought about it,

"To far" he agreed "Wives have never been a part of this, I apologize," he said but they both knew he didn't mean it. Greg Marino had murdered the wives and children of traitors to the Family. Joey would never let his wife be harmed by Marino men.

After he ushered Marino out and connected with Cain's voicemail he cursed himself and sat down to form a plan. He pulled a sheet of blank paper in front of him and willed his plan to take form. Joey was a great planner, this he could do, he thought as he started writing.

CAIN

The next morning Cain woke and as promised made breakfast of scrambled eggs, pancakes and bacon. Cherie walked out in his t-shirt which made him smile. She had legs for miles. She hadn't wanted to talk about her day last night, only wanted to feel alive, twice. He had been more than happy to oblige.

"You know." she said over breakfast, "I never saw anyone get killed until yesterday. The way she did it like she was going to carry on a conversation with him and then Bam he's dead, it was so easy for her." Cherie sounded both awed and uncertain. "She's different from any girl I have ever met"

"What's she like?" he asked, eating his bacon. His earpiece was back in place but he knew Alice wasn't on the call. He had been listening for her all morning. He bet she was still asleep after how hard yesterday had been on her.

"Self assured," Cherie said "She came in with Shawn Holmes zip tied in her trunk and passed out. She was dressed like she had come from a club short skirt and low cut top and stilettos. She had me get tools that Billy Senior had said I would need." Cherie paused and stopped eating looking sick. "He handed me torture tools like it was nothing" tears pricked her eyes "And Alice used them, she had us move away from her and she pulled the guys teeth, and sliced his face and arms. Gave him a new piercing and when that didn't work she just sat and talked to him quietly. That's when he started screaming details. I was talking to you at the end of that part so not sure what she said but from what Phillip said, she looked cool as could be, talking to him like she was ordering a coffee. Covered in blood all over her outfit and boobs." That part apparently really grossed Cherie out. Cain could imagine it and had seen similar seating arrangements. Derrick, the one Anton murdered, had been that guy for them. Now they would have to call in someone from the other families to assist with that. Maybe they could use Alice if she would fall under their umbrella.

"Sounds like a terrifying woman," he said softly "You said she looked younger than you?" he asked softly.

"Yea, she's gotta be like eighteen or nineteen, twenty at most. I offered her my flask and she said she didn't drink and Billy made a joke about how she broke all the other laws, what was one more." Cherie said "Billy and her are friends, he hugged her after Anton had been shot, she didn't seem upset by it either. She leaned into him like he was holding her up then just snapped out of it. I asked Billy if they were a thing and he said no he has a girlfriend. That didn't stop him from ordering everyone to stay ten feet or more away from her and he would walk the distance like some sort of guard." good to know she did have a friend but why then didn't she confide in him?

"Do you tell people I'm your boyfriend?" Cain asked, trying to maintain a casual conversation. He knew if he kept probing she would get suspicious. Peppering questions about the Woman in, around their casual talk would be best.

"I tell them I have a man but not who," she said looking a bit nervous. "Do you tell people about me?"

"My nearest and dearest, Joey knows and his wife Carol, a few of my friends know. The kids I tutor know. I mention you in casual conversation as my girl." he said knowing it's what she needed to hear. It was true he had mentioned her to a lot of his friends as the girl he was dating. "No one questions me on who I see or who they affiliate with." he shrugged. He didn't know why it stung she hadn't called him her boyfriend to her friends.

"That's sweet," she said, leaning over and kissing him. He deepened the kiss tasting the maple syrup she had used on her pancakes. He heard her silverware hit the counter as her hands clung to his biceps. Right then his cell phone rang and he pulled away with a scowl.

"We will finish that in a minute," he said answering the phone, it was Joey. "Have you spoken with Alice?" He asked immediately.

"No, it's eight in the morning and I have Cherie over." there was a pause.

"Call me when you talk to Alice and make it this morning," Joey said, he sounded agitated about something.

"What's going on? You ok?" Joey paused again. It wasn't like him to be so demanding first thing in the morning. Something must have changed.

"We will talk later. Catch it" Joey said which was a phrase he only used when something was wrong and they needed to meet just the two of them. "Two hours" he hung up.

"Everything ok babe?" Cherie asked when he got off the phone.

"Yea baby Joey needs me, something is going on. What have you got planned for today?" he asked, clearing his plate away and loading the dishwasher with the pans he used to make breakfast.

"Billy Senior has a debrief for us all this morning after he talks to Alice about the new areas we will be covering but I doubt she will put me in one of those. She and my Dad are tight and they keep me close to home. I'll be at the bar most of the day." he nodded.

"I'll swing by tonight," he said, kissing her soundly. "I gotta jump in the shower and head out."

"Ok I'll see you tonight," she said, picking up her purse and grabbing her clothes to dress... He liked that she didn't linger. She knew they both had business to attend and when it was time to go she left. He jumped in the shower and out within five minutes and clicked his earpiece to connect to Alice.

"Morning Cain" she said and he could hear background noise.

"Morning, are you busy?"he asked.

"At a coffee shop doing homework," she said and then paused. He could almost feel her cringe at the honesty. Another slip in her perfect armor.

"You in school Alice?" he asked, loving this small detail "what's your major?"

"Nice try, Boundaries" the double meaning there lingered before she continued. "I was thinking the six-seventy-eight as a splitting point. You would get the entire southern area and I'll take the North," she said.

"That doesn't sound like an even split," he said.

"I did more work than you." she countered. She was brisk, kicking herself for letting details about herself go.

"I'll bring it to Joey. How are you doing this morning?" She paused and thanked someone for her coffee. She sounded breathy and the male voice was flirty. A tide of jealous energy beat at his chest. Who was this flirting with Alice?

"I'm on a call right now but can we chat after?" she asked the man who agreed. "I'm fine"

"Sounds like it" he knew he sounded like a sulky child. He had no reason to be jealous; he had just sent his extremely beautiful girlfriend out the door. So that he could call Alice. Damn his own luck.

"Don't worry, you're the only one that can boss me," she replied, making him smile. This was the weirdest relationship he had ever had. "Besides Cherie already told me she was staying the night with you, we have to live with the reality of our situation. I don't know if we will ever meet in person. We have a business relationship and a very odd friendship." That was one way of putting it.

"Yea ok, just don't like the image of you with anyone else," Cain said sullenly. He didn't know how to explain it but he felt like she was his already. Cherie was a fun girl but her laugh didn't make his heart stutter the way Alice's did.

"What do I look like in your mind?" she asked, curiosity filling her voice. Cain was dressed and pulling his boots on when he sat back in his chair.

"Chestnut brown hair with green eyes, pale skin. Five-five with soft curves. Tight body." he said slowly "Am I close?" he asked.

"Not remotely," she laughed at him. "I like it, that woman sounds sexy and alluring. I like that you think of me like that. Let me know what Joey says."

"Will do, study hard Alice." she sighed at this detail.

"You will be my undoing Cain" she said softly. Her voice held fear and excitement. "I hope not," he said softly. She paused for a moment before hanging up.

Cain arrived at an office park where he knew Joey would be. They had a few places to meet up linked to a few code phrases. He sat on a park bench and glanced around. He saw Joey casually walking down the sidewalk and he sat next to him.

"Marino is planning to move back to New York, leaving his son in charge of Nevada." Joey said quickly "This would mean me stepping back, we all know Marino is the strongest and he was in charge before so people may accept it. His family started all of this and he started the expansions. He made comments about Carol, the girls and the kids." Cain felt the rage pouring off of Joey when he said this.

"What?" Cain said in shock. They would lose everything they had worked for. The community. "How can he just decide this? What about us? The community won't stand for it. The violence has fallen drastically since you took over and our streets are safer."

"He would make me his second and you a Lieutenant. He would bring a few of his high performers out here but most would stay with his Son. He wants Alice to heel and fall under him. He sees her as a threat." Joey said. Alice, Cain hadn't thought of how she was going to react. "This will mean war with Alice," Cain said softly.

"I told Marino that my men have a debt to Alice and her crew so we cannot go against her. It would be dishonorable and he agreed. She has too many people to go at her head on, he would be doing shadow work and going after just her." Joey said "The question is, how do we use Alice to get rid of Marino?" Cain looked at Joey. He could see Joey was planning something and he wondered if Alice would survive it.

"I think she is going to be pissed that Marino didn't leave," Cain said, "We let her know what is going on, and we monitor what Marino is doing." It would be tricky but it was the only way he could protect her and Joey at the same time. "Marino knows I talk to her on this thing," he motioned to the earpiece. "I'll keep that up but in his eyes there will have to be a point where she and I have a falling out." Joey nodded slowly.

"This has to be handled carefully. I am going to work the other end and see if convincing him to move to Florida would be best as they need help with not only turf, but their people are defecting." He said evenly. "Marino mentioned a trip was needed so he plans to fly down in a week or two if things haven't improved." He hesitated "He knows about the shipment so he knows that we are going to lose that if this isn't handled perfectly. I don't like how she has positioned herself. She did this with intent" Joey was bitter at this point. He knew Alice had lured them into business with the thought of taking over. She had been all cloak and dagger and they hadn't seen any of this coming.

"Yeah she did, I'm pretty sure she's been planning this for a long time. I don't know how we missed her all this time." Cain watched Joey, his mentor and the best father figure he had ever had. When it came down to it he was going to be pulled between Joey and Alice.

"From what I hear" Joey said evenly "She only had about thirty in her crew until recently. She started recruiting hard as soon as Anton popped back up. Something changed around that time that she was able to come out of the shadows." Joey sat pondering what it could be.

"I'll try and find out," Cain said with a sigh. "I found out she's in school today, said she was doing homework" Joey looked unsurprised.

"If she's as young as we think then it's not surprising she's in college, like you should be. I'll ask Erin if she knows anyone who fits Alice's description but Erin only takes online classes so not sure if she socializes with any of her classmates." Joey rubbed his face "I'm driving her to Theo's race today so I can make it a casual question."

"How is she doing? I haven't heard about her in awhile." Cain said, trying to leave on a positive note and bypass the college conversation again. That life wasn't for him.

"Good, busy. I don't know how she does it. She has two majors she's going for because she says she didn't know which one she really wanted to do. She's working almost full time at a cleaning service. Plus she bought a foreclosure recently that she's trying to DIY back to life. When I see her she always looks exhausted and stressed. Carol says she doesn't know

how to cook so she's living off of fast food and take out so we try and make big healthy meals for her. Girl is driven." He said "She still flinches when I lift a hand around her though or if I enter a room quietly she will just freeze like she's being hunted. She's working with a therapist and got her doing some exercises to help her with that."

"That's probably why she only takes online classes" Cain said "she would be jumping out of her skin with a bunch of guys around her."

"Yea" Joey agreed "She's got some guy flirting with her for months now, he's asked her out twice and she is shy. Just go to the coffee shop where he works to talk to him." Cains mind shifted to Alice that morning talking with some guy. "Carol is trying to convince her to invite him over for dinner with us so she won't be alone and can be more comfortable." Cain dismissed his previous thought. No way Alice was afraid of men, not with how she handled herself this week.

"That sounds nice, have you looked into this guy?" he asked, leaning back on the bench.

"Yea solid kid, going to law school. In the Army Reserves. Part Italian but his family is from Texas just moved here last year. Patrick Miller, you should talk to him, we could use a good lawyer." Joey said.

"Patrick Miller, ok I'll get with him this week," Cain said easily.

"I need to get back, we pick up the kids in an hour. Oh, what's the boundary?" he asked.

"She put forth use the six-seventy-eight as a split because in her words 'I did more than you Cain' " Cain said with a laugh "showing her age there" Joey laughed.

"Yea, that sounds like my girls arguing over who cleaned their room better." Joey laughed "Sounds fair as long as we get the entire south side of it to include the flushing meadows beach that touches the water."

"I'll bring that back to her," Cain said, rising and offering his hand. "With the cross country meet I'm assuming homework will be late?"

"It's Friday night Cain, they can get to their homework tomorrow." Cain nodded and smiled.

"Cherie will be excited. I'll check in with the guys, do a money collection and drop it at your place while you're gone. I can drop in on Patrick this morning. What cafe does he work at?"

"It's called Flowfi, they have wifi that she uses. If you see her, don't let her know what you're up to."

"If I see her I'll buy a coffee and leave and come back later," he said with a shrug. Joey nodded and they parted ways.

Cain thought of their situation. Attacked or uncomfortable on all sides. Joey was caught between a rock and shit place with Marino coming back here. Using Alice against Marino would be wise but with their hands tied on trying to help her. She may turn on them as well, take her shipment and her people and clean them out.

CHAPTER FIFTEEN

ERIN

$\mathcal{E}$rin had just closed her laptop with a smile at Patrick, who was waiting on a customer when he glanced her way. He had asked her out and she had agreed to meet him for a late dinner that night. She was getting back from the race by seven so she would be on her first official date at eight o'clock that evening. She was anxious but knew Carol would pump her up all afternoon. She had a call with her therapist prior to that to discuss it.

She felt guilty because of all the flirting she did with Cain, but he had Cherie. They had never met in person and she was going to keep it that way. She shouldn't deny herself simple pleasures and Patrick was a simple pleasure. Did she have the same strength of feelings for Patrick that she had for Cain? No, she didn't but she figured Cain was more domineering and could have his way with her if they were to meet in person. Patrick likely wouldn't be that way. Maybe he could help her with her fear of men. He was kind and patient. She had come a long way since living in the apartment with her parents. She had overcome a lot and was changing her life for the better.

Erin slid her laptop into her backpack and started packing away books when she saw a black SUV pull up in front of the cafe. She looked around for a moment and cursed that there was only one exit and sure enough Cain was heading this way. The windows were tinted so he couldn't see inside. She sent a silent prayer that he would go next door for something. She slung the backpack over her shoulder and bolted for the bathroom just as Cain stepped inside. She hid for ten minutes when she finally peeked out of the bathroom. He was sitting close to the front counter talking to Patrick who looked slightly concerned but a little hopeful.

It was now or never, she walked casually out of the bathroom and nodded at Patrick who inclined his head but didn't make a move toward her. She looked out the window as she walked past Cain and Patrick and out the door going down the street. She walked three blocks before turning to look over her shoulder. She was alone, with no tail. She headed back to her place to drop her stuff. She had to get ready for the drive to the cross-country race. She had told her crew their orders already, but she was waiting for calls from the realtor on the closing of that extra forty acres as well as Cain's response from Joey, who she would be spending the day with. Life was getting a little too closed in, she thought entering her house and disabling her alarm.

Thirty minutes later Erin was in the back seat of a SUV with Josie talking her ear off about school and dance class. They were preparing for a Christmas show. This dance class was also part of a theater group so they went for Broadway musical style shows. They had turned A Christmas Carol into a show tune. She was going to enjoy it only because Josie apparently had a beautiful voice and got the part of the Ghost of Christmas present that got to sing about Tiny Tim's struggles. It was an epic tale according to Josie.

Her cell rang and she answered it glancing up front to see Joey's eyes on the road and Carol humming to the radio. "Hello" she said, holding a finger up to Josie who didn't make a sound. They had been doing this for years now so she knew she couldn't make a sound.

"Alice, we need to talk," Cain said. He sounded aggravated, something must be wrong.

"Give me an hour," she said, glancing at her smartwatch. "I'll call you back" the clipped tone he had told her he was serious. He had never sounded like that with her. She glanced at Joey who was eyeing her in the back seat. "Everything ok?" she said in a lower voice.

"Not really, Joey and I are concerned," Cain said in a grim tone. She held Joey's gaze for a moment longer and glanced at Josie with a soft smile as Josie looked up in concern.

"Ok I'll call you back" she used her soft sweet voice that you would normally reserve for a boy. Carol's ears perked up as Erin hung up.

"Everything ok honey?" she asked, glancing back.

"Yea Patrick just needs to chat before our date tonight. He sounded stressed." She lied quickly.

"You said he goes to law school right?" Joey asked "Maybe he's struggling a bit, might need to study or get a pep talk from you, guys need that sometimes." He said, reaching for Carol's hand. Carol smiled at him with love in her eyes. That was something to yearn for, she stared at their linked hands for a long time. Wishing she could have a life like them. Though she couldn't cook, or decorate or keep house the way Carol did. She would have liked that kind of life.

"You two are good together," Erin said before she could stop herself. They both looked shocked at this observation and she flushed.

"Thank you Erin" Carol said "It took a lot of work and a lot of fighting to get where we are. Relationships aren't always easy." Erin nodded, smiling at Josie who was looking at her with wonder.

"What's going on in that mind Josie?" Erin asked, smiling down at her sister.

"Do you think you and I will have a marriage like Carols or like Moms" she asked looking serious. "The kids at school say you marry your father and I don't want that" her voice was small.

"You marry whoever you want, and don't worry if any guy you date is even slightly like Dad, he won't be in your life for long. I promise," she said, hugging her sister. "Besides Dad isn't your only father figure, you got Joey here and look at how he treats Carol. You're going to have eight years of Joey showing you how a man should treat a woman." Erin locked eyes with Joey in the mirror and they both knew at that point that the kids would never live with her. Tears filled her eyes briefly but she blinked them away.

"Then I better make sure I treat Carol like the Queen she is, and Erin's right I would never stand for anyone to mistreat you Jojo" Joey's voice sounded hoarse and he was blinking a lot too. He loved Josie, she could see it in his eyes. Carol was beaming at them and Josie smiled as she pulled away.

"So what is your favorite line in the play?" Erin asked Josie to change the subject. She let Josie chatter on for the rest of the drive. They got to the course and she was impressed with the park set up. It was going to be a beautiful run. She greeted Theo and wished him good luck in his first race. The racers lined up and the little pop gun went off and they were off. She watched him go in the middle of the pack as they raced forward. She excused herself to return Cain's call as they waited the twenty to thirty minutes or so for the racers to come back to the finish line.

The connection was made to his earpiece, and she heard Cherie gushing about some customers at the bar that afternoon. Oh she hated to interrupt but this was the only time she would have today.

"Cain" she said softly "This is the only time I can give you until really late tonight," he told Cherie he had to step away for a call and she understood.

"Hot date?" he asked as he moved away and she could hear his footsteps.

"You wish" she said "whats going on?" Cain proceeded to describe the Marino issue and the proposed solution for keeping her safe temporarily. "Well that's inconvenient" she sighed after he finished describing the conversation Joey and he had earlier that day.

"Yea, he knows about the shipment but we kept the location and distribution to just a few trusted guys but with the expansion, it will be hard to continue that. If he is taking over he will want to know his source." Erin thought about the dangers of that.

"If he sees me as a threat what is the likelihood he would want to continue to take my product? It is your biggest money earner." She knew this because she had done the math on what they charged their customers versus what she charged them.

"I'm not sure but we have been holding that line item out of our accounting that he gets to see. When this happens he will want you to fall in line." Cain was silent for a moment before he added "We value the relationship we have with you and don't want to endanger that." That made her concerned. That meant they were willing to turn on Marino for her. Maybe use her to overthrow Marino. Cain had offered partnership earlier but she didn't want to be under Bonetti. She needed to be in control or her anxiety would go sky high. She had worked too hard and gone too far to fall in line.

"I appreciate that," She said slowly. "That will hold for now. What did he say about the boundaries?" she leaned back in the grass and watched Joey and Carol holding hands with Josie between them. They were up at the finish line looking down towards the path the runners would come down. She stood and headed a little way down the path with a few of the other dads that she knew would run next to their kids, yelling and cheering them on.

"He accepts with the knowledge that the entire coast area that touches the highway belongs to us." she sighed.

"Can I barter rights to utilize a small part on certain days? She asked back. "I will ask," he said.

"Thank you, get back to Cherie I gotta go" she said, seeing small bodies in the distance as the runners were coming in. The yelling was starting and she needed Cain to not hear it.

"Call me when your night is done even if it's late." he bossed her, making her smile.

"Bossy" she said back "Yes sir" with that she hung up on his answering laugh. She got down to the line with the dads and she watched the first six boys race by when she started running. She cheered and yelled and Theo pushed fast passing the boy in sixth right at the line. His coach, Joey, Carol and Josie all ran at him thumping his back and shouting over the crowd. She smiled at the scene and joined them.

"You're fast," Theo said to her. "Wanna race?"

"Only after you go run another three miles," she said smiling "Great job Theo!" she hugged the sweaty boy and grimaced at him. "You're gross"

Erin had a nice date at a local Italian restaurant for dinner. She wore a mid length skirt and a nice blouse that teased at cleavage. Her heels were high but that was the only kind she owned. She had hired a personal shopper to help with her more grown up wardrobe and they had favored high skinny heels. Patrick was sweet and liked to talk about his dreams and goals. He had political aspirations that could be useful, if she got him to join her organization. She also hadn't flinched all night even when he had reached across the table to take her hand. She had felt the panic and breathed through it focusing on his kind eyes.

"Was that one of the Bonetti guys talking to you today?" she asked when there was a lull in the conversation.

"Yea just introducing themselves, asking about my college plan, that kind of thing." He said. He sounded like it was no big deal but the pride at being approached was in his eyes.

"You thinking of getting mixed up with the mob?" she asked, tilting her head. Most Italians in their neighborhood knew if you were approached it meant you were either being recruited or being charged. Patrick didn't have money but he did have a future that was useful.

"I'm thinking my law school is going to cost a lot, so will my eventual election campaign." She nodded at this. Patrick was an opportunist like most politicians.

"Have you ever thought about going for another group? Led by the girl boss?" Patrick scoffed lightly. Well that was offensive, Erin thought watching him her face guarded.

"She may be terrifying to most, but she's new and Bonetti and Marino have been around forever. They are established and once they tire of dealing with her they will get rid of her easily." That hurt, Erin thought as she sipped her soda. Get rid of her huh? She would see who would get bumped off. Though she wasn't prepared and it was supposed to wait years before she took on Marino.

"So you think she's just a one hit wonder?" she asked, her head still tilted. He grinned at her and nodded. Oh, he would regret that one day. She was going to make it her mission to show him that she ruled New York.

"Bonetti is the way to go, mark my words" he said "If they extend an invite I'll take it." Oh this could be useful, she thought.

"So if this works out with you and me, I'd be dating a made man," she said in her flirtiest voice.

"Yea, that would be nice," he said, tracing a finger down her cheek. She flinched at the surprise contact. Then blushed hard at his surprised look. "You don't like to be touched do you?" he asked.

"It's not that, you just surprised me," she said softly, digging into her pasta. She sighed to herself, she had been doing so good at not flinching tonight.

"I noticed you do that a lot," he said, watching her "If a man comes near you, shrink back and flinch if they move too quickly." She had thought she was getting better at that. This is why she worked in the shadows. You don't flinch in front of your team if you're not seen by them.

"Yea, I'm working on that," she said, sitting up a little straighter. She could feel her anxiety spiking. Breathe, she ordered herself, just focus on your food and let this pass. It was working. She felt her heart rate dropping and the flush leaving her face.

"One day will you tell me why?" he asked, taking a bite of his food. He looked like he was genuinely concerned about her. Sweet and kind Patrick, she thought, this is why she came here. To try and be out with a kind man.

"Maybe one day" she said, smiling at him. He was nice. He was naive but he was nice. Maybe nice could be enough for a little while.

By ten-thirty she was back home and in her pajamas of a tank top and pink pants with bears holding hot chocolates.. She laid on the couch and turned on Star Trek. She called Cain as ordered. She heard moaning and she muted the TV. Cherie was moaning and Cain let out a short grunt. She sat silently intruding on their intimate moment and tears filled her eyes. She hung up and knew he would hear the soft catch of breath she let out just before she hung up. She hoped he would just never mention it, as she sat holding her knees, tears rolling down her cheeks.

He wasn't her boyfriend but she felt like he was hers. Even after coming home from a nice date with a nice boy who liked her a lot. She felt like she belonged to Cain and he belonged to her. Their late night talks had gone too far. She could not fall in love with someone she was afraid of. When she thought about Cain she was afraid of him. He had a reputation for being loyal and strong. He was Joey's right hand at twenty-three which was unheard of. She needed to real herself in and be happy with the nice, naive boy she had just been on a date with. Within five minutes, her phone rang. It was Cain. She took a deep breath and answered the call with silence. She needed to stop crying now.

"Alice," he said with concern in his voice. "Are you ok?"

"Yea," she said softly, her voice only wavered lightly, clamp it down girl! She told herself silently. "You should go back to Cherie, it's rude to walk away right after sex"

"She's in the shower," he said brushing that off, he sighed and she could almost feel him pacing. "I'm sorry," he said.

"No, I'm good Cain really, just a long day with lots of surprises." He sighed and groaned.

"You're concerned about Marino?" he asked as if trying to determine the root cause of her voice.

"Of course I am" she snapped at him, then sighed, it wasn't fair for her to act like a jealous child. She had been pushing Cherie and him together because Cherie liked him and it was useful. "Sorry, if he moves back eventually he will either turn you against me, or demand that I work for him and absorb my crew. Marino only cares for his top people, not for all his families and men. He screwed a lot of people when he left before. Bonetti didn't realize he left some people behind. Or maybe he intentionally did it because he didn't like their style. A lot of people got hurt. I will never work for Marino. So he will try and kill me." she said this matter of factly. "Now it's a game of how long can I outrun him." She could see Cain's face clear in her mind looking down at her as Marino pulled the trigger and ended her life. Right now she knew she couldn't win, he had gotten too interested in finding her too early. By helping Joey to protect her siblings from being in danger she had put a target on her own back. She was stupid, she thought bitterly, kicking herself.

"This sucks," he said in the most aggravated guy voice she had ever heard. She laughed out loud at this.

"Yes it does"

"We have already told Marino that we cannot go against you as we owe you for the Anton thing," Cain said, his voice sounded lost, like he was flipping options in his mind and coming up blank. Join the club buddy, she thought bitterly.

"So you're not helping either of us then" she mulled this over in her mind and thought it was at least fair.

"It ties his hands, he can't use our men to go after you. He's only bringing two crews with him as he doesn't want to cripple his Son. So you will have ten guys looking for you." she sighed.

"Any chance you'll give me names and descriptions?" she asked with no hope.

"I can't do that. I will tell you if he's getting close. There may come a time where we will have to take a break from these calls." This hurt her heart but she sat back and thought of Cherie. This wasn't fair to her, Erin knew Cain had feelings for her and for Cherie. She would miss the calm that came from him bossing her.

"I can appreciate that" she said "I need time to think, I will call tomorrow night." She knew she sounded sad again.

"Let me know if you need anything." He offered. She grunted and hung up. *I need you,* she thought bitterly. She sat thinking about her situation. Marino was someone to fear. He was old-blood Italian. His family still had connections in the old country. She needed an ally that was not Bonetti. Though the Bonetti crews would be leaving her alone she knew eventually she would be found. Until then she would grow her presence in the North and reach out to someone she hoped she could call on.

She went to bed after two hours of planning.

Greg Marino walked the living room of the new house he purchased down the road from Joey's. His wife was already ordering furniture and decorating it as she had flown in the previous night to move out. He stood in what would be his office looking at the ten men in the room with him. They had all proven themselves at finding people and getting bloody. They had all proven loyalty to him and his family.

"We have a couple things to go over. I assume your families will be joining us in the coming days and weeks. Take the next two weeks to get adjusted and your family settled. Then we will depart for a short, and I mean short trip to Florida. Lanza needs assistance and we will clean up his mess. I have had my nephew Nicki move down there to be the new number two and help right the ship but they need muscle and my presence." the men grunted in response.

"When we return we will be hunting for this Alice woman. She is used to working in the shadows. Her own crew only just saw her face for the first time recently. She gave them a fake name that was made up by Bonetti's number two Cain. For now, Cain has agreed to continue his calls with her and try and help us locate her but the Bonetti's cannot go against her without it being openly dishonorable to the neighborhood. She is like Robin Hood for the people in this area so we have to do this quietly."

He paused surveying the men in front of him. None of them were known for being gentle with anything. He had brought his most loyal, most merciless men that he had in his employ.

"Is Derrick Caruso still around?" Jeffers asked from the front of the group. "He was always loyal to you and if given the choice he would work for you. I know he thinks Bonetti is too soft."

"Caruso was murdered by Anton, who was taken out by Alice. She did us that favor. I want her alive, I want to try and reason with her. She will bend the knee and work for us. She has something I want, that should belong to us." Marino wanted that supply. It was worth its weight in gold. As a customer he had gotten his hands on some of it and there was no better product that he had ever had. The men all agreed to working with some stealth but he knew it wouldn't be long before Alice knew he was hunting her.

As the meeting broke up and the guys departed Marino looked out a window at the darkened street below. He had wanted to go to Nevada because New York was too hot. The feds were closing in and his children were small. The move had been smart and he had taken everyone of value.

He knew that people were going to be raw towards him for how he left. He had broken up the people and promoted some sending them to other areas. He left Bonetti behind thinking he would take the fall with the feds. He still wasn't sure how Bonetti got out of the noose that was tightening fifteen years ago. Marino turned when he heard someone enter the room and smiled at his wife.

"Veronica, are you ready to go back to the hotel for the night?" he asked. Her black hair curled gently around her pixie features. This was how a Mob wife should look. Delicate petite and mysterious.

"Yes dear," she said, offering a hand to him. He took it and led her from the house. His wife would never think of trying to interfere or give an opinion on business matters. Her job was to take care of the kids, the house, and his needs. If he told her to clean his shoes she would do so. A good submissive wife was like a treasured servant only for you. No one else could mistreat her but she was his property. He did love her more than his most prized possessions because deep down while she was submissive to him, she loved the power she held over the other wives.

Not like Bonetti's wife, slipping him slips of paper or whispering in his ear. He knew Bonetti talked to her about business. Marino grimaced at thinking about having a woman run things like with Alice. Her emotions are taking control. The fact that she could not seem to stop talking to Cain was a clear indication that she should not be running an organization as complex as she had. She had put herself in the middle of a conflict that had nothing to do with her for what reason? No one knew, and that troubled Marino.

What if she was trying to tempt their men over to her side? What if she had a side deal with Bonetti? The hate in that man's eyes lately angered Marino. Bonetti had every right to hate Marino and he knew it. He set him, planted evidence to throw the feds off himself, and then fled. Sure it was cowardly but it was what needed to be done. He would suffer Bonetti and slowly cut him out. Jeffers was his real number two and they both knew it. It would just take time to ensure a smooth transition. Hopefully, by then he had Alice under his umbrella as well and could have his cake and eat it too.

After they returned to the hotel Veronica took his shoes off and stowed them before preparing a drink for him and hanging his suit jacket. Now that he was back Veronica would now be the wife in charge which meant that she could get Carol Bonetti in her place rather quickly. Veronica may look meek but with other women, she could be brutal. Before Carol and Joey had been newly married with young children themselves and Veronica had been busy with his own children. Over the years in Nevada Veronica had picked up a few tricks to making both the women and their husbands fall in line.

"Dear heart," he said sitting in a chair by the desk. "Now that we are back you need to contain Carol Bonetti. She keeps giving Joey advice and stepping out of place. You need to show her how a woman should behave." Veronica smiled at him with that full beautiful smile.

"I will darling, thank you for letting me know. Should I do this before or during your trip to Florida?" She was eager. The woman always wanted to be in control of someone since she had no control over him.

"Start slow while I'm in Florida, then when I am back you can go all out. I will be here to back you up then and make Joey stand down. She has two little kids now though, not too extreme. It may be wise to start a ladies' group for the wives. Teach the wives and daughters a rightful woman's place." He slapped his lap in summons and she appeared by his side so he could trace her legs up her skirt.

"That is a wonderful idea, love," she said, moving to sit on his lap as directed. There was no more talking after that. The woman always distracted him from coherent thought, but any woman would when they bent to your will so willingly.

CHAPTER SIXTEEN

CAIN

Over the next few weeks life had fallen into this kind of rhythm that Cain was sure was the calm before the storm. Cain spent his days doing his job for Joey, his early evenings with the kids doing homework, and his evenings with Cherie who all but lived with him now. She didn't comment on his nightly disappearance to chat with Alice on the patio, who had become distant. Their conversations were rarely longer than five minutes. She was seldom flirty but she ended every call the same way. He would order her to call him the next night and she would say "Yes sir"

Marino had officially moved a block away from Joey and he was back in control of the family. Joey had bent the knee to keep the peace and he was the number two. Cain though was just another Lieutenant among the many. He had been cut out of all high-level meetings unless Marino wanted an Alice update.

Cain recalled the day Marino tried to send his guys with him to pick up the shipment. Alice had left a typed note with her signature at the bottom. The arrangement was the same. Cain was to handle all contact and pick-ups. Bonetti's men were to distribute the merchandise. She was ensuring that Bonetti was taken care of in this merger. As Halloween was days away the annual masked ball was being held at Bonetti's home. He had invited Cherie who was thrilled and had texted Alice for approval.

Though Maniro was looking for her, Alice had expanded and word was out that she had an alliance with the Irish. She was now stronger than any crime family had been since Al Capone had been arrested. Joey's FBI contacts also had nothing on her which astounded everyone. Cain sat back on his couch with Cherie curled against him. She was comfortable, the kind of girl that filled the seats of the wise guy wifes. He knew she wanted a commitment and Joey was encouraging it. He heard the click of his earpiece and got up walking to the balcony.

"Cain," she said in the same tense voice she had been giving off for weeks now. "Alice. Heard about the Irish today," he said

"I needed numbers. Marino is sniffing around. He questioned Cherie today, did she tell you?" Cain glanced back inside at Cherie who was pretending to not be listening by straightening the throw pillows she had bought for his place.

"No," he said, "what happened?"

"Marino went to the bar asking what I looked like if she knew my real name. Offered her a spot with him. Used you in the offer." Alice sounded pissed "She alerted on her watch and The O'Reilly's got there quickly and kindly escorted him out. Is he telling you to poach my people?" she demanded.

"No, I didn't know. Marino knows if he needs Cherie he should ask me." Anger coursed through him "I will talk to him." He felt like putting his fist through Marinos skull, for chasing Alice and bringing Cherie into it. There was a method to living in this lifestyle with some decorum and Marino approaching another man's woman was unprofessional. Even if Cain was losing interest He knew he didn't want to marry Cherie, but he also didn't feel the need to move on. Alice was a fictional option and he didn't know the effect a breakup would have on the already tense organizations.

"She's solid, I think. She sounded like it was tempting but I only got second-hand accounts." Alice sounded put upon with this information. "I am distancing myself from my people, going back to how it was prior to the Anton issue. These calls will also be stopping for the most part. I would like to do a weekly check-in rather than daily."

"No," he said. He needed to know she was safe. He had not only grown used to but needed to hear her voice even if it was pissed off.

"Why?" She sounded sad. Like she was losing something she needed.

"I just need to know you're ok" his voice sounded light but the meaning was clear.

"This isn't fair to Cherie or to my person. We are both involved with people, and Cherie loves you." He knew she had told him but when he pictured his future it was with someone different. Someone he had an image of that he knew one day would be in front of him.

"I know," he muttered, "I'm supposed to invite you to the Bonetti Halloween masquerade." she laughed her deep rich laugh and he felt his entire body relax. "It's been so long since I've heard that." His voice was deep and gruff. He missed their all-night conversations but she wasn't wrong about them both having someone else. She likely was distancing because hers was getting serious, which burned his ass.

"I'll see if I can swing it" she giggled to herself with sarcasm dripping from her voice. "I'll bring a date. I approved Cherie's going so you can enjoy your evening. Keep her away from Marino."

"I will," he said softly. He would be making it very clear to Marino that going after Cherie was out of bounds. "I want these calls daily."

"Twice a week" she countered. "We both need space."

"Fine" he acquiesced, not trying to hide the bitter voice.

"Cain, I wish that one day the Romeo and Juliet thing we have going on could meet in an epic way where you could rescue me from the evil wizard, but we live in the real world. Let Cherie be your Juliet and know that I will be ok ruling the world alone."

"I thought you had someone," he said.

"They are temporary," she said and his chest loosened immediately. He hadn't realized how tight it had been since finding out she had someone. He thought of Cherie and knew that she was temporary as well. A big part of him wanted to tell her so but he didn't voice this.

"You have my cell, you can always text me and I'll keep this earpiece on just in case." He said and she chuckled.

"Cain, eventually we are going to stop talking. Marino will force you to turn on me and when that day comes the connection between us will be broken." he sighed, growling at her in response, looking out over the streets below. He wondered idly where she lived.

"We aren't there yet" He turned and found Cherie at the door listening to his conversation. She looked jealous and angry.

"We are getting close," Alice said, "I will contact you after the Halloween ball, enjoy yourself." There was a long pause as she waited.

"Call me on Halloween" he bossed the way she liked to hear his voice firm and in control. He heard her soft sigh in response and felt the sadness of the moment.

"Yes sir," she said, hanging up. He felt like he just lost something amazing. Cherie on the other hand, looked like a storm was brewing.

"Alice approved of you going to the party," He said, trying to avoid the fight that was heading his way.

"Are you sleeping with her?" Cherie demanded. This stumped him completely and he laughed.

"How? I don't know what she looks like, her real name, or how to find her. So how on earth would I be sleeping with her? Plus she practically shoved us together. She asks about you every time we talk." Cherie looked taken aback but still had a storm in her eyes. "Why didn't you tell me about Marino?" Cherie took a step back throwing her hair over her shoulder.

"He just asked some questions and wanted to talk. I didn't tell him anything useful about her or you. He did point out that it was odd that you would be the contact and not Joey himself. Made out like you two have some sort of relationship. You hear from her more than I do or even Billy." This was news to Cain, he knew they talked daily but the fact that her number two didn't hear from Alice daily was interesting.

"Yeah well, that's stopping now that she knows Marino is trying to poach her people. She's been offended, Marino wants to force her to bend the knee and he will use you or anyone else in her organization to do that. She's distancing now so any working relationship we had is now gone." he said and was all but shouting at her. "Don't be jealous over a voice on the phone."

"She's not just a voice, she's my boss and she is stronger than me. She is smarter than I am and younger. I swear, if I never see that redhead again I will be happy because from what I just heard you love her. I have never heard such tenderness in your voice." he was shocked both by the venom in Cherie's voice and the words coming at him.

"No I don't" he lied, his voice quiet to her shouting, calm to her volatile. He needed to keep Cherie where she was, with Alice, Cherie could do untold damage to Alice if she went with Marino. Cain decided to protect Alice from Marino at this moment. He knew how to get to Cherie and he would use his knowledge. "If I loved her I wouldn't be with you" Cain moved before she could react, pulling her against him. "I wouldn't want you" he ravaged her mouth, smothering her protest. He pushed her against the wall of the living room. He kept devouring her mouth and in his mind's eye he saw a redhead with blue eyes looking up at him with a sarcastic grin 'Boss me' she said as he ripped Cheries top down the middle sending buttons flying. He was a bad, bad man, he thought carrying the woman to his bed. "Tell me, are you jealous now?" he demanded, slamming her to the bed and ripping her panties from under her skirt. His lips trailed down Cherie's body until he found her sweetness making her groan. "Answer me" he demanded, devouring her flesh.

"No" she cried "Not jealous" She was lost. He smiled and he climbed her body and slammed into her through the gap in his jeans. He held her down as he dominated her. As she shouted his name he pictured his red-headed vixen as he came collapsing on top of her.

"Let me know if you need a reminder," he said rolling with her so she lay on top of him. She giggled and cuddled close to him and waited for him to drift off.

CHERIE

Cherie waited until Cain was snoring lightly like he always did. No matter the words or sex he threw at her, Cherie wasn't stupid. Cain and Alice had feelings for each other. Billy had suspected it weeks ago when he had suggested she stop talking to Cain and Alice had laughed it off. Listening to their call Cherie knew that at least on Cain's end, he loved her. Cherie picked up her clothes and dressed silently. She grabbed her purse and headed out the door.

She stopped at a bodega, bought a new burner phone and pulled Marino's card out of her purse. He answered on the third ring. She was going to get even with Alice and ensure Cain would never get to see the little whore alive.

"It's Cherie," she said softly. "I think you're right about Cain and Alice. He has feelings for her. She broke it off with him tonight. Said she doesn't want you poaching her people." she took a deep breath while he waited in silence. "I have to be very careful if I am going to help you find her. She is evil and will kill me."

"Don't worry Cherie, we can do this carefully. Keep this phone on you and text me anytime on it." Cherie sighed deeply. She was doing this to hurt Cain but also to protect herself. If Marino was back for good as Cain had told her he was then she had to pick the winning team. She was old enough to remember life when Marino ran things. Her father would likely not want to go back to Marino but she could make her own decisions. She needed to move out and on with her life anyway. She would make herself a made, successful woman.

"I'll find out where she will be and let you know. She's distancing herself from everyone right now, so it may take time." Her fate sealed, she hung up the phone and drove home to try and plan how she would make this switch easily.

Cain stormed into Marino's office without waiting to be announced. He noted Joey in one of the chairs and

Marino didn't look surprised. "Cain" he acknowledged as Cain slammed his hands on the desk and glared.

"You confronted my girlfriend about her boss?" he demanded "and didn't tell me? You offered her a position with you and tried to use me as a fucking pawn" he spat the words out. Marino did not look surprised or offended. "You disrespected me" This had Marino pausing.

"I did not intend to disrespect." Marino said solemnly and he bowed his head slightly "I apologize for any disrespect that was felt." This was a big issue for anyone in the family. Disrespect was a big issue and for a boss to show his men this was an insult. "I did not want you to be put in the middle. She seemed interested in my offer and it would be a less complicated relationship."

"It would bring open hostility between Alice and us. We would lose the shipment, she has an alliance with the Irish and her reach has extended out of Queens. She's in the Bronx and Brooklyn and you want to open hostilities? She knows you went to Cherie, she has canceled our daily calls. She is pissed going back to our old arrangement of no contact. That means she has pulled support if we need assistance." Marino listened intently, his face not changing. This was why he was a good Don. You couldn't read him unless you knew him and Cain didn't know him very well.

"Sounds like she's running," Marino said to Joey who shook his head.

"Sounds like she's angry and getting ready for a war. A war we can't win even if we call in reinforcements." Joey said evenly "What did she say to the invite to the party."

"She laughed at me and said 'Nice try, I'll see if I can swing it'," Cain said, throwing himself in the chair opposite Joey. "I am going to give her a day or two and try to connect when she's had time to calm down." he refocused on Marino "If you want anything from my woman you come to me. I would never go to your woman behind your back, give me the same respect." Marino nodded slowly.

"You are a brave one Brescia," Marino said "Not many would charge my office like this."

"The only reason I didn't lay you out is because I respect Joey Bonetti too much to disgrace him. You crossed a line not only on a personal level but a professional one."

"It will all be moot soon," Marino said evenly "I should have Miss Alice in a few days my men are closing in on her. We know the college she attends and are watching all her men. As soon as she makes contact we will have her. Then she will have a choice, bend the knee or be dealt with." Cain felt his blood chill as he nodded his head in agreement. He had to warn her.

"That's good to hear, do you have a description yet?" Joey asked, looking at ease in his big chair.

"A vague description, a young girl between eighteen and twenty doesn't drink or smoke, hair color is either dark brown or black with blue eyes." Joey leaned forward at this and looked at Cain.

"We should tell the men to look out for a woman with that description. Observe and report to you immediately if we can bring her in; it would be best for everyone."

"Got it. I will blast that as soon as I leave here." he looked at Marino "Where do you want her delivered when we do find her?" Marino sat back in his chair and considered Cain.

"You know I have been on the fence about you," he said slowly. " These daily calls and Cherie being on her crew, I questioned your loyalty which is why I cut you out. Joey here has been telling me I was wrong this entire time." Cain looked over at Joey surprised. "You really wouldn't put a woman over the family, which is rare. Women have the ability to warp our minds. It happened to me with my wife and to Joey with Carol." Marino nodded to Joey who smiled lightly. Cain doubted Marino felt this way about his wife as he had seen them together. She was basically a high-class servant, bending to his every whim.

"Neither Cherie nor Alice is my wife. Cherie has been clear about her goals, if we make a permanent commitment she would be out of the game as a housewife. Alice won't tell me her real name and I have been in communication with her only on Joey's orders. I started dating Cherie under orders to get information and I have repeatedly given the info I have gotten. I have never given anyone cause to question my loyalty" Cain was fuming at being cut out. He would have done the same thing if he had been Marino but still, it was humiliating to go from number two of an organization to just another soldier.

"Well if you are open to it, I will let you back into our daily meetings," Marino said once again, bowing his head slightly.

"I would be interested," Cain said, getting comfortable in his seat. They spent the rest of the morning discussing business as usual. The expansion effort in the south. True to her word Alice had no one in South Queens. Every time Alice made a deal she kept it and Marino

seemed to be the one pushing the boundary. He was rescinding the agreement for her to use the coast once a week. Now if her people showed up they would be turned away. Joey cautioned that this could be just another point for her to start a war with them. Marino seemed to be driven by the need to find her, this woman who had become so powerful so fast and he wanted her blood. Cain listened to the way he spoke about the impending trip to Florida with disdain and thought that it was lucky he was leaving. The next few months without him would be a little less stressful, hopefully.

CHAPTER SEVENTEEN

ERIN

*E*rin saw Marino men everywhere she went in Queens. They were in her territory often and her men politely escorted them out. Someone had described her to them that was not wholly accurate but was close enough. Each day that passed more people were being questioned about her. Billy had told her to stay away for a while and so she had taken a trip to the house she was having built on that forty acres in West Virginia. She focused on homework and monitoring the situation from afar.

She had driven back that morning to get ready for the Halloween Ball that she had been told was mandatory by Carol. The kids were excited they had never been allowed to go but their parents had gone every year. She had taken the kids' trick or treating and kept close to home. She pulled out the dress Carol had gotten her and cringed; it had a full back that was subtly sheer and would hide her scars, hopefully. The dress clung in all the right places. She coiled her hair into a pile on top of her head letting red curls trail down her cheeks. Her makeup was powerful under the mask highlighting her dark blue eyes. Her pale skin and red lips made her look like a modern-day siren. She turned her back to the mirror and could only just make out the brand if she focused hard on the spot. Hopefully, no one would ask any questions.

She was worried about her ability to be in a crowded room with people milling about. She had warned Patrick they may not be able to stay long because of claustrophobia. The majority of the party would be men all much larger than her. Plus standing in a room hoping no one called her Alice was a risk. Her anxiety was high, and she yearned to call Cain and have him calm her down. Just hearing his voice brought stillness to her world. She closed her eyes and remembered him telling her to call tonight. She would call after she left the party.

She got to the party with Patrick on her arm and introduced him to her siblings. Theo was sizing Patrick up and decided he was not a fan, though he was polite. He introduced a girl from his class Susan Walker. A pretty girl with black hair and gray eyes that just stared up at her in awe. The amount of people in this house had her flinching at random movements and she felt like her chest was tight. There was a reason she had wide-open spaces in all her buildings. She had never been in a room with so many people. Patrick traced his hand down her back and looked concerned as he felt her scars. She was grateful he was there, he was normal and kind. She leaned against him, catching him off guard.

"A lot of people in here," she said in his ear.

"We can go, if your siblings have similar issues we can all go for a burger or pizza." Patrick offered and she smiled. He truly was a good person and he really seemed to care for her. She wished she could care for him as much but something held her off. Cain's laugh flitted into her mind and she knew what held her off from loving Patrick.

"No they are having a blast, they didn't have it as bad or as long." She said vaguely. She shook hands with a man who introduced himself as Jeffers, a friend of her father's. He leered at her and made Patrick uncomfortable.

Patrick nudged her when Marino came in with his wife on his arm. They both wore blue masks with feathers. He went straight for Joey and Carol to chat. "Cain!" Josie shouted calling out to Cain and Cherie who were wandering about the food tables. Her eyes widened and she looked at Patrick.

"You want to meet Marino?" she asked, suddenly making Patrick light up. She raced for Joey who looked up in surprise as she walked up to them. Marino turned and locked eyes with her in surprise.

"Erin, you remember Greg Marino" Joey said, raising an eyebrow.

"Yes, good evening Mr. Marino and Mrs. Marino, Joey Bonetti and Carol Bonetti" she curtsied slightly. "I wanted to introduce Patrick Miller, my boyfriend." Patrick shook hands with Marino and Joey. "Carol, can I borrow you for a moment?" she asked looking over her shoulder at where her siblings stood with Cain looking around the dance floor. Carol followed Erin out of the room into the kitchen leaving Patrick making small talk with Joey and Marino. "What's going on honey?" she asked with concern, filling her eyes.

"I'm a bit claustrophobic with all the people here," she said and when a waiter lifted a tray she flinched hard. "I wanted to introduce Patrick, he's been recruited by Joey's people. He really wanted to meet Joey. I need to go, can you grab the kids for me?" Carol's eyes were full of concern as she nodded. Carol stepped out just as Cherie walked in looking confused and froze when they locked eyes.

"Ali" Erin put a finger to her lips.

"You never saw me, you look beautiful Cherie," she said "Have fun tonight, and if you can dance with Bonetti for me, and tell him I said I liked his mask." Cherie nodded, smiling before nipping out the door. The kids came bursting in moments later. Theo looked concerned. She made her excuses and Carol retrieved Patrick quickly.

"We wanted you to meet Cain," Josie said "I can go get him"

"No he's here with someone, it wouldn't be appropriate. I will meet him one day I promise! You two are doing so well! I will see you tomorrow." She hugged them both and Patrick high-fived them before they left out the back. Patrick's car was pulled up by the valets and as he opened the door for her she glanced back and saw Cain looking down at her. She grinned and got in the car.

She invited Patrick to her house for the first time that night. He was amazed that she had a two-story walk-up. Now that she owned this area it was getting cleaned up and housing prices were going to rise. Patrick had been patient and she had finally stopped flinching when he moved around her.

Erin admitted to herself that she was bitter that Cain had Cherie. He slept with her and enjoyed her. She had never let anyone close enough to enjoy. She was too self-conscious of her body. As Marino was closing in though, she felt the probability of her dying was more and more likely. She didn't want to die a virgin. She wanted to feel that kind of pleasure. Patrick was comforting and kind to her.

Her bedroom was half done and he walked up to her safe. "What do you keep in here?" he asked.

"In this neighborhood all of my valuables" she laughed as he wandered. "I need to make a quick call and I need to get out of this dress. Will you stay?" she asked, heading for her closet.

"Yea, if you want me to," he said, heading for the door. "I'll put on a movie," she nodded, grabbing her phone. She dialed Cain and heard the party still in full swing. "You look good in a suit," she said, laughing in his ear. "The white mask though, I always thought of you as a dark night"

"Where are you?" he asked as the noise died down. He must have been running outside.

"You saw me. You were so close to me we could touch" she said remembering he had been at the table within inches.

"You're crazy, you know Marino has a description of you."

"I was invited if I recall," she said "You can tell Joey and Marino that it was a pleasure speaking with both of them tonight. Handsome men, tell Marino I don't think the blue mask went with his suit and Joey's handsome as ever." he cursed and she laughed as she peeled the dress off and took off her thigh holster.

"Don't get caught" he ground out at her.

"That's inevitable but I will enjoy taunting them and you while I can. This counts as my call tonight, I will call tomorrow to discuss other things."

"Tomorrow," he said

"Bossy, yes sir," she said, hanging up. She slid into pajama pants and a t-shirt with no bra or panties. She had decided tonight she would let Patrick make a move. When she got to the living room his suit jacket was off and he was grinning at her.

"You're beautiful," he said, pulling her into his arms for a kiss. It was a soft sweet kiss that held the promise of more. Patrick would be gentle with her, she knew this. "Thank you for introducing me to Bonetti and Marino. That was something I never expected. Your brother and sister live with the Bonetti's, are you related?" she winced at this and moved to the couch.

"My parents were killed in the line of duty. They were not the nicest parents and Mr. Bonetti feels so guilty that he didn't realize how badly we were being treated. So he's trying to make up for it. I won't move in but he has them and they are doing so well over there." She knew she sounded sad when she said it and he wrapped an arm around her.

"Erin, you amaze me," he said, kissing her again. She climbed up his body slowly deepening the kiss. Patrick responded and then stopped when his hand went under her shift and felt her back. "Were you burned? He asked, tracing the lines.

"Whipped" Erin felt ashamed as she admitted it and turned her back to him. She removed her shirt and let him see the marks. She could only imagine what he was thinking, how ugly they were. This was a huge mood killer. She felt him trace a line, then another, then another, he was counting them. He felt the knot that had been the heel of her mother's stiletto on one bad evening. His arms came around her and his face was buried in her hair. He kissed her ear and held her hands that covered her breasts.

"Thank you for trusting me" he whispered, turning her to him. They kissed slowly and took every move slowly for the rest of the night.

Her phone was ringing when she awoke in her bed with Patrick wrapped around her. "Hello," she said as his grip tightened and he groaned snuggling.

"Not alone?" Cain asked his voice deep with a hint of jealousy. She kissed Patrick and got up before answering.

"Is your bed empty?" she asked back.

"No comment" he responded "Joey and Marino would like to sit down."

"No," she said, moving into the kitchen. "Marino has been very open that he wants me on my knees in front of him and from what I am hearing even then I will be stripped of my areas, my men, and my standing. I am a woman in this lifestyle and the families are old school. I'll be lucky not to be displayed to the highest ranked and whipped raw." She shivered at the thought, he knew her history and had seen the pictures thanks to Joey.

"Sit downs are how we resolve these issues. We need your connection for the supply." She was frustrated with this. She knew he was sitting with Joey and Maniro but didn't care. "If I send Billy Senior?" she asked, an edge to her voice.

"It would be seen as a sign of disrespect," he said evenly.

"Then I decline out of self-preservation with my full respect to Bonetti and Marino. No one knows what I look like, that is the only card I have." she heard Patrick getting up. "I have to go unlike you. My significant other doesn't know what I do." She hung up as Patrick came in.

"Who was that so early?" he asked shirtless in his boxers.

"My boss," she said "Tiffany called in sick so I got to pick up a shift today."

"Nice, I work the afternoon shift today," he said, kissing her on the mouth. "Your house is half torn apart you know," he said looking around.

"Yea I'm fixing it as I have time but as you know, I don't have much time."

"I have time" his arms snaked around her pulling her close. "My Dad did a lot of construction back in Texas. If you want I can help." he offered, kissing her throat.

"I think I would like that," she said, her head falling back. He lifted her and she giggled as he carried her back to the bedroom.

"What time do you need to be at work?" he asked.

"I have an hour," she said as he kissed her softly. This was nice, to be wanted like this. Patrick was a sweet thoughtful lover and did everything slowly. Probably because he knew how much she jumped around people.

"I can work with that, does your shower work?" she froze.

"No, I shower at the gym a block over." he laughed and kissed her again.

"Then we better be quick" and with that, she was lost in the physical pleasures of her temporary boyfriend.

Erin was approached by Marino's men three days later, they were questioning everyone who had spoken to Bonetti and Marino at the party. Two hulking men stood towering down at her at the cafe while Patrick stood in between them.

"Did you talk to Bonetti about talking to me?" she asked as Patrick wrapped an arm around her.

"Why would we?" they demanded "You fit the description of The Woman"

"How?" Patrick asked "She's a redhead, not a brunette or black-haired girl. She has blue eyes not green and from what I heard The Woman is like five-eight she's definitely not that." Patrick was getting heated and she smiled shyly up at him.

"Joey Bonetti is the custodian to my siblings which is why I introduced my boyfriend to him and his wife. It was lucky Marino was there because it was of course an honor for Patrick, new to the family to meet the boss. If you have any questions about me, you tell Marino to call me himself. I don't have to answer to soldiers when my siblings live with a Don." her tone sharpened and her stance changed. Internally she cursed herself, she shouldn't be acting so confident. Both men stepped back from her. "If I were The Woman, don't you think Joey Bonetti would know? I'm the daughter of one of your soldiers Derrick Caruso"

Both men gave vague apologies and headed out quickly. Patrick kissed her and smiled, "I like it when you get heated, it's like you change into a different woman." He kissed her again as his manager snapped her fingers at him and he rolled his eyes. She finished her homework and packed up. She was running out of time, she needed to stop taunting them. Radio silence was called for.

She called Billy and Cherie to let them know the new order of things. They were pausing the expansion of their area to focus on maintaining their new vast area. Building ranks and setting up systems to insulate themselves.

Over the next few months, it was an epic game of cat and mouse. Erin more than once rounded corners as Marino's men came looking for her. She knew she had a leak in her ranks after the third time because she had only informed four people that she would be at the pier for a meeting. Erin cursed as she thought about her options: Billy Senior her number two and a stable father figure to her. Billy her best friend, Cherie the first person she promoted, Philip one of the most loyal men she had ever met, and Benji who had redoubled his loyalty and work ethic after she got him back from Anton.

She had a routine with Patrick, he came over three afternoons a week and helped her work on her house and every other Sunday he accompanied her to the family dinner at the Bonettis. She had to admit with his help the house was coming together. The upstairs was complete to include the safe room that he helped her install. He hadn't questioned it, just said it was smart for the affiliations they both had.

He had also taken a personal affront to her bathrooms and demolished the upstairs one first and renovated the entire thing for her so that they could shower together. The other four nights he was working for Joey and Marino. Marino had to take off to Florida for a month to handle some issues down there. This meant that for that month his men had gone with him.

She had stopped all communication with Cain, which had been painful but necessary. She had also managed to avoid meeting him in person because she knew as soon as he heard her voice he would know. This had caused her to have to miss two of Theo's races.

Now it was the beginning of summer as May brought summer rains. She sat outside on her front steps in the rain enjoying the steamy humidity, trying to form a plan to find the rat, and for the first time in a long time dialed Cain. Not the earpiece she doubted he wore it anymore after so long of nothing but his cell phone.

"Who is this?" he answered menace in his voice.

"Well don't you sound happy" she purred back.

"Alice," he said and the room that had been full of male voices quieted at once. "Are you busy?" she asked in her most flirty voice, knowing the answer.

"Not too busy to talk to you," he said, his deep voice making her insides clench.

"Oh, but I think you are selling my product like crazy, upping the amount needed two months in a row. You didn't come alone yesterday," she said, her voice mocking him. He had brought Patrick which irritated her that Patrick was using her to get higher in Joey's organization. She was growing annoyed at a lot of things Patrick was doing, he was changing more and more every day. He was turning into a Mob man which was not what she wanted. Marino had been mentoring him for some reason and Marino had some wild opinions on women's places. Patrick had taken to trying to implement some of these new views with her. Her favorite so far had been her sitting at his feet while they watched a movie together.

"You're right, I should have asked first," he said, his voice sullen "I appreciate you not blowing us up."

"I thought about it, you're lucky you're cute, that is your only chance next time I blow the boat. I have a leak in my organization giving Marino tips. Do you know who it is?" she asked knowing that in a room full of men where she was likely on speaker phone he would not answer. She just wanted him to know and Marino to know she knew as well.

"No, I'm not aware of anyone giving information on you," he said his voice surprised there was a grunt and she could feel the tension she had just created.

"Is Bonetti there?" she asked. She hoped not, he may recognize her voice but at this point, it was too late. They would all know soon enough who she was.

"No, he had a family obligation" Marino answered back.

"Marino, the man, the myth, the legend" she mocked, sarcasm dripping off her tongue. "How does it feel to chase a ghost?" he stayed silent "To my knowledge it has never taken you this long to find anyone."

"You're not wrong, are you ready for a sit-down?" he asked, his tone brisk.

"We both know I have embarrassed you. We both know how this ends," she said, her voice falling flat.

"Do you think you will win this little one?" Marino asked. Little one? He was calling her a child. Oh, screw you, buddy.

"No, I don't old man," she said easily, fuck you, she thought bitterly "But I have obligations to attend to and people to protect. When you left and abandoned your men, did you ever consider what would happen when they came upon hard times?"

"I left Bonetti in charge" he returned.

"No, I know the agreement, you left Bonetti with the knowledge that he was not able to step up due to the feds being at your door, leaving them at his door, and a treaty with the Irish for two years. Two very long years Marino that decision is what created me." She heard the collective intake a breath "You caused this and if and when you do kill me the best supply you have ever seen will go to the Irish and my proxy will declare war and you will die. So let's save Italian lives here and just leave each other alone"

"You know I can't do that," he said evenly.

"Too bad, Cain?" Erin's voice didn't falter as her chest tightened. She looked up at the sky and let the rain fall on her.

"Yea, Alice?" His voice was deep and controlled.

"It was so good to hear your voice and I am sorry this will be our last conversation." she hung up and hung her head. She broke the burner phone and trashed it as she walked down the street. Letting the rain darken her hair.

Erin didn't know where she was walking; she just needed to walk. She found herself at the bar across from the dock where this had all started the night she murdered her parents. She spotted the Marino men staking out the boat and sighed. She would have liked to go out on the water and just be alone.

Usually, she was amazing at laying plans but now things were just hazy. She could win a war, she would have to win a war but how to do it without Marino using her siblings as tools. He was close to finding out who she was. She had heard the newest description of her and it was pretty accurate. Red hair and lots of it, she had taken to wearing it in a bun since then. Blue eyes, short with a big rack. She laughed at that one. Crazy and violent wrapped it up.

Every plan she started to make she stopped because her siblings could be used. They all ended with Marino discovering who she was and using them. She could not risk it, they had been through too much. She started to jog back to her place. When she got in she typed up instructions for what to do after her death. Erin knew who could tie the families together after she died. It was a startling moment to realize you had accepted your death was close and inevitable.

CHAPTER EIGHTEEN

CAIN

The men all sat shocked at the phone call that just took place. "She sounds young," Marino said to Cain.

"Yeah from what I was told she is around twenty, but smart. Do we have a mole?" Cain tried to pump excitement in his voice. The truth was his chest hurt like his heart had just been ripped from him. The last conversation? He hadn't heard from her in months but he always assumed he would hear from her again. She had stopped answering the earpiece when he tapped the button and even set up a mocking voicemail that he could leave messages, which he did, once a week.

"Yes, one of her LTs, we have gotten close a few times, she's not wrong she is a ghost." Marino spat "I don't like that she blames me. We need to look at who was left behind fifteen years ago and what became of them." Cain nodded, sitting back. Marino dispensed orders to the men in the room and dismissed them.

"Cain, hold up," he said as the others left. "She sounded sad when she said goodbye to you."

"We had a very flirty, friendly relationship over the phone," he said "It was a game for both of us but she is a woman and she started to have feelings which I believe is why she broke it off," Cain said, playing to Marino's misogyny. "I will put my earpiece back in and see if I can contact her again. She knows she can't maintain this, she doesn't seem to want a war so I wonder what that is."

"Agreed, try and get that relationship back. I would like this to be handled as quietly as possible" Marino looked distinctly uncomfortable with all he had learned.

"She's not wrong though, you will display her as defeated before it's over?" usually this meant calling the LTs and Dons together before killing with an audience, and while they waited there was torture and pain.

"I have to, the amount of time and drama she has caused calls for it," Marino said.

Cain raced to his loft, grabbed his earpiece, pressed the button, and heard the clicking sound. "Cain?" her voice was small but firm and he heard the clicking of a keyboard on her end.

"Alice you need to run," he said instantly "Run far and fast so he can't get to you." she laughed lightly. Oh, he hated that laugh that hit his gut and made his heart twist.

"I can't do that," she said "When all things are settled, Billy Senior will come to you with my final requests. I would hope that you would honor them. I have a family that will hate Bonetti for this and you need to help them past that. They will need to know you and I were friends. Tell them that their sister crushed on you hardcore"

"Don't say that" his voice broke, she was giving up. "You're a strong woman you can stay alive for them"

"I will do my best but I am being betrayed by someone and my luck will run out. Are you keeping your earpiece in again?" she asked with desperation in her voice. He felt the same desperation.

"Yes," he said, his throat closing on him.

"Ok I will call you later" she sighed.

"Call me tonight" his voice was stern.

"Bossy, I like it, Yes sir," she said with the laugh that he remembered.

Over the next few days, he got caught up on what the most recent description of Alice was, redhead with blue eyes. He had felt Patrick stiffen next to him Sunday morning when he had heard this. He had similarly stiffened when he had heard the voice on the phone.

He was heading to the Bonetti house to celebrate Erin's birthday. He was finally going to get to meet the mystery sister that Josie and Theo loved more than anything. It was a surprise party for her. Cherie had blown it off saying she had better things to do. They had been fighting a lot lately and he felt it was time to sever that relationship.

Cain entered the room and smiled at Josie who bounded up to him. "At school today a fortune teller came," she announced to him.

"Is that so?" he asked sitting at the bar in the kitchen "Yeah I asked who I would marry and she gave me the initials J.R. I asked her who my sister would marry and she gave me the initials C.B" She giggled and blushed "Then you will really be my brother."

"I would love that, doesn't she have a boyfriend? And whose initials are J.R? I need to talk to that young man." He asked, glancing at Carol.

"He bailed on tonight's dinner. Had some legwork to do for Marino" she sounded upset "Not all boyfriends turn into husbands. JR is still a mystery but we will keep an eye out for anyone with those initials" she added with a wink. They hung out for forty minutes before there was a knock at the door. He turned around on his stool and when the kids yelled "Surprise" he joined them in a much smaller voice.

The woman in front of him was a little pixy, maybe five foot two, a hundred pounds but her dark red hair was tied in a messy bun on top of her head. Her blue eyes shined up at him, her hourglass curves tempted him a little and he reminded himself she was nineteen four years younger than himself.

"Erin, this is Cain, a psychic said he would be your husband!" Josie said, bouncing over.

"Yea and if a psychic says it then we gotta do it" Cain jokes, "You got a white dress?" The girl looked shell-shocked for a moment, her eyes moving over him and her eyes locked with his as a smirk touched her lips.

"Bossy I like it, Yes sir," she said, giving him a small salute with her hand. He paled out and stared at her. No way, no way was The Woman, his Alice, a nineteen-year-old who had her siblings living with Joey Bonetti. He looked up at Joey who immediately moved to him. He felt like he had been punched in the gut as he looked from

Joey to Carol to the kids then back to Erin who was busy listening to the biggest and best news that wouldn't wait. Erin glanced back up to him and now she had a taunting smile on her mouth.

"Cain, what's wrong?" Carol asked as Cain looked from Joey to Erin. He was in shock and had to shake himself out of it.

"I think I surprised him," Erin said, moving up to him. He shook his head momentarily and looked at Joey confused. How did he not know?

"Yea sorry, my mind just went blank." His voice sounded hoarse.

"You're pale as a sheet," Joey said, watching Cain closely. "Did you eat today?"

"No that must be it" Cain kept coming back to Erin who had a mocking smile on her face. Carol handed him a whiskey and ushered them to the table for snacks. Erin sat next to him with the kids across from them. Joey and Carol sat at either head of the table. Carol served roast with corn on the cob and Macaroni and cheese which Josie informed him was Erin's favorite. He couldn't keep his eyes off her, she ate slowly savoring every bite. She talked to the kids and joked. She listened to their school weeks and she mentioned her homework assignments. She took her napkin and dabbed the side of her mouth and when she placed it back on her lap she touched his thigh. He didn't jump but took her hand and squeezed softly.

"Cain, don't you think Erin is pretty?" Josie asked and he smiled.

"Most beautiful girl in the world," he said "Well second only to you" he winked at Josie who giggled. He entwined his fingers with hers and held on. He had never imagined he would find her in the Bonetti house. After dessert and she said goodnight to the kids she hung around to chat with Joey and Carol. She mentioned that Patrick had been blowing her off lately, and thought that was pretty much over, and Carol gave her sympathy. She didn't seem that upset about it. Each time they passed each other they brushed or grazed each other.

It was like some slow dance just for them. He raised a hand to Joey and she flinched so hard that she almost fell off her stool and he reached out to grab her hand. "Erin," he said, holding onto her openly in front of Joey and Carol.

"It's ok I do that sometimes. Habit" she said apologetically and he now understood why she was so distant with everyone. She may rule the world but she feared men and she had reason to. She moved into his arms and gave him a hug which shocked Joey and Carol who stood speechless. "It was a pleasure to finally meet you. I want to thank you for working with my brother and sister. They mean the world to me and knowing you're looking out for them means everything to me." she said, breaking away. The double meaning for only Cain had his heart clenching. She was giving responsibility for the kids to him, he could read it clearly in the embrace.

She walked around the counter and hugged Carol thanking her and moving to Joey who hugged her and stared at Cain and Carol his shock evident. "You two have been the biggest blessing me and my siblings could have ever been lucky enough to get." Carol burst into tears and Joey cleared his throat. "See, my therapist was right, I could make you cry with a hug. I haven't meant to be this hard. I'm doing my best."

"It's been our pleasure," Joey said

"Alright I've made everyone cry so I'll take off now," she said pausing once more to study Joey, Carol and finally Cain. She walked out the front door and Cain made his excuses to leave the now tearful kitchen. He followed Erin out, two blocks to her car. He got in the passenger seat without a word. They didn't say a word as she drove straight to what he assumed was her house. He followed her into the two-story walk up and as soon as the front door closed and she reset her security alarm he had her in his arms.

"Take off your weapons," he said, pulling her sweater off and spying her shoulder holster. He tossed his shirt to the ground and placed his gun on the counter. Her holster came off and clattered to the counter. He picked her up and kissed her hard "Where?" he asked, pulling at the button on her jeans.

"Back room on the left," she said, moving her mouth down his neck. He groaned and slammed her into the bedroom wall.

"Nice place," he said, tossing her on the bed. "Pants off" he demanded and kicked his boots off. She stood up and shimmied out of her jeans and panties and he just stared at her naked body. "Your perfect" he breathed trying to commit her perfect breasts and hips to memory. Her trimmed pubic hair made a heart shape that made his mouth water. She blushed as he just stared at her. This woman, the voice in his ear, all the months of flirting and sharing their lives all came to this moment.

He dropped his pants and picked her up again. He wanted to be everywhere all at once. He trailed his mouth down her throat to her breasts taking his time with each one. Her purr of pleasure made him growl while he sucked her nipple into his mouth. He traveled down her slim waist and nipped at her hip, he noted a small scar there, She gasped and he continued his journey down her body. "Look at me," he said as he hovered over her most delicate flesh. She looked down, her dark blue eyes shining with pleasure. He ran his nose up her center and inhaled. "You are perfect," he said again as he grabbed her hips and pulled her to his mouth. The moan that left her was earth-shattering. She tasted of honey so sweet that he didn't want to stop. She fisted his hair and pulled hard until he crawled up her body.

"I need you," she said against his lips, tasting herself as she kissed him. He slammed into her to his hilt. He paused, enjoying the feel of her so tight. She moaned out his name as he gripped her hands and started to move.

Hours later they lay in each other's arms, they had come together three times already and showed no sign of stopping. He traced her scars but didn't ask, he knew from Josie and Theo what had happened to this woman.

"You are amazing" he whispered against her hair.

"So are you" She traced a tattoo on his arm, the symbols for the elements he had gotten in jail when he had been bored. "I knew if we saw each other in person we would end up here"

"You are even more beautiful than I imagined," he said, tightening his grip. He needed to protect her. He just got her in his arms and he needed to see if this could work. "We need a plan," he whispered.

"I am all ears," she said "My current plan is that when I die, you take over for me and run my crew under Joey with the hope that with my men you can get rid of Marino" She rose on an elbow and looked down at him. "I was never meant to have a long life, I thought Joey would kill me when he found my parents," she said, sitting up completely and looking around. Her parents? He thought, sitting up, Anton supposedly killed her parents. Suddenly he thought about how she had been merciless with Anton and Shawn Holmes had picked up and moved the day he got released from the hospital.

"Anton didn't kill your parents did he?" he asked as she stood up naked in front of him. She turned to walk to her closet. He watched the scars move on her back and the brand on her shoulder. What had she lived through to become a warrior and more ruthless than most of the men in New York?

"No, they hit Josie for trying to clean me up and stole five thousand dollars from me. After that, they beat me, whipped me, and branded me." She didn't sound upset about it, more resigned than anything. He looked at the scars on her back and noticed the scars on her legs and a brand on her shoulder. It was an Irish family crest.

"You were branded?" he asked, rising to touch the scar. She jumped at his sudden touch and stilled. He had been told about this but seeing it was disturbing. He felt a sudden urge to kill Derrick all over again.

"Yes my mother's family crest, my father wanted it known even if I left that I was not fully Italian, I was half Irish. The last one was a bad beating because I tried to leave. He was going to kill me until my Mom said something. Then he changed his mind and branded me." she said softly. He lowered his mouth and kissed the mark. He moved and kissed every scar he could see. He turned her around and kissed the scars on her belly and thighs.

"Let me protect you," he said, standing and taking her hands. He lifted them above her head slowly and kissed her deeply. He felt his body stir as he twisted her arms behind her back. He moved slowly, sat on the end of her bed and pulled her on top of him. "Ride me," he said, sliding inside her.

CHAPTER NINETEEN

ERIN

They spent the entire day Monday in bed together. They handled work from their phones and even had Patrick pick up the shipment. She had never felt so protected and perfect in her entire life. Her body came to life under Cain's expert hands. She had no idea what she had been missing for the last ten months.

Cain kept having bouts of deep thinking where he would be trying to find a solution to their problem. The only solution was the likely impossible one. Erin would have to kill Marino, and that would lead to a fight with his son and the other two families. It would cost a lot of lives and she didn't want that. So she was giving up in a way. She would not move forward or back so she was waiting to be caught, she thought to herself with only slight bitterness. She had finally found out what a good strong love could be and she seemed destined to lose it all.

"What are you going to do about the mole?" he asked.

"I need to find out who it is, they don't belong in either organization," she said, tracing her finger through his chest hair. "I have a plan for that"

"Joey needs to know," Cain said again, this was a common comment.

"It puts the kids in danger if he knows. If he has no idea it protects him and the kids. The reason all my plans get scrapped is because eventually, it does have to come out who I am. As soon as Marino and Joey know it's over. Marino will use the kids against me. I will come in and he will torture and kill me with you and Joey watching." She had explained this already but Cain thought Joey would be able to come up with a plan. She was tired. She had taken on too much with school classes, legitimate businesses, and then trying to run an organization. She had compartmentalized everything so that no one knew all the plates she had spinning. She walked to her safe and pulled out a large binder. It had all the details Cain would need. She set it on his lap as he sat up. She had finished putting it together the week prior.

"What's this?" he asked, opening the top flap.

"That is my entire organization," she said easily "My legit businesses, the 'shipment' as you call it. The processing center, my prescription contacts, all of it." he flipped through the folder and looked shocked.

"This is a lot of moving parts, why the cleaning service?" he asked after another moment.

"I needed a legit job that was age-appropriate that would get Joey to leave me alone," she said laughing. She had gone to great lengths to get Joey to leave her alone. The dispensary was the most profitable and was floating the delivery business she had just started to enable her people to get into areas they normally wouldn't be able to.

"You created an entire business to get Joey off your back." Cain had to laugh at this.

"Yea Maria the manager, basically runs it and has been growing it very well. They are going to make a profit in their first year of business," she said with pride in her voice. She had to smile thinking of the hassle she went through just to stay close to the kids, she had not anticipated Joey becoming their guardian.

"You're giving this to me because?" he asked, looking her over. She went to her closet and slid on an oversized T-shirt. He wasn't going to like this conversation but it was needed.

"You need to have it when Marino finds me, Billy knows he is to report to you and the men will follow him. That's how I know he isn't the mole." She said Billy would have told them that Cain would be running things if she died which would have given them a false sense of security. That left three possibilities but she only really suspected one.

"He's not going to find you" he almost shouted at her.

"We both know he will, I cannot run forever" Erin responded evenly.

"You know you have a reputation for being brutal and always protecting your people and here you are handing your people over to someone else and just accepting that you're done. You're lucky the neighborhood can't see you giving up" his voice was harsh and she stared at him shocked. How dare he say she was giving up! He had no idea how exhausting it had been to evade Marino for the past few months.

"Fuck you," Erin said holding her ground. Cain rose from the bed, his look pinning her to the spot. Her body immediately went into defensive mode. Flashes of beatings she had taken came into her mind as she backed away and hit the wall next to her safe. She tried to keep her defiant look on her face but she knew the fear was still there.

He stopped at the look she gave him and looked confused for a moment then dawning came into his features. "I forgot about your past," he said, grabbing his pants and pulling them on. "I will never hit you," he said softly. "It's really easy to forget your past knowing what you do for a living." she watched him wearily as he dressed. "Let's make a plan to protect you while maintaining this" he lifted the folder. "My first thought is you need insulation" What? She couldn't think of business right now, her mind was in survival mode, it had been for a long time. She had finally accepted what was going to happen and here he was trying to play white night.

"You can try," she said, rolling her shoulders and trying to visibly relax.

"You said you know for a fact Billy Senior and Junior are not the mole, what about your other LTs?"

"Cherie, Phillip, and Benji." she supplied, pulling on some jeans. "Benji, I would bet, has been loyal ever since Anton. He has always been a strong leader for me."

"So Cherie and Phillip, how do we determine which one it is?" he asked. He had a feeling it would be Cherie but she had every opportunity prior to this to betray

Alice and hadn't. When they had begged for a description she had not given one, apart from the slip about the hair color.

"I planned to tell them each that I will be in different locations at the same time and see where Marino's men show up," she said with a sigh. "Just not sure how I will know where they show up."

"I can find out that part" he offered and she stared at him. This was a pivotal moment, Cain was offering to help her, really help her. This was him betraying Marino openly and this put him in massive danger. This was also a betrayal of Joey which was a huge issue. Everyone knew Cain was loyal to Joey above all else.

"Say we win " she still didn't go near him. "What happens if I kill Marino?"

"You're safe then"

"No I'm not" she laughed "His Son and the other families will be expected to act. Joey will be expected to bring me in. Are you going to betray Joey?

"No, Joey has been forming a plan to use you against Marino but your cutting off contact with me made that difficult. Now Marino is so suspicious of Joey he doesn't let us be alone together most days. He keeps Joey chained to his side all the time or sends him on errands and keeps me close. It looks like you need to do some back-door deals with the other families to oust Marino. He isn't well-liked, being respected is not the same thing as being liked." Cain clarified when she just glared over at him.

If that was possible, who should she go to first and how would she go about getting to them? She couldn't exactly leave her siblings to travel to Arizona and Florida;

these wouldn't be quick one-day trips to West Virginia, these would require sit-downs and multiple meetings with all the pomp and whistle that the family would put you through.

"I'll think about that," she said softly. "First we need to get rid of the mole"

Two days later Erin sat in her living room with Billy Junior and Cain. Billy had never been to her house before and when he had entered to see Cain his eyes got wide and his hand went for his gun. It had taken a lot of explaining to get Billy to relax a bit around Cain. Billy still sat in the farthest chair with his gun on his hip holster like some modern-day cowboy.

"So you two have been in a friendship for almost a year?" Billy said, looking between the two of them as Erin handed him a cup of coffee. "You didn't tell me"

"You know I keep things tight," Erin said evenly "He came up with the name Alice by the way" She smiled over at Cain who grinned back. Billy looked between the two of them in shock.

"You're doing it aren't you?" he demanded in the most high school voice she had ever heard. Erin couldn't stop the smile but shook herself out of it. She was supposed to be a boss, not some teenage love-sick kid.

"That is none of your business" she snapped. Her voice was sharp and unquestionable. "Nothing has changed"

"Other than sleeping with the enemy," Billy said sullenly.

"Enough" Erin snapped. "Sleeping with the enemy has perks, we have a mole and you two are going to help me find them." Billy leaned forward, his face going mask-like.

"How?" he didn't question how she found out or who it was, he just wanted to know what to do. This is why Billy was an amazing LT. He was always down to do what he was told and he was smart enough to know when he couldn't push things further.

"We think it's either Cherie or Phillip" Billy sat back uncomfortable.

"Cherie?" he asked, which surprised Erin as she thought he would be more concerned about Phillip as they were close "I don't think it would be Cherie," Billy said shifting a bit.

"Are you sleeping with Cherie?" Cain asked out of nowhere and Billy blushed.

"A bit" Billy admitted and Cain went stony.

"Well we are going to test her anyway and I appreciate your honesty," Erin said, moving over to Cain and resting a hand on his solid shoulder. "Cain, you will be present at Cherie's test, and Billy, you will be on Phillips. I think we should do this today." Cain inclined his head slowly as did Billy. Both men were very uncomfortable with this situation and both knew that the risks would be high.

"What are we doing?" Billy asked, breaking the silence.

"We are going to plan a meet in two very different locations and see where Marino's men show up. Where is Cherie right now?" she asked the room.

"She should be at home," Billy said.

"She's at the bar this morning doing inventory" Cain corrected "I'm the other guy she's sleeping with" he informed Billy who paled. Yea that was a slap to both of them, she was in love with someone in a relationship with one of her people. She was the other woman and it felt crappy.

"I see, get around huh?" he couldn't seem to stop the words and Erin cringed.

"Cain and I just happened and Cherie and Cain have been going out for almost a year since I came out in public at least." Billy nodded.

"I knew there was someone secret in her life" He shrugged "You still going to be a thing?" he asked looking between the two of them. Erin felt her insides knot at this.

"I'll be ending it with Cherie next time I see her. I only want Alice, er, Erin here" He corrected looking up at her. "Erin Caruso" he smiled "You are going to turn the world to fire when that gets out." She blushed and smiled.

"That was the point," She said "Right Billy?"

"Yea we are changing the game!" he agreed, happy to be in on the conversation.

"Alright let's get to work," she said, rolling out a map of the city on her coffee table.

Two hours later Erin was on a conference call with Billy and Cain who were both monitoring the locations of the meet for Marino's men. Cherie stood at the docks while Phillip waited at a cafe. Both were eager to see her and agreed to meet quickly. Her nerves were on edge as she listened to both men check in and chat back and forth as they got to know each other. They were very similar in a lot of ways she mused, both liked cars, football, and baseball. Both were loyal and strong. Both made her laugh and were protective of her. Billy would die for her but she had reservations about Cain. He was a strong man who had worked for Bonetti for a long time. He would die for Bonetti. That is where they differed.

"I got something," Cain said softly. "Marino men waiting down a ways" Billy cursed at this.

"I got nothing over here, Phillip is just sipping his coffee waiting."

"Ok both of you get out of there," she said softly, her heart clenching. She had liked Cherie. A nice strong woman like herself. "I need time to think" She hung up on them and grabbed her school stuff. She went to the coffee shop and sat down at her regular table when Patrick sat across from her looking pissed.

"You're lying to me," he said evenly.

"About?" she asked the hair on the back of her neck standing up. She slid her backpack back on and kept her hand near her gun just in case.

"You're the Woman," he said plainly, not accusing just outright saying the truth.

"And when did you decide this?" she asked.

"I knew the moment you had that call with Marino. I was in the room. You flirted with Cain and sounded so sad when talking to him. So I watched and I waited and I kept trying to get into that safe of yours. Finally got the combination last week and saw your binder. You're giving everything to Cain." He was on a roll "So I started asking around, there are a lot of rumors about you and Cain. You two have a weird thing going, so I ask myself.

She knows I work for Marino, yet she kept me around. Why is that?"

"You didn't work for Marino when we got together." Erin said slowly "And if you recall I did ask if you would consider working for me," she said knowing this was an admission "You said I was a one trick wonder if I recall"

"You're a killer," he said, sounding disgusted. "I've heard what you did to Anton and his crew."

"I did what was necessary. Marino is a killer too, this is the life you chose and you're going to judge me for being better at it than you?" she stood then, knowing this was the end of them which was also necessary. "I liked you. You were normal and calm and nice. You made me feel safe but the longer you've worked with the family the more you have changed. I miss the comfort I felt with you but that's been gone a long time."

"I should turn you in," Patrick said with anger and hurt in his voice.

"I expect you will be highly rewarded for that," she said softly and with that walked out of the coffee shop. She took off at a run and slammed through her door dialing Cain.

"Alice," he said, making her aware they were not alone.

"You with Marino?" she asked.

"Yes"

"You tell him he can fucking keep Cherie, I ever see her again she's dead so he better hide her good. She no longer works for the bar or for me."

"Understood," Marino responded. "You can end this now, just come in."

"Oh you're going to know who I am by the end of the day I'm sure. My boyfriend just confronted me with who I am and he works for you" Cain gasped and Erin hung up on them. She grabbed her go bag and was out in her garage instantly. She drove fast to her safe house that she had purchased weeks prior. No one knew about it and the documents hadn't been in her safe. She lit up her monitors and watched her house. Knowing it would be ransacked by Marino soon.

Her cell rang and she answered quickly it was Phillip. "Hey boss you never showed."

"This escalated, Marino is going to know who I really am today." Phillip was silent for a moment.

"What can I do?"

"Cherie is out, inform Billy Senior and the crew, get her area covered, and let everyone know she is captured or kill on site. She is a mole for Marino. Radio silence to her father until we know if he can be trusted. I am at a safe house now."

"Will do, what else can I do?" He asked and she could hear him moving on the other end of the line.

"I have a loose plan but it's going to require moving fast and being articulate." She said and he laughed.

"I aced my public speaking course." He said back, making her laugh. "Can I know your real name?" Phillip asked.

"Phillip you already know it, Erin Caruso, we were in third grade together." he was shocked for a moment.

"I thought I recognized you from somewhere." he said slowly "Are we at war?"

This stopped her dead, there was no way around it, she had to officially go to war with Marino. "Yes, inform the crews. Marino men only, not Bonetti. Phillip, I need you and Billy, Billy Senior, and Benji at my safe house now." she rattled the address out.

"Yes Ma'am," he said before hanging up.

Thirty Minutes later, Billy, Billy Senior, Benji, and Phillip sat in her safe house flat above a bodega six blocks from her home. They saw the monitors, a single cot and a small kitchen that was sparsely stocked with canned goods and dry pasta and six cases of water bottles.

"Boss this isn't a way to live, let me get you some groceries," Billy Junio said with disgust in his voice looking at the store-bought pasta.

"Not now, Billy you are going to Nevada, and Phillip you are going to Arizona, and Benji you're going to Florida. I want your next in line acting in your place here. We are going to make backdoor deals with Florida and Arizona. Phillip, Luca is the father of my little brother Theo. You are to inform him that by making a deal of non-aggression towards our family he is protecting his own son."

All four men looked shocked at this. Yes, her family was more tied up in this than they knew. Benji, you will inform Lanza that the new crew in his area for some reason isn't messing with his crew but is protecting their interests thanks to me as I have kept in touch with Shawn Holmes and given strict direction for his people." More shocked stares.

"Yes boss," Benji said after a moment.

"Billy Junior, my friend," Erin said slowly. "You are going to be moving to Nevada and taking over the Nevada operation from Marino's son. Take ten of our best men with you and cloak and dagger your way into his office. I need you there and him at your mercy by tomorrow night at eleven pm, you will force a call to Marino from his son. We either end this now or a lot of people are going to die."

"I have always wanted to go to Nevada." Billy Junior said looking at his Dad who nodded.

"Billy Senior. You are going to be my second until things are settled here. Then if you would like, you can go to Nevada and help Billy Junior." the older man's chest filled and he nodded. "First flights out on all accounts. Get your teams on alert to only go after Marino men. We are taking this war to them. Billy senior, get in touch with the Irish and update them on what's going on. Any assistance would be appreciated. Officially my name is Erin Caruso, it is wonderful to finally have you all know who I really am." All four men left after shaking her hand. This was it, Erin thought to herself as she watched her most loyal leave her side. She was going to be all alone soon.

CHAPTER TWENTY

CAIN

*I*t took two hours for him to break away from Marino, who was waiting impatiently to be informed of who she was. Cain knew that she had been discovered by Patrick who was now going to leak her address. He drove over to her house to find it locked and empty. He dialed her cell again and it went to voicemail. He looked up at her camera. "Call me" he demanded and walked back to his car. He went to the cafe where Patrick was still working and the kid looked pale and depressed.

"Patrick you good?" Cain asked, sitting down with him.

"I know who the Woman is," Patrick said "You got a thing going with my ex?" he asked Cain outright.

"Your ex?" Cain said, succeeding at sounding surprised. "It can't be, weren't you dating the Caruso girl?" he asked, poking the bear. He wanted to watch this little fucker squirm. He knew it was petty but he had touched Erin and held her and now was going to turn her over to be slaughtered by Marino.

"Yea she's the Woman. I broke into her safe. She's handing everyone over to you. How did I miss you two being that close?" Cain imagined if Erin wanted to keep a secret from her boyfriend it wouldn't be too hard since her entire life was a secret from everyone. Cain wondered if he would be able to discover all her secrets if they made it through this.

"We aren't," Cain said, trying to look stunned. He hoped his face looked appropriate. "She's very short on the phone with me. I've been trying to charm her forever to get anything I can. You're sure about this?" He asked, leaning forward. He wanted to reach out and close his hands around the man's throat but held back.

"Yea she didn't deny it when I confronted her, just said I would be rewarded when I turned her in." Cain felt like he was being gutted, why was she throwing in the towel? They had a plan and she was just giving up. He sat back in his chair.

"Sounds like a white flag to me," Cain said "What are you going to do?"

"I am done here in twenty minutes then I am going to Marino, will you come with me? Show a united front. I can show him pictures I took from her folder with her entire organization outlined." Cain sat thinking for a moment of the irony that this guy wanted him to be moral support in turning in the woman he loved. If Patrick knew he would probably try and hit him. Cain nodded and watched as the guy stood up and went behind the counter. He finished his shift and they both got in Cairns SUV and drove to Marinos. He listened to his earpiece and the silence that made his anxiety spike. Where was she?

Joey thankfully was not there and Marino listened intently before shifting his eyes to Cain. "Caruso?"

"Yea Derrick Caruso's daughter you've met her a couple of times." Cain supplied "I think it's best to keep Joey out of this until it can't be avoided." Patrick glanced up at Cain at this.

"Agreed. Patrick, thank you for bringing this to me. I want you to lay low for right now. She is already coming after the mole we had in her organization and now that she knows you know she will likely turn on you." Marino was being cautious which showed how much Erin intimidated him.

"She had a chance to kill me. She had her hand on her gun the entire time and she didn't, it was like she was giving up. I think I hurt her by confronting her and she seemed sad." Patrick said, not wanting to be waylaid. "I'd like to help find her, she has humiliated me and I would like retribution."

"She has humiliated all of us, Son," Marino said standing. "She will pay for all of this. Cain take him home for now." Cain nodded and put a hand on Patrick's shoulder. He led the guy back to his car and drove him home. The entire drive he considered places he may find Erin. He hated that Patrick knew her more than him.

"Where do you think she's hiding?" Cain asked Patrick.

"I don't know, she's a liar and a fraud." Patrick sounded angry and hurt. "I took her virginity, you know that. The Woman was a virgin until a few months ago.

Leading all these people, killing people, vicious and pure all at the same time." Patrick sounded love-struck. "She used to flinch anytime anyone got near her. Took me months of just talking to get her to not flinch when I was near her. She's supposed to be this big scary boss and she flinches if you move fast."

"Interesting combination." Cain agreed "I knew her father, she's a product of that man's faults."

"I heard about him from some of Marino's guys. Sounds like he was the best at getting information but was a dick to everyone. That's why Marino left him behind. They said he was a good warning for everyone. You can be the best but if you're shit to work with then no one wants you." Patrick said, watching Cain.

"That is some good advice," Cain said, pulling up in front of Patrick's apartment building. "Stay put and if she calls you, call me immediately." Patrick nodded and left.

Erin called an hour later as she watched Marino's men in her house. "My siblings?" she asked.

"Are safe, Joey doesn't know yet. Where are you?" he asked. Cain felt both relief and tension as he sat waiting for her answer. He needed to see her, to hold her, and make sure she was safe.

"Safe," she responded infuriating him.

"How can I protect you if I don't know where you are?" he asked with anger in his voice.

"I am protecting you by not giving you the knowledge. They busted my safe and have that folder you're going to be called in."

"What happens now?" Cain asked, holding his phone so tight he was shocked it didn't shatter.

"Now it's war," she said evenly. "Stay safe and keep Joey safe." she hung up on him and he growled as his cell rang again. He barked into it only to hear Cherie's voice on the other end.

"Baby what's wrong." oh this was just fucking perfect, he thought bitterly. Perfect timing to end this and get rid of this bitch once and for all.

"Are you sleeping with Billy?" He asked without hesitation and she paused.

"Yes," she said, anger in her voice. He could feel her riling herself up to fight with him.

"Then I'm not your Baby anymore. Get your shit out of my place by the end of the day. Oh and I hear welcomes are in order. Great job turning on your old boss, now I know you're a snake, and trust me even though you're under our protection you will never rise in this family. We don't trust rats even when they rat to us." He hung up on her and punched his steering wheel as he drove to Joey's for homework.

Cain was tense and stressed as he paced Joey's office. Carol and Joey just watched him and waited. The kids had long gone to bed and Cain had waited for how to tell Joey about the situation which he now had to do whether Erin wanted it or not. After his tenth lap around the room, he threw himself into the chair across from Joey.

"Ready?" Joey asked, smoking his cigar.

"I know who the Woman is," Cain said right as his earpiece clicked.

"You know who the Woman is?" Joey sat up almost dumping his cigar onto paperwork.

"Cain don't," Erin said pleading in his ear. He jumped, when had she called him?

"I have to," Cain said back, "It's Erin Caruso." Joey sat frozen and Carol paled. She stumbled over to the couch to sit down staring at Joey in alarm.

"No," Joey said after a moment "It can't be" Cain could see the clues clicking into place as Joey came to the realization.

"It is, I knew the moment I heard her voice at the party the other day," Cain said, watching Joey's eyes glaze out lost in thought.

"She hugged you," Carol accused. "She had been talking to you for months, we have never seen her go to anyone like that and she hugged you, and you left with her" Carol was making these leaps fast. "Did you sleep with her?" Carol asked and he heard Erin groan.

"So happy I'm not there" she muttered to him and hung up. He didn't respond to either woman.

"Did you?" Joey asked, rising from his seat, all fatherly aggression. Cain hadn't thought about this aspect of the conversation. He had assumed they would immediately jump in to help him not accuse him of sleeping with their proxy daughter.

"She's not your daughter," Cain said, standing from his chair and retreating. Joey was going to murder him, Joey for months had droned on about how the girl was afraid of men, finally not flinching as much around him. He could see Joey's mind whirling as he rounded the desk and had Cain backing into the wall.

"You slept with the Woman? You found out in my kitchen who she was and didn't tell me? I am supposed to protect her!" Joey all but shouted. The walls felt like they were vibrating. Joey pulled back and hit him in the gut hard. Cain felt his breath leave him. He hoped Carol would come to his aid but when he glanced up Carol looked furious and was not moving to stop her husband. "She's my responsibility and my enemy and you don't tell me?" he sounded betrayed and Cain felt guilty.

"I never meant to betray you, I fell for her before I knew her name. I was jealous when she mentioned she had someone. I relied on her calls probably just as much as she did. And she doesn't need your protection or didn't. Her boyfriend Patrick, outed her to Marino today." Carol let out a strangled sound and sat quickly again and Joey paled again. Cain sucked in a breath and straightened when he was sure Joey wouldn't hit him again.

"She's dead" he muttered, "he has her?"

"No, She just yelled at me for telling you, she's safe but won't tell me where," Cain said trying to sound as reassuring as he didn't feel. "In her words 'it's just a matter of time, she knows she's going to be caught, she's just trying to do as much as she can while she's still here."

"What's her plan?" Joey swept his desk clear and pulled out a fresh pad of paper. He started writing ideas as fast as he could.

"Currently set us up to take over her crews to protect you and the kids and hopefully we can take out Marino after she is gone." Cain said, "I spent all of yesterday trying to come up with a plan."

"Tighten security on the kids," Joey said to Carol who nodded and exited the room. "I won't have Marino use them against her."

"Thank you," Cain said slowly. "I propose we help Erin as we can be brother organizations with hers and no one would have to bend the knee."

"How?"

"I told her she should make backdoor deals with the other families in Miami and Arizona so that way there would be minimal retaliation. With her not letting me close anymore I say we make those deals. You know Miami will go for it and Arizona could be brought around."

"I'll think about it, Arizona is Theo's real father so we could have an advantage at getting him onboard," Joey said, sitting back in his chair. Cain was shocked at this news but Joey went on, "She has been difficult since the moment I met her. Hated me for so long. She hugged me the other day and I was so proud of her, of me winning her over. That was her saying goodbye wasn't it?" Joey asked, "You sticking with her?"

"It wasn't intentional but she's it for me though. She's my Carol" Joey froze at these words.

"I hope for both your sake you're right and we can all get through this alive," Joey said, dragging deep on his cigar. He pulled out his cell and dialed the burner that went to Erin. Her answer was short. "How could you do this to us?" he asked her without a preamble. There was a response he couldn't hear and Cain rubbed his face as they spoke. He knew this woman would be the death of him. She was dangerous and reckless. She was exciting and smart, beautiful and strong. He was in love with her and now he needed to save her from this situation.

"One day you will have to sit down and explain everything from start to finish." there was a pause "What do you mean you owe me a million dollars?" his face reddened "You're going to explain this to me one day." He got off the phone and looked at Cain.``Is this how you feel after dealing with her like you have a lot of information and there's nothing you can do to stop anything?"

"Yes, that is exactly how I feel." Cain said, "She's been driving me crazy for months on this crap." Joey sighed "I asked Marino to keep you in the dark about who she is and he agreed"

"She wants us to lay low and stay out of the way. She just ordered me to 'Joey stay low and keep Cain and the kids out of the way' the brass on this Woman." Joey said, growling low in his throat. Carol came back into the room and rested her hands on his shoulder. He leaned back into her hands and looked up at her.

"We need to back Erin in this fight. Make the calls" This was not a suggestion, this was an order. Joey locked eyes with his wife for a long moment and something passed between them. He picked up the phone and dialed Luca Marone in Arizona.

The next day after several failed attempts to get ahold of Erin, Cain sat in Joey's office. It had taken a lot of discussion and Carol kept slipping a notepad across the desk to Joey as he handled his calls but he had a verbal agreement with both Arizona and Miami to no longer back Marino if it came to an internal conflict. It was a surprise to know that Miami was in a meeting with Benji from Erin's organization when they called. They would not back either man and stay neutral to ensure the organizations were fair. Arizona had already spoken with Erin, still going by Alice, and had been civil with her. She was making moves of her own which made Cain happy.

"She's not answering me anymore," Joey said evenly. Cain nodded in agreement.

"What's the next move?" Cain asked as Carol came in with a tray for lunch for them both.

"Marino just pulled up," she said softly, moving to answer the door. Joey and Cain rose and Marino looked surprised to see Cain there.

"Cain, Joey good to see you."

"Greg, nice to see you, please come in and have a seat. Carol just made us some lunch. Would you care to join us?"

"No, I need a favor. We found out where Alice is getting the shipment from and I want you to send some men down to scope the place out and see who's running it. My sources say she owns everything but she's not working the land." Joey looked surprised and so did Cain.

"That's great news!" Joey said standing up and offering a hand "Yes I can send some men out today where is it?"

"West Virginia " Joey looked from Marino to Cain shocked. "I know, she's smart for someone so young."

"Yea cut out a supplier you make all the profit," he said easily "I'll send Fazzari out with a few of his guys. Lorenzo will get the details we need." Marino handed Joey a piece of paper with the details on it and looked at Cain.

"Cain I would like you to go over to a factory I found that may be her processing place. You can't go in hard or it'll ignite but we need to know what's going on in there." He pulled out a second sheet.

"Yes sure, I'll head over now, I was just letting Joey know I broke up with Cherie so I can start doing homework with the kids on Wednesdays again," Cain said thinking quickly.

"Yea she said you broke things off, smart, she's got loose lips," Marino said easily. "She's under our protection now I have her hiding out as Alice made a threat against her former Lieutenants life."

"Busy woman," Joey said, glancing down at his paper. "Looks like we are closing in on her though," Joey said, his poker face in place.

"Just a matter of time," Marino agreed. "Joey, call Miami and Arizona and let them know to be on standby for when we catch her. We should all meet the woman who caused all this aggravation" Cain locked eyes with Marino as Joey made words of agreement. He felt hatred for the man in front of him. The smile on his face held a bit of menace that he hoped would be misconstrued.

Cain headed to the warehouse and scoped it out when his cell rang. "Yea," he said, not looking at the caller ID.

"Cain" Erin sounded winded.

"Erin you ok?" he asked.

"Yea just avoided some Marino guys near my sister's school. Was hoping to get to say bye for a while," she said, her voice soft and sad.

"You can call anytime during school time and I will put you on with them," he offered.

"Yea got an interesting text, why are you at the warehouse?" she asked, sounding like she was jogging again.

"Marino has your binder, he's also sending guys out to West Virginia." she cursed at this and groaned.

"What are the odds I can get you not to do that?" she asked and he heard a door slam and some shouting.

"I'm under orders to check it out, what are the odds I can get a guided tour?" she laughed softly at this.

"Cain, I'm on the run right now, I can't go anywhere my people know about thanks to Cherie and my binder. You can knock and try" he grinned. "This is probably goodbye Cain," she said softly.

"Don't say that."

"I have to, you need to think about yourself and Joey and the kids. Promise me you will protect them." she sounded more out of breath.

"I promise, where are you?" he asked, getting back in his car.

"Out in Hollis Hills a ways away from you. Billy Junior may call you tonight if he can't reach me. I hope you can improvise." She cursed and there was more shouting and the sound of running. "Love you," she said before hanging up. He cursed and dialed Joey as he revved his engine and raced off to Hollis Hills.

"Yea Cain we are here." Cain ground his teeth.

"Hey, this warehouse is what a processing center looks like. She's got people and inventory all in there. It looks like they package it here and load it into the boat. I would be curious to know how big her operation in West Virginia is to handle this much product."

"Big from what I could see in her binder," Marino said back. "Where are you now?"

"Heading home for a quick shower got a bit dirty doing recon." he lied running a red light and hugging a turn to merge onto Highway twenty-five.

"Good work Son," Marino said before Joey hung up. Son, he wasn't Marino's Son and he wished he would stop calling him that. He would like nothing more than to put Marino on his knees in front of Joey and Erin. He would love to have him on his knees in front of him. He dialed Carol immediately.

"Cain?" her surprised voice came on the phone.

"They are chasing Erin, she went to say goodbye to Josie at her new school in Hollis Hills and they spotted her." she gasped "I am heading there now to try and get her out of there. I couldn't tell Joey with Marino there."

"I will let him know. Do you know who her second in command is? Can you call him and get her people out there? Or I can call if you have a number?" He could hear the desperation in her voice as she was trying to move quickly to find solutions. Just then he heard a doorbell and Carol cursed. "God Damn Veronica Marino is here."

"I will call her second in command, deal with Veronica." he hung up quickly and dialed Billy Senior. When he didn't answer he called Billy Junior. When it rained it poured, if Veronica Marino was there that could only mean bad news for Carol.

"I'm not in New York," Billy Junior informed him, sounding tense. "I have a mission to accomplish just getting off my plane."

"What mission?" he demanded, taking the off-ramp at Twenty-Second Street.

"One that will hopefully save Erin," Billy said, hanging up.

Three hours later he was cursing Erin as he drove the streets of Hollis Hills again and again. He missed homework time with the kids. He had missed dinner and it was getting closer and closer and closer to him losing his mind. She wasn't answering her phone for anyone. It went straight to voicemail which made him curse. Where was she? Fear gripped him as he revved his engine and peeled out towards Joey's.

His cell rang and he answered Marino who was ordering him to an office park they rented out. He pulled into the parking lot right after Joey and they got out feeling uneasy. Neither man spoke as they walked into the building and were shown to a large warehouse area at the back of the building. After rounding rows and rows of inventory for whatever business was renting the space currently, they saw her.

Hands hanging from a chain from the ceiling head down. Her red hair fell from what used to be a bun on the top of her head. Her feet touched the floor on their toes. She was breathing hard and blood was all over the ground. The back of her shirt ripped and whip marks red and dripping.

"Joey, Cain I would like you to meet Alice in the flesh." her head jerked up and they saw her blue eyes shine up at them.

Billy Junior- 9:00 PM EST- 6:00 PM MST

Billy Junior stood in his hotel room with his men and smiled around them. They all looked like wiseguys which he thought was pretty tight. They had the plan they had come up with on the plane ride over. Erin had bought out the entire plane for a direct flight to Las Vegas. She was banking on them not being known to be spotted.

"Two hours," Billy Junior said and two at a time went down to the casino that Marino the Son would be walking into shortly. He went to the same club in the same casino every night. It was where he operated which was inconvenient. The best place to grab him was on his way in or out. As they had a deadline it had to be before.

Billy exited the hotel room last and went slowly down the hall with Rooney, his top guy. He was tall with sandy blonde hair that defied gravity in lush waves. He was twenty-eight years old and an AC repair tech in the legit world who moonlit for them when needed. Rooney was fast and deadly accurate. "We got this boss," Rooney said comfortingly. Billy wondered if he looked nervous. He had never killed before or been in a gunfight. He felt wholly unprepared for this fight but he would do it for Erin. For their people and all he had worked so hard for. He would earn his own territory tonight.

Billy opted to take the stairs, no surprises coming off elevators for him. He may have seen too many mob and heist movies. He and Rooney made their way to the club and he glared at Gerald Marino already sitting in his normal booth in the back corner. Guy was a cliche, Billy thought bitterly, and he was early.

"We have to move, get him to his office in time to make the call," Billy said, looking at his watch. The

Marino office was twenty minutes away by the car that they had waiting for them. Who knew how many men they would have to go through to get into the office to make the call?

He counted at least six guys, armed, spread out in the area near Gerald. Gerald himself had thick black hair in a slick-looking suit with a vest. What kind of douche wore vests? Billy thought to himself, never catch him wearing a vest. "Rooney, spread 'em out. I need you to get to him, you're the only one that can." Rooney grinned at Billy and wrapped his arm over his shoulder turning him towards the dance floor where bodies mashed together in sensual waves.

Rooney took his arm back and wandered off leaving Billy to watch the crowd. He moved slowly up to the bar next to one of Geralds's guys. A short stout man with a pinky ring and slicked back hair. He looked mean and Billy grinned at him. Billy moved first, sliding his gun into the man's ribs. He didn't jump, merely looked at the gun.

"You know who we are, kid?" the older man asked.

"Yea, I need to borrow your boss," Billy said and the man lunged at him. Billy pulled the trigger and the shot started chaos. Rooney grabbed Gerald as his other guys and Geralds fought with fists and weapons. He watched as Cid went down and he cursed, launching himself at the man who took his friend down. These were all his friends and Billy would die for them. Rooney walked Gerald out the back with Billy and the rest of his guys on their heels. The car was waiting just where it was supposed to be. They got in the cars and pulled away from the curve. Gerald was cursing and spluttering. Billy punched him in the face twice and he shut up. He looked at his watch. They had fifty minutes to get into his office and make the call. Vegas traffic was a mess of course, Billy cursed as he watched the minutes tick as they drove slowly toward the office building.

They pulled up in front of the sleek gray buildings with dark glass. In the dark of the night, it was deserted and they forced Gerald to swipe his entrance card and get into the building. "You own this building right?" Billy asked and Gerald glared at him. "I can ask nicely or I can use force?" he offered and Rooney cut the back of the man's ear with his knife.

"Yes I own the building, the men in it are mine they will kill you," he said and Rooney poked the now bleeding ear.

"If they do that I will kill you," Rooney whispered. Billy grinned and they forced the man into the elevator and up to his floor. Billy looked at his watch and raised his gun. As the door slid open two men stood waiting. Billy shot one, Rooney the other. Don't think, Billy said to himself as he pushed Gerald into the office.

"What do you want, do you know who my father is?"

"Yes, your father is why we are here." Billy said, glancing at his watch "And in ten minutes you're going to make a call. Let's discuss what comes after."

CHAPTER TWENTY-ONE

ERIN

- FIVE HOURS EARLIER-

Erin sat in her safe house watching Marino's men tear her home apart. They got the rest of the stuff out of her safe and started just trashing the place. Not that she had much in the way of things but what she had was stuff she had worked hard for. They took the binder and her paperwork. Nothing that would lead them here.

She got confirmation that Benji spoke to Miami and Phillip was meeting with Arizona currently. She knew Joey had called both places as Miami had relayed the information to Benji. Billy had landed in Nevada and was scoping the building to get to Marino's son now.

"I can do this Erin, you stay safe." Billy had said hanging up. She knew it would be a matter of hours before her safe house was found. She had purchased it under her sister's name which would be easy to find. She armed herself and decided to head to Theo's school first.

She found Theo by his locker during break. He was surrounded by friends and they all stared at her in shock. Theo seemed to know something was wrong so he ushered her into an empty classroom.

"I have to get out of town for a while." she said "Marino is going to find me soon, probably today." Theo gave a slow nod. "You are going to stay with Joey, finish school, and get out of this lifestyle. You're better than all of this. I want to be clear, Joey is an ally, he will protect you." Theo nodded.

"Joey is a good guy. I told you," he said, tears pricking his eyes. "Why did you have to do all this?" Theo asked.

"Because someone needed to both help and hurt them and I have done that. I helped enough to make them dependent on me and will hurt them when I am gone," she said, wrapping her arms around him. This hurt, worse than any beating she had ever gotten. Her brother, the bastard son, was her only confidant at least while they lived together.

"We can't do this without you," he said, his voice filled with raw emotion.

"You can Theo, you have a good thing going with Joey and Carol. Joey found out about me yesterday and he seems to be trying to help. It may get dangerous and I need you watching over Josie." He squeezed her tiger. She clung to him back and savored the feel of her little brother. "You are the strongest kid in the world."

"Cain would protect you. I know he would, you should go find him." he put in.

"We got together in the end. He's taking over my crew and if it makes you feel better I do love him." Theo pulled back and looked up at her in shock. She smiled at him realizing he was as tall as her now. He was growing still, he would be taller in no time. She didn't want to miss seeing him turn into a man. "You and Josie were right, he's perfect for me." Theo grinned.

"Then why are you leaving him?" Theo asked, his voice bitter "Why are you leaving us?"

"Because I have to. Marino may kill me but I am making it to where he can't touch you and Josie or Cain and Joey will kill him." Theo shuttered lightly "Promise me you wont stop thriving. You can be sad for a little while but don't let this warp you."

"Like you did?" he asked, anger now replacing sadness and shock.

"Yea don't be like me" she laughed, messing his hair up lightly. "I'll be watching over you," she said, hugging him again. "I am going to go try and see Josie."

"This Goodbye?" he asked fear, lacing his words.

"Yea I think so," she said, tears pricking the back of her eyes. "I love you, Theo, you are the best little brother a girl can ask for. There is not one thing in this life I would do differently. Every beating, every early morning school drop off, it was worth it just being your big sister. I am so sorry I wasn't able to protect you more." He hugged her again hard.

"You always protected us, I could have handled the beatings but you always protected me," he said burying his head in her neck.

"That's what older siblings do. Now it's your turn to protect Josie for me." he nodded as she let him go. "Be good Theo" she said before leaving him in the classroom and heading out of the school. She checked her phone and saw a text that Cain was outside her warehouse. They were moving on her operations.

Theo's school was only three blocks from Josie's but just as she stepped up to the school a truck pulled up with Marinos guys. They spotted her and she took off running.

She skidded into an alley and pulled a dumpster behind her as she dialed Cain. After a brief back and forth as she ran from building to building avoiding the men she jumped a fence and headed into an apartment building. She raced up the stairs with the three men close behind her. God they could run, they were faster than her which was obvious as they kept almost catching her as she made tight turns and dashed into doorways. She busted into an apartment at the end of the hall to find it thankfully empty. She heard them run by shouting as she started down the fire escape quickly. She got to the bottom and rounded a corner racing down the street toward her car when she heard the taser discharge and felt her entire body spasm with pain. She hit the ground hard and passed out.

Water was splashed over her entire body as she jerked awake now cold and wet sitting tied to a rolling office chair. They caught her, Dammit! Erin thought as she glanced up. Marino sat in front of her glaring at her. She glanced around the room and didn't recognize anyone apart from the men who had chased her.

"Alice, I believe?" he drawled slowly. She inclined her head to him but didn't say anything. "You and I are going to have a long conversation" he pulled out a knife and flicked it open and then shut. She watched the knife not him mesmerized by the blade wondering where he would hurt her first. She marshaled her mind and after a quick tug on the restraints realized there was no escape at the moment. She stayed silent. "Leave us," he said evenly to his men who all filed out of the room.

Marino turned her chair so she could see a desk filled with her weapons as well as some torture tools she recognized. *This is going to suck* She thought to herself as he moved his hands over the implements. "Bend the knee"

"No" her voice was strong when she said it. He brought over rope and tied one wrist tight before clipping the zip tie and tying her other hand. He punched her hard in the gut as he unclipped the other zip-tied hand and pulled her to the floor.

"You know the beauty of knowing your history and meeting you at Bonetti's? He showed me exactly how to punish you. Or how did your father say it, bring you to heel" He hooked the ropes to a chain and raised her arms so she was on tiptoes and cursing. She tugged at the ropes. Putting all of her body weight on them hoping they would loosen. They didn't. Think Erin, are they hooked? She looked up at the ropes and they had been put into a giant clip. She stood as high as she could and tried to open the clip as Marino watched and laughed lightly. After a moment she stopped and took a deep breath. There was no escape, she had to play for time. He wouldn't kill her until the Dons arrived. They couldn't get here before eleven. Billy don't fail me now, she thought as she turned slowly back to Marino.

"He used the word 'tame' before he whipped me." she spat kicking her legs out at him. He dodged easily and moved behind her. Then she felt the knife slicing the back of her shirt and bra. He spun her around so she could see the table again and saw the whips and canes lying on the table. *Oh, this is going to hurt* she thought to herself as he grabbed a whip. He lashed out and struck her back and she closed her eyes as the torture began.

"You know your father was the best at what he did. If he hadn't been such a low-class person to work with I would have taken him and you to Nevada with me. I thought Bonetti would have had him killed just to get rid of the embarrassment that could be Derrick Caruso."

Erin stayed silent, he would not get a conversation, not until she either had backup of some sort or his phone rang at eleven o'clock. He circled her and she heard the sail of the whip and closed her eyes.

Hours later after several breaks for Marino and some of the men utilizing the canes and of trying to humiliate her by trying to whip her jeans off she was exhausted. The only thing she would say when he would tell her to bend the knee was a gradually weakening "No." She heard the doors open again and heard more footsteps and wondered what would be used next. She raised her eyes to see Joey and Cain both pale and shocked. Tears pricked her eyes now as she watched Cain taking her in.

"Erin" Joey sounded shocked and out of breath. "No" he stumbled toward her and looked at Marino "Greg please, she's one of ours," he stopped just short of her looking at her bruised face. No punches, just open-handed slaps to make her spin for their amusement.

"She was one of ours" he lashed out with the whip and slashed her back again causing her body to stiffen but no sound left her mouth. "She never yells out, it's oddly unsatisfying, like a cruel challenge to get her to scream," Marino said. "I am hoping you can motivate her to talk to us. I need to know some things."

"What things?" Cain's voice was horse and hard all at once. He looked like he had been kicked in the nuts. Erin saw every flicker of pain on his face as he took her in. He was pale though his color seemed to be returning. She could see the anger building and burning in his body. She drank in the sight of him, he gave her strength and she found her feet stilling the swaying she had been doing. He was her calm, she could handle this until the phone rang.

"I need to know how this happened. She's very detailed about everything she's running in this binder" he said motioning to a table that held her binder. "But not about where she got the capital."

"How do you want us to get that information?" Joey asked, his voice harsh as Marino sliced with the whip again. Her eyes closed this time and her lip trembled. It was humiliating to be whipped in front of Cain. She hadn't thought about being tortured in front of him and wished she could make him leave.

"I was hoping you could bring in her siblings," Marino suggested.

"No" All three of them shouted at once. Rage filled Erin and she pulled hard on the ropes and lifted her legs kicking out and catching Marino in the shoulder. Marino smiled and turned her toward him. This was a mistake,

Joey and Cain both gasped when they saw her back all but shredded. Her jeans ripped at the tops and a new brand on her other shoulder. A big 'M'.

"See that's all she says, I say bend the knee, I get a 'No' over and over, it's infuriating," he said pulling her hair back but he loosened his grip and his face was close. She pulled back and head-butted him in the nose. He cursed and stepped back momentarily.

"Leave them alone" she spat in his face and he slapped her hard sending her spinning on her toes thanks to the ropes. After cleaning his face and giving her five more lashes that had her hands clenching and feet lifting from the ground. She saw stars as she opened her eyes looking at the ceiling.

"She's a woman, '' Cain said, stepping in between them "I know she's been an annoyance to you but she has never been violent or done anything but help us. This is not how we should be treating her."

"You think you can make her bend the knee?" Marino asked, Erin laughed, which made him groan.

"Shut up Erin" Cain spat "You think pissing him off will end this quickly but it won't"

"Bossy" she mumbled and her lids closed as she focused on breathing and not passing out. She used what was left of her reserve with her failed assault. "What time is it?" she asked Cain who had moved closer to her.

"Ten-thirty in the evening," he said looking at her glazed eyes.

"Good" she sighed and took a deep breath "Almost over"

"This is the most I've heard all day," Marino said, moving her around to face him. "Are you ready to tell me what I need to know?"

"Sure you will be releasing me soon anyway" This stunned all the men in the room and then Marino laughed and slapped her hard again. She felt Joey and Cain tense. "What was your question again?" she asked after she stopped spinning on the spot dangling from the chain.

"How did you build this business without Joey Bonetti knowing?" She took another deep breath and felt Cain's hand on her hip lightly holding her steady which was amazing. She was getting dizzy from all the spinning.

"How did I get started?" she repeated and turned to look at Joey. "I stole from you," she said to Joey, her face going red. "There was a deal you made years ago that my Dad was supposed to collect on. A million dollars and my dad picked up the money and was mouthing off to my Mom about it and getting drunk. Then as usual he got too drunk and he beat my ass because all of us kids were being too loud that time. So I took the money and I hid it and I had to decide, do I turn it into Joey and try and get him to get rid of my Dad or do I take it and build something amazing, that Joey relies on, makes money from and burns his world down with it. To call you here" She turned her head away from Joey back to Marino. " So that I could hurt you the way you hurt me. So, I took it and made my plan. I researched, studied and worked hard. I was invisible and when I heard about Cain here the rising star I was seventeen I thought he was cute. I made a fake bomb, put it on my boat and made the deal of a lifetime that I knew Joey would jump at. I convinced the Mexicans to go to my land, to work for me, and to manage my West Virginia ventures. See I am an all-encompassing boss. I only require loyalty, not heritage."

Marino barked a laugh at this. "So you stole from Joey and got your old man in trouble to get us over a barrel." he said "Why did you come out in the open?"

"I killed my parents, so there was no need to hide anymore," she said evenly with no remorse. She felt like a weight had been lifted as she said it.

"You killed Derrick?" Joey said, turning her to face him. He had anger and hurt in his eyes.

"He hit Josie, he never did that before. It was always me and maybe Theo but never Josie. She was to be protected, but when I came to, I saw the bruise on her face. I was bloody and broken and this little angel was cleaning me up with a bruised face. So yes I forced them to the docks, got on my boat, and took them out to drop in the ocean. Not far enough apparently. I appreciated Anton for taking the blame. His timing was impeccable for me. Both for an introduction to me and for taking the blame." she sighed deeply. "When you showed up at the apartment I thought you would kill me. Thought you were as horrible and evil as my father said. You took the kids, you were kind, Carol was kind.

"The day you called me into your office to tell me you found their bodies I thought you were going to know that I did it. I thought 'Oh crap the jig is up I'm dead' but you so easily blamed Anton. I do regret that you saw those pictures that night." she said, turning to Marino "You're a dick" he laughed again.

"If you weren't such a conniving bitch I think we would get along. Tell me how is this my fault? How did I create you? Why were you going to call me out here?" Marino spat, he sounded genuinely concerned about this. Good, he should be, hopefully, Billy would handle his side of things soon otherwise her time was about out.

"When you lived here before you left for Vegas, do you remember my Dad?"

"Of course, I remember Derrick, he was the best at what he did. He was unpleasant to work with though. Had a mean streak and always wanted the violent option. I judged him as not good enough to associate with in Nevada. He was really good at cruelty though.." Marino said, sitting back in a chair by the desk of weapons. "That's why you're so good at it, come by it naturally."

"Yea he worked at the old factory that I bought, the one that you had Cain scope out earlier" Marino's eyebrows shot up and he glanced at Cain but she kept going "I got cameras, Ring doorbells are a wonderful thing. Well after you left almost immediately they fired him for fighting because you weren't here to protect him and Joey was not managing the way you did. No one would hire him and Joey had him on collections which he said was small-time stuff and didn't make him enough money. He stepped up his game on drinking and then my mom stepped out with Luca Morone when he was out visiting and helping Joey. When she got pregnant with Theo that's when the beatings started. You sent Luca rather than come yourself to help out. You left your people and it's just a happy circumstance that you ruined any chance of happiness that I had in my life. My therapist says I have an unhealthy obsession with making things equal between you and me and that I should be more forgiving. I don't agree. Thank you for the referral Joey, he's very discreet." she said all this in a rush as her back was starting to burn. Her shoulders were on fire and her toes hurt from trying to hold herself up. Come on Billy, she thought, I need you to make it at eleven.

"So I abandoned my people and your dad was a terrible person and that was my fault?" Marino said, evenly rubbing his thumb along his lower lip. "I concede that I left at a time that was not great and mistakes were made" his voice was firm "but you went a bit far here. Bend the knee work for me and this all stops," he said evenly standing from his seat.

"No" she breathed out as he growled in frustration at her. "You bend the knee and work for me" she responded, her head laying against her arm as she looked at him.

"I don't think you're in a position to make demands," Marino said evenly.

"What time is it?" Erin asked looking at Cain who was drinking her in, his eyes burning.

"Almost eleven," he said evenly.

"Oh good," she said "almost over"

"You keep saying that," Marino said, shaking his head and spinning her around. "This isn't ending until you bend the knee."

"No," she said and heard the whip sail through the air but there was no blow. She opened her eyes to see Cain had disappeared. Joey too. She turned and saw Joey pulling the whip out of Marino's hands and Cain facing her, blood showing on his neck where the whip hit him.

Tears pricked her eyes and he kissed her softly. He lifted the rope, unclipped it from the hook and lowered her to sitting on the floor when Marino's phone rang.

"You will want to answer that it should be your Son." Marino and Joey froze. Marino reached for his phone. "Speaker if you would," she said, trying to stand but failing. Cain assisted holding her on the sides of her hips to not touch any open wounds.

"Dad," a deep voice said through the phone. "I don't know how this happened"

"What happened Gerald?" Marino asked, standing as well. Erin had Cain help her move to her weapons and raise a gun pointing it at Marino. No one moved. She was so proud her arm was holding out, and Joey slowly stepped away from Marino which was smart, she thought. No telling if her arm would handle a shot like this.

"They killed five of our guys in the club. Two in the office so far..." there was the sound of the phone being taken away.

"Put Erin on the phone." Billy Junior's voice was hard and angry through the phone.

"Now Billy you sound upset, is Gerald giving you trouble?" Erin responded in a shaky voice.

"Boss, you sound rough." She could hear the grin on Billy's face as he spoke. Relief fills the void. He did it, they were safe. Relief flooded her body and she leaned on Cain lightly.

"I'm bleeding but I ain't dead" she responded, making Billy laugh. "I believe we were deciding who was going to bend the knee," she said moving slowly out of Cain's arms to Marino who had paled "Or should I hang you from the rafters for a while?" Marino dropped to his knees slowly with anger and hatred in his eyes. She could feel the heat radiating off of him as he hit the pavement.

"Don't hurt my son," he said in a hard voice.

"I would never hurt someone's child, but here's the thing. I can't have you hanging around seeking retribution, and Billy, you see, he's earned a territory and since Nevada seems to be available I think Billy will take over Nevada, and out of respect your son can be a footman." Marino paled "Billy does that sound fair?"

"Thank you boss!" he said softly.

"I'll send Benji to be your second. Gerald, I will be sending your father back to you as a civilian only. If you want to remain in my or Billy's employ you will not allow him to step out of line and he will never leave Nevada again. If he is found to be promoting discontent he will be killed along with your Mother and your sisters. You will be killed last Gerald as I believe in punishing the person responsible. You are now responsible for your father, he's retired permanently."

"I understand," Gerald said, his voice deflated. She took the phone from Marino and pressed the gun to his leg.

"I feel like I owe you something for all the trouble you have caused me. You know I had realized after the whole Anton thing that I could work alongside Bonetti here. He's a good man, he cringes at the bloodiness that you and I can just sit in. That's who should be running the family, a good man. She fired the gun into Marino's leg and he shouted in pain gripping the now bleeding limb. His men came racing in and she pointed the gun at his head.

Marino rushed through an explanation and all the men bent the knee. "See Cain?" she said, sitting on the desk and putting the gun down. "I can be reasonable" Cain laughed and he shook his head as she turned her gaze to Joey. "Truce?" she asked softly.

"Truce" he agreed, holding out his hand. She shook it and smiled.

"I would love to have a sit down sometime next week to discuss a merger of sorts. I believe a psychic said that I have to marry Cain." Joey burst out laughing at this as Cain moved in to let her rest against him.

"Are you proposing? He asked her.

"No, I am just doing what Josie told me to." with that her eyelids fluttered closed and she passed out.

CAIN

Cain and Joey carefully loaded Erin into Cain's SUV and drove to Bonetti's house. Joey called in his on-call doctor and when they arrived they stood holding Erin between them to stare in shock. Carol had Veronica Marino tied to a chair with a gun on her. Carol was bleeding from her arm and mouth and her hair was disheveled. Veronica on the other hand had a broken nose and was wheezing.

"Tell me we won, otherwise I am going to kill her just so that when Marino takes me down it will be worth it." she was furious, and when she lifted her eyes and saw Erin she paled.

"We won, Marino was shot, and they are all going back to Nevada under new management," Joey said, leaving Erin to Cain and moving to his wife. "What happened here? Where are the kids?" he asked, taking the gun from his wife and looking her over.

"What happened to Erin?" she asked, rushing over and ignoring her husband. "Let's get her into her room." Cain followed Carol as Joey stayed with Veronica who was trying to talk through a wad of dishtowels in her mouth.

"She won," Cain told Carol. "She's in charge now, or really she and Joey are in charge. She had a plan and it came through but she's lost a lot of blood." Cain laid her gently on the bed face down for her back as Carol started hovering.

It turned out Veronica had come to according to Carol "teach her the rightful place of a Mafia wife" and when Carol had laughed in her face the woman had hit Carol in the face. She then took a knife and sliced her arm before Carol "took control" of the woman. It was a shame, according to Joey, that Veronica did not know that Carol was well versed in not only fighting but taking out the trash, so to speak. Carol had disarmed her, beaten her, and tied her to the chair. She had been lecturing her on the true purpose of the Mob wife, and how Veronica had failed to fulfill her true purpose. The kids had come home and she had ordered them pizza to eat in their room and stay out of the way.

Carol was terrifying, Cain thought, as he watched the doctor work on Erin. The whip marks were bad, her entire back was covered. The brand was not as bad as it looked but it would be permanent.

Word was already spreading as Marino's men told Bonetti's and Bonetti's told Erin's everything that had happened. A new fear of the woman who could be beaten and whipped but utter no sound and then take over all the organizations with a phone call was putting the fear of God into the wise guys of New York, Nevada, Miami, and Arizona.

The Irish had already connected with Billy Senior who stood stoically in the corner of the room. They had offered respect and assisted with getting Marino on a plane and out of the city.

CHAPTER TWENTY-TWO

ERIN

Her mind felt like it had been through a blender, nothing connected. Her back hurt and burned and itched. Her mind floated away from the pain. Josie's face circled in her mind a worried look on her face. Don't worry. Erin thought. Theo's voice reached her momentarily.

"I bet she egged him on. She used to do that to Dad, taunt him to get him talking, buy herself time, and usually caused it to..." Where did he go? Erin thought and why couldn't she open her eyes?

Cain's face, close to hers. "Erin, I need you to wake up. Now" he tried his bossy voice. She liked that and smiled but didn't feel her mouth move. He wanted her to get up and he had said it just the way that calmed her soul, taking the choice out of it. She needed to open her eyes or say something.

Pain seared her back as she felt the full scope of her body. She was weak and had tubes attached to her. She listened to the beep of a heart monitor and voices. She was laid on her stomach so that her back would heal, most likely and Cain sat next to her talking to Carol who she assumed was in the doorway. "It's hard to imagine how hard she had to work to keep everything going that she had with no one to talk to about it," she muttered suddenly.

"Yea, she is tough and strong," Cain said, yawning, "she needs to wake up," he said, squeezing her hand in his. That strength, she needed his strength.

"I heard you're splitting time between Joey and her group and staying at her place," Carol stated fishing for information. Erin smiled and felt her mouth twitch. She could do this, she clenched her thighs and didn't feel any tubes down there so felt she might be safe to sit up if she could get that far. First, let's open our eyes.

She studied Cain from the bed, he hadn't shaved in a few days and had a full-fledged beard and mustache combo. He looked rugged and tough and sad. She wanted his laugh, his charm, and his flirting.

"Yea, she was fixing it up herself so I am trying to fix it up at least the construction parts." Well isn't he cute, working on her place? Living at her place? She was sure Billy Senior was doing most of the work. She thought about what she could say to this and thought of the house and what she lacked decorating ability.

"Have Carol decorate it for me," Erin's voice said softly, Hey it worked! She thought She twitched her arms lightly and was proud they worked. Both of them jumped and stood up hovering over her. She started to move her arms up slowly to her chest to push herself up. Each move hurt, her body was achy and stinging all over.

"Erin" Josie shouted from the hall, obviously eavesdropping.

"Hey kid!" Erin said, trying to sound awake. "How long have I been out this time?" she asked as her sister danced up to her. Cain shot Josie, a warning look that made Erin smile even more.

"Two days, you're a mess," Josie declared. Erin laughed lightly and saw Cain relax slightly and she caught his eye before glancing down.

"I don't have a shirt on do I?" she asked, Josie shook her head. "Get me one" she ordered her sister who promptly ran to a suitcase that was at Billy Senior's feet. Billy Senior stood still, catching her eye and smiling lightly. He looked like he had aged a lot in the time she had been out.

"How are you?" Cain asked once she was sitting up on the bed. Stupid question she could see he was kicking himself for saying it. What was she going to do about him?

"Dandy," she said sarcastically, squeezing Josie's hand. "Two days, what did I miss?"

"I sent Benji out to Billy with five crews after I reviewed your binder. Marino went along and is on house arrest to our standard. Cain and I have been managing stuff waiting for you. Theo got second in his cross country meet yesterday and Josie's decided to take up horseback riding." Billy Senior filled in quickly and efficiently from his corner where he gave her the space she had always needed, until recently.

Erin rose from the bed, her loose sweatpants hanging from her hips as she stood up and hugged Josie only grimacing when her back was squeezed. Her eyes scanned the room pausing on Carol for a moment then meeting Cain's eyes.

She felt overwhelmed, all these people cared about her and waited by her bed. She had known the love of her siblings and that had always been enough to make her keep going. He was what calmed her and she squeezed his hand lightly as he held her steady.

"Sounds like an eventful two days." She said moving to the doorway with Cain's assistance and spotting Theo who grinned at her, she grinned back and moved to just in front of Cain. He looked down at her their vast height difference way more obvious now. "I'm sorry you had to see that," she said to him and she leaned her head against his chest. He put one hand on the back of her head and gripped her arm. He would forever have those images in his mind. She wanted to forget and could if she didn't see her back but anytime she was with him he would see and be reminded. Her scars made her hideous but he was looking at her like she was a prize.

"I'm sorry it happened," He said, pulling her head back and lowering his mouth to hers. He kissed her deeply to Josie's yelps of excitement and Theo's grunts of approval.

Cain drove Erin home that evening and she walked to her now mostly clean house. Cain had all but moved in as his clothes now hung in her closet and a cat was running around her house. "Make yourself at home," Erin said as he helped her onto the couch. The cat jumped onto the couch next to her.

"This is Lady, she likes your stairs." He introduced, as Erin started to pet the waiting cat. "I do believe a psychic said we were getting married," he said casually as he crouched down to take her shoes off. "Usually I would ask your father for your hand but since I don't have that option, I asked Joey, who approved." with that he pulled a ring box out of his pocket and set it on her lap.

Erin froze one handset on top of the cat who was demanding attention, the other on the arm of the couch. He was crazy, they hardly knew each other at all. They belonged to separate organizations. "You're crazy," she whispered, opening the box.

"Crazy enough for you?" he asked as she looked at the diamond ring shining from the velvet box.

"I think so," Erin said, sliding the ring on her finger. "We have a lot to figure out, you know," she said as he kissed her.

"I know, but tonight all I want to do is hold you and watch Star Trek." She laughed and when he sat on the couch she laid across his chest and snuggled into his safe and comforting arms.

"You know I have had that fantasy more than once about you and I." He laughed deep in his chest. It vibrated her ears and made her smile. "I love you," Erin said into his chest. "I don't deserve you, but I love you."

"You deserve so much more and I will make sure you get it," he said, holding her close. "I love you, Erin Caruso."

Erin knew without a doubt that she had found her person and that Josie was right. She would marry him.

Five Years Later - Erin

*E*rin and Carol sat in the sitting room of the walk-up she had bought as a teenager and Carol cradled the baby in her arms. Joey and Cain stood with Theo in the corner talking business. Erin watched Josie, now a sixteen-year-old girl, serve the men drinks and bring cookies over to Carol and her.

"You know being the wife of a Don is a wonderful thing," Carol said to Erin who groaned. It was like digging a knife but she knew Carol was right. Cain already run her organization for her at least for the past nine months. "Joey doesn't make a single major decision that I don't know about, his office is bugged so that when high-level meetings happen I can listen in and when needed I bring in a note but since you have that nifty earpiece you could just use that." This shocked Erin.

"Really?" She said, astounded.

"I come from a very old Italian family and the women may have our place but we still have a voice and as long as you use it wisely you can make the major decisions while taking little to no risk and protecting all the babies you're going to give me to snuggle." Carol said, snuggling the little girl wrapped in swaddling. "Ella really is a beautiful name"

"Thank you and I like that idea, it would cement the partnership between our organization and the families," she said watching as Josie stole the baby from Carol and sat down snuggling the sleeping infant. "Besides I don't think he could manage all of the legit business as well as the illicit ones. So I can focus my energy on them and taking care of Ella"

"I think you will do alright and if you ever need to talk I am here," Carol said, smiling over at her. The men came to join them right as the doorbell chimed. The housekeeper Charlotte let in Patrick who was looking sullen and sheepish. Cain came to sit next to Erin who was now holding the baby.

"Look Ella, it's our Lawyer Patrick, what can we do for you Patrick?" she asked, smiling up at the face that was no longer that of a young college student but that of a young stressed attorney.

"I got a job offer today from a defense firm," he said shortly "I would like to take it."

"Why?" Cain asked as Erin ignored them.

"I want to be a defense attorney. It is more lucrative." Patrick said slowly.

"Do you no longer hold political aspirations?" Erin asked, raising her head. "I seem to recall grand goals of being the president someday"

"Well yes, but currently I am too young." Erin nodded at Theo who grabbed a folder from the coffee table and handed it to Patrick,

"For my plan, I have you in a congressional seat in five years but that is dependent on you being a prosecutor and rising through the ranks. Can you hold out five years to sit in Congress and then another five to make it to the Senate?" she asked, looking him dead in the eye. Patrick looked taken aback.

"You have a plan?" he asked, his face showing the shock and censure he was feeling.

"Of course I do, I started making a plan the day you told me you were a law student in that coffee shop." he blushed and looked at Cain who smiled down at his wife. "My plans are long-term and require a lot of patience but they almost always work out. So no drinking more than two glasses of wine or scotch a day, no hookers or escorts, and no drugs. Don't bring a scandal to you and you will be in office in five years, three if a city council seat opens up, which, if Garcia keeps up his scandals it might." she said tilting her head to look at the baby.

"I can do that," he said, excitement back in his voice.

"So turn down the defense firm and stay on track." the baby giggled up at her mother. "Also you will be reporting directly to Cain from now on. He is taking over my organization as I am stepping back to enjoy motherhood." Cain jerked and looked at her more intently but stayed silent. Patrick stammered a congratulations to Cain and soon left.

After everyone returned to the Bonetti house Cain sat by Erin watching their daughter on the baby monitor. "You don't have to step down."

"I want to step out of the light. I can still help you make big decisions but you can handle all this. I can help manage the legal businesses to keep the feds off our backs and you run the families with Joey." Erin said, leaning into him. "Carol says she bugged Joey's office and that's how she knows what to put in her notes to him." Cain looked shocked and blushed.``Thinking about all the stuff you've said in there now? Stuff we've done in there?" she asked her mind flashing back to when they snuck away from Thanksgiving to Joey's office to have sex the year they were married. Cain nodded, grinning at her.

"I can't believe he didn't tell me. '' Cain said, "I guess that's a husband and wife secret," he said, stroking her cheek. "I like that but I would rather have you in my ear," he said easily.

"You say that until you're in a meeting with the baby crying with me," she said laughing as he turned on the TV and started Star Trek for them to watch together as they did every night before bed.